Yevgeny Usti<br>
Nations, leane<br>
with both hanc

"A comet, Do<br>
to strike terror into our hearts. ~~~~ ~~~~~~ ~~~~~~<br>
preparing to dismiss another impossible claim on the world's limited resources. An unmanned probe, sending back pictures, might indeed be a good idea. But a manned expedition? Out of the question.

"But, sir, allow me to explain." David Kondratieff felt the sweat on his palms and tried to keep calm.

"In eighteen months' time, this comet is going to provide the most spectacular sight in the heavens since the dawn of civilization. But that isn't what I'm concerned about. Three and a half years after that the comet will return. And it's going to come very close indeed.

"It could very well strike the Earth."

# JOHN GRIBBIN

### and

# MARCUS CHOWN

# Double Planet

**VGSF**

## ACKNOWLEDGEMENTS

Thanks to; Mary Gribbin, who shared her ideas and encouraged us; Dr Alison Jolly, who grabbed an incomplete version of *Double Planet*, devoured it with the relish of a starving person and came up with a whole load of helpful suggestions; Ashley Grayson, for all his efforts in the US; Malcolm Edwards and Faith Brooker, for their faith in the book; Charles Sheffield for his encouragement; David Brin, for his helpful advice on the nature of comets; Karen Chilver, without whom *Dragon-Drawers* would have had even more death and destruction!

VGSF is an imprint of Victor Gollancz Ltd
14 Henrietta Street, London WC2E 8QJ

First published in Great Britain 1988
by Victor Gollancz Ltd

First VGSF edition 1989

Copyright © John Gribbin & Marcus Chown, 1988

*British Library Cataloguing in Publication Data*
Gribbin, John, 1946
Double planet.
I. Title    II. Chown, Marcus
823'.914[F]

ISBN 0-575-04599-X

Printed and bound in Great Britain
by Cox & Wyman Ltd, Reading

To Arthur C. Clarke,
for switching both of us on
to science fiction in the first place.

# Prologue

"Don't go too far, Jan." Frances Reese's warning was still ringing in Du Toit's ears as he cut the jet pack and attempted a landfall a kilometre from the cluster of spacecraft. The terrain a hundred metres below was largely hidden, cloaked in mottled shadow, but it was unlikely, in such low gravity, that he would come to grief by dropping blind. Still, there was no sense in taking chances. He peered down into the gloom, trying to make out something as he fell in a long, leisurely arc towards the surface.

He had had to get away, get some precious solitude, and even mother-hen Reese had relented, grudgingly, when he'd told her, in all seriousness, that he was set to explode. It was true; make no mistake. He might have been the most even tempered and phlegmatic spacer on the long flight out to the Dragon, but intolerable pressure had built up inside him like a head of steam, until he didn't like to think what he might do to any of his crewmates if he didn't crack a release valve, and soon.

Du Toit felt the metal claws on his boots snag the surface, and flexed his legs to take up the momentum. The Sun was directly overhead, forever at zenith now that the comet was no longer spinning, but it was still too distant and dim to illuminate the surface properly. But some detail was visible close by. Where the ice wasn't streaked with dust it seemed to glow eerily as if from an internal light source, deep down

7

inside. He'd seen the same ghostly effect on Earth, walking across freshly fallen snow on a starry night.

Du Toit turned off his helmet light and felt himself poised between the stars and the faint Sun and the glowing surface of the comet. He seemed to be in a valley, or at least a depression of some kind, cupped in a giant hand carrying him through space. He had to remind himself that this really was a world, with a substantial surface area, with hills and cliffs, mountains and crevasses. It was difficult to reconcile this reality with the image of a tiny speck – for that was all it had been – that he had watched for three months in the Hoyle's 50-centimetre finder.

When he clicked the full beam of his light back on, the cone of illumination lit up a wide cleft with sheer ice walls towering on both sides of him. The wall to his right had to be fifty metres away, but the left-hand wall was just a few strides from him. His gentle landing, floating down almost parallel to the ice face, could so easily have become a tumble down the nearly vertical face. Back home they'd call the feature a kloof. Du Toit's kloof! How about that? He would talk to Reese on his return and request that they name it after its discoverer. He had no idea how long the feature would persist in the heat of the Sun once the ice started buckling and boiling off into the vacuum, but it was the nearest he would ever get to immortality.

He began walking parallel with the ice walls – long, loping, comical strides, each of which ended in an awkward manoeuvre he had yet to perfect, in which he corkscrewed the claws of one boot into the ice to gain purchase for the next stride and to ensure he didn't bounce off into space. All this was unnecessary. He had a jet pack and, if he floated away in the minuscule gravity of the comet, all he had to do was orient the nozzle and trigger a short burn to nudge himself back down to the surface. But that would be cheating. He wanted to walk, or at least practice what laughingly passed as walking on this oversized snowball. He had spent too much time, these past few months, floating inside a spaceship or tethered to one or another of the vehicles, directing the burns that cancelled the angular momentum of the comet. He wanted the pretence of normality, and that was why he was out here, doing silly walks on a chunk of primordial ice between the planets.

In two days' time Reese would order the big burn which would change the course of this ponderous iceberg of the vacuum. Only a couple of hours before, they had finished orienting the fusion engines. So Reese had given them all a much needed forty-eight hour break from their daily toil. And he had taken a walk in the dark rather than oblivion in his bunk. Sleep wasn't what he needed. No, he needed a breath of fresh air. Metaphorically, of course.

The kloof had tributaries, narrow fissures which swallowed up the light of his helmet beam. Du Toit stopped and peered into one. He could see at least a hundred metres into the crack, which stretched downward into the comet, maybe to its rocky core. He would never know, since a sharp bend interrupted his line of sight. Better watch out for crevasses, he reminded himself. His quest for solitude had taken him out of radio touch with the ships. That, perhaps, was unwise. But he would be careful.

He swung his helmet beam out of the crack and began examining closely the wall of the kloof. It had a curious texture, looking like fabric; narrow sinuous runnels were criss-crossed by dust veins. He pressed the palm of his glove against the wall, and convinced himself that he could feel the roughness. He had a good imagination.

Thoughts of scientific investigation slid from his mind as he imagined the great bulk of the comet, a sleeping Dragon waiting to be warmed into life as it neared the Sun. This was a landscape that no other eyes would ever see, let alone investigate scientifically. He moved on, trying now to think of nothing at all, to blank out all the tedious events of the past months, using the walk to recharge his mental batteries.

Breathing deeply, and leaping along rhythmically as he learned the trick of the twist in each step, he began to fall into a meditative, trance-like state, and felt fatigue seeping out of his bones. He glided to a halt, cupped in the bowl of ice, and turned slowly to see how far he had come. It was then that he felt the first, faint rumble beneath his feet.

Du Toit froze. His pulse rate and a dozen other physiological signs somersaulted off the scale. What was that? Movement where there should be no movement, deep down inside the comet. The Dragon was coming to life – but much too early, it shouldn't stir for weeks yet. For an age he stood motionless, with only the flutter of a muscle and the beating of his heart preventing the complete fusion of his awareness with the structure of the comet. He felt himself fusing with the ice, imagining layers upon layers of icy crystal plane stretching down into the cryogenic core. He felt that he could detect any microscopic slippage of these crystal planes. Poised on the knife-edge between comet and space, he felt for the heartbeat of the vacuum – but the rumble had stopped. With sudden relief, the answer came to him. The fusion engines! Reese must have been testing the main drive. Of course!

Then the world fell apart. Literally. He was thrown loose from the ice and found himself floating in a shower of splinters as the comet convulsed beneath him and a great gaping canyon opened up before him, barely ten metres away along the floor of the kloof. A rising berg of ice, tens of metres across, nudged him to one side as it moved ponderously upward and out into space; Du Toit saw he was heading for the nearest ice wall, and fast. A spacer's instinct made him lunge at his tool belt, activate the emergency grapple line. There was no time to see whether the explosive harpoon buried itself in solid ice or powdered snow. The stars were obliterated, eclipsed by a moving mountain of ice. Then he hit, and darkness closed in.

When he awoke, he was floating. But the grapple line had held. Thank God. His head was muzzy and his left elbow bruised and stiff. The suit had not been pierced. But when he triggered his jet pack, nothing happened. He was alive, but his principal means of propulsion was useless. He hauled in the grapple line, hand over hand, until once again he could hook his boots into the surface and "stand" on "solid" ice. How long had he been out? The needle on the gauge showed thirty minutes of oxygen used; given that he'd been unconscious and breathing shallow, that meant maybe an hour had passed.

What had happened? The massive quake couldn't have been anything to do with Reese. The Dragon, dormant since the birth of the Solar System, had hiccuped. They knew it would happen when the heat of the Sun got stronger – but not this soon. They were still out near Mars, and the Sun was too feeble to melt off even a film of surface ice. Perhaps it was a result of the outburst of activity during the first pass of the comet near the Sun, months before. But, surely, it had had ample time to settle down again. No, it had to be the fault of the expedition, somehow, with heat from the engines and the change in stresses caused by halting the comet's spin combining to release an old pressure along a line of weakness that had been there since the beginning of time. But that was no excuse.

He began to pay out the grapple line, crawling now, not leaping, over the kloof floor. Something else was wrong. What was it? His fuddled brain tried to take stock of the surroundings. The Sun! Where had the Sun gone? It should be directly overhead; it had been before the quake. Where was the Sun? Scrabbling frantically onward, slipping and sliding on the ice, digging his toe claws into the ice to stop himself, Du Toit reached the canyon he had seen open up in the kloof floor. But it was no longer a canyon. There was nothing on the other side.

Trying hard to swallow panic, he craned over the edge, and found the Sun. It was down a sheer face of glistening ice. How could that be? How – then his brain finally understood, and Du

Toit felt a cold hand seize him in its grip. Surely it couldn't be. He closed his eyes for a moment, but when he opened them the scene was still the same.

In the light of the distant Sun he saw rubble and ice, great blocks of the stuff, occulting the stars; a flotilla of calved icebergs setting sail upon the sea of the vacuum. With him riding on one of them.

# 1.

David Kondratieff had been one of the first people with any real influence to learn about the comet. It took a pretty spectacular item of genuinely scientific news to justify disturbing the science adviser to the Council – his real role was administrative, trying to decide how best to employ the depleted technological resources of the world to the ever pressing problems of food production. News about new crop strains, techniques to combat drought, better rainfall forecasting in the monsoon regions – things like that went straight to his desk. But gone were the days when scientists had unlimited budgets to probe the structure of matter, or the depths of space. Gone too, since the Incident, were many of the large computers that would have made his task so much easier.

Nigel Cooper, the Director of the Canary Islands Observatory, dropped the package in personally with his bi-monthly report.

"This might be your sort of thing, David."

He glanced at the title on the tape! *Comet Osaki-Mori. Aquisition and Orbit.*

"A big one? Naked eye?" Nigel nodded. Kondratieff tossed the tape on his desk. "Fill me in quickly, Nigel. I'll view the tape at home – when I get home." A wave of the hand indicated the stack of material in his "in" tray.

"Okay. We got the news first from Japan, of course. They're still doing sky survey work with their Schmidt camera. And we've been taking quick looks with the 2-metre almost every night over the past month. Can't spare too long on it, because of the work on Holly objects – all that's in the main report. But it's big all right, definitely a newcomer, and from the orbital information we have so far it should pass close enough to put on a good show. We won't have the final orbital details for a couple of weeks yet – it's being quite seriously perturbed by Jupiter. But with luck it will be better than Halley. We'll be glad to help publicize the event, get video crews down to photograph through the big telescope, and so on."

"And to drum up some favourable publicity for yourselves, eh, Nigel?" Kondratieff smiled. "You don't have to worry about influencing me, you know; and it doesn't really matter what the public think. If you want to get your budget increased, you'd better find a way to convince the Council that discovering a comet is something to make a song and dance about."

"It won't bring any more rain to East Africa, will it?"

"It's not got any short term benefits, David. But it's one helluva good opportunity for some real work on the origins of the Solar System. Maybe the Council could spare the resources for a probe, to bring back some samples."

"A probe? Now I know you're losing touch with reality down there on the island. I have enough trouble justifying all the shuttle flights I schedule as it is; Ustinov knows perfectly well we're running those little packages from your friends at MIT up into orbit, counting cosmic rays or whatever it is they do, and he seems to think that sometimes I'm timing the flights to suit MIT, not to maximize our cover of the crops. It doesn't pay to tell politicians the whole truth, but I'd need a pretty convincing story to get official approval for a comet mission, and official approval is what I'd need."

"I know, David." Cooper stood and extended his hand. "I mustn't waste your time with my madman's schemes. Let's be grateful that we've got a friend like you to help us keep the observatory running, and to smuggle those not so secret packages up into orbit. Anyway, if nothing else this might bring the opportunity for you to come down and see us at work."

Kondratieff stood and shook the proferred hand. "Maybe." Releasing his grip, he waved again at the stack of work. "And then again, maybe not. But keep me posted on this comet, Nigel. If it comes close enough we'll try to get one of those little packages up above the atmosphere at the right time to take a peak at it."

Linda Regan didn't much care about the comet, one way or the other. Of course she knew about it, in a vague sort of way. The newsfax had been full of the story for days. An unrepeatable scientific opportunity, it said; and the spectacle of a lifetime, far better than the disappointing return of Halley's Comet a couple of decades ago. But a fat lot of good that would do Linda.

In six months time she would be eighteen, legally an adult and with a lifetime of opportunity ahead of her. Only, there were no opportunities. Her mother had broken the news that morning.

"I'm sorry Linda. There's nothing I can do. They've cut the ration again and we don't have the money for the unrationed shops. Maybe next year things will be better."

"But next year's no good, Mum. It's my eighteenth *this* year. You promised I could have a party."

"I know." The tall woman brushed back a strand of her dark hair, just beginning to be streaked with grey, and sat down by her daughter at the breakfast table. She reached for Linda's hand, trying to comfort her, but the hand was quickly withdrawn. The girl gazed intently at her drink, stirring the brown liquid into a swirling pattern, and pretending not to listen to her mother's words.

"I really thought things were improving after I got the job. But it's no good them keeping prices steady when they keep cutting the quota on what we can buy. Maybe it's better in Russia or America. But the rest of us have to do what we're told."

"It's not fair. They've got resources to send spaceships to Mars, but they pretend there's nothing for the smaller countries. I bet they all have parties. Why do we have to do what we're told, anyway?"

"Oh, my baby." This time the offered hand was taken. "Sometimes I wonder, too. But your grandfather knew even worse times. Things are getting better. And I don't *really* think they've got a better ration than us," she added gently, "there just isn't much to go round."

Yevgeny Ustinov knew only too well how little there was to go round. As Secretary to the Council of the Reunited Nations, Ustinov, as much as anyone, was the ruler of planet Earth. The Council invariably took his "advice"; and the world bowed to the wishes of the Council, as much through lack of any idea what else to do as through fear of the decaying stockpiles of nuclear weapons. Symbolically, the RN's administrative headquarters – the World Government – was located in Reykjavik, Iceland. Not exactly neutral territory, in terms of the old loyalties, but at least located geographically in between the two land masses of the northern hemisphere where the former rivals held sway. The symbolism, thought Ustinov, might have been better if they had picked somewhere on the equator, midway between the North and South, for that was where the real differences in the world lay today. And then at least he wouldn't have had to endure these bleak northern winters. But then again, at least the bleakness of the location kept even essential visitors down to the minimum and left him free to concentrate on the task in hand. As long, that is, as he didn't allow his tired mind to wander off in daydreams about relocating the Council on a tropic isle.

His visitor had stopped talking and was waiting, expectantly, for the Secretary's response. Ustinov leaned back in his chair and rubbed his face with both hands, the fingers lifting his old-fashioned glasses from the bridge of his nose.

"A comet, Doctor Kondratieff, is hardly something to strike terror into our hearts in the twenty-first century, you know." He smiled wearily, preparing to dismiss another impossible claim upon the world's limited resources. An unmanned probe, sending back pictures, might indeed be a good idea. A show for the people, to take their minds off the absence of bread in their bellies. But a manned expedition? Out of the question. Why couldn't these people understand that they couldn't return to the twentieth century, and that what little effort could be spared for work in space had to be geared to practical ends, weather forecasting and monitoring of cropland from near orbit. After the fiasco of the O'Neill colony, surely anyone could see that deep space was a waste of effort, even though the technology to reach Jupiter did still exist.

"But, sir, allow me to explain." David Kondratieff felt the sweat on his palms and tried to keep calm. It had been hard enough to get this audience, and on what he said now rested the only chance of deflecting the newly discovered comet from its path.

"You must appreciate, sir, the difficulty of predicting the precise fate of this object. It is a first-time visitor to the inner

17

Solar System, and its orbit has taken it close past Jupiter. Usually, these things dive in from space, rush past the Sun, and head out once more, never to be seen again. But the deep gravity well of the giant planet has deflected this comet. The result is that it is dropping into a stable orbit which will go only a little closer to the Sun than we are, before swinging out past Mars and then dropping back towards the Earth's orbit.

"In eighteen month's time, this comet is going to provide the most spectacular sight in the heavens since the dawn of civilization. But that isn't what I'm worried about." Kondratieff hurried on, before the Secretary could say what was clearly in his mind, that heavenly displays, no matter how spectacular, were of no interest to him. "Three and a half years after that – three years and one hundred and twenty three days, to be precise – the comet will come back to our part of the Solar System. It will become what we call a short period comet. And it's going to come very close indeed.

"I said its closest approach to the Sun is just inside Earth orbit. I should have said 'just inside the orbit of the Earth and the Moon.' The Earth and the Moon follow a complex path around the Sun, as you can see in this holo." He gestured to the wall screen, where Ustinov's desk was displaying the images from the tape he had dropped into it at the start of their conversation. "Most people think the Moon circles the Earth, but it doesn't. All we can say about the comet's orbit is that, left alone, it will intersect this double orbit a little under five years from now, just when the two planets are there. It may pass harmlessly by. But it could very well strike the Earth."

The presentation was faultless, Kondratieff was sure. The facts spoke for themselves, and the computer animation of the comet's orbit piercing the interwoven strands of the orbits of Earth and Moon around the Sun was the icing on the cake. The probability of disaster might seem small. It *was* small. But as the report spelled out the effects would be immense. A small risk of an immense disaster; in actuarial terms, the only sane course of action had to be to reduce that small risk precisely to zero, if at all possible. And it was possible.

"If this comet strikes the Earth it could be the greatest disaster in sixty-five million years, since the death of the dinosaurs. Far worse than the Incident. We know the Earth has been bombarded from space over the eons, and we are pretty sure now that these bombardments explain why suddenly thousands of species of life were wiped from the face of the Earth in massive extinctions. Sixty-five million years ago, it wasn't just the dinosaurs that died but hundreds of other species. And the best explanation is that the cause was a giant meteorite striking the Earth – the Enever effect."

"I know all this." The Secretary leaned back and waved a hand dismissively. "That disaster was caused by a huge lump of rock, but a comet is merely a snowball. And it may have been a disaster for the dinosaurs, but not so bad for us, eh, since it opened the way for the mammals!"

Kondratieff, not for the first time, cursed inwardly the Secretary's habit of viewing pop science for light relief.

"Of course, sir. I'm not suggesting a disaster on that scale. But this dirty snowball still has a mass of $10^{18}$ tons – that's a billion, billion tons of ice and snow. It's the biggest thing to come into the inner Solar System since civilization began." He had a flash of inspiration. "And remember what happened in 1908. The Tunguska Explosion. Trees were knocked down all over Siberia. That was caused by a fragment of comet exploding in the atmosphere, not even a whole snowball. If it had arrived a few minutes later, the rotation of the Earth would have placed Leningrad directly under the explosion. That's what even a small fragment of a comet can do, and we are dealing here with one of the biggest."

He watched Ustinov ponder the implications. The Secretary stood and walked to the large window, gazing through the thick triple glazing into a black night which offered no view more preposessing that the swirl of cloud and snow in the lights from the building. He certainly had heard of the Tunguska event, and his family came from Leningrad. A meteor – or a comet – striking the ocean could throw up clouds that would circle the Earth and bring a new Ice Age, the report said. A whole world like Iceland in winter. No more tropic isles. He shuddered and turned from the window. "David Kondratieff, you are a rogue. I don't know if you are really concerned about this comet striking the Earth, or if you simply see an excuse to revitalize the space programme. No, I don't mind." He raised a hand to stop Kondratieff's attempted interruption. "Either way, you are right. We cannot afford to take the chance. Things aren't easy here. It is all we can do to keep things from falling apart as we stumble from one crisis to the next. But if we stop trying to solve the problems, then we stop being civilized human beings. I can't promise you much, but if you can get this crazy scheme of yours off the ground, then you will have my support. But I hope you have thought it through. I fear that, win or lose, this may be the end of our spacegoing capability."

The audience was clearly at an end. But it had turned out as well as Kondratieff could have hoped. Better get out quick, before the old man could change his mind, and get the wheels turning officially. Once a project like this got started, it would take more than a change of heart by the Secretary to overcome its inertia.

"Thank you, sir. I am aware of all the implications, and I have prepared an outline plan in case of your approval. May I . . . ?" He left the question hanging as he moved towards the door.

"Yes, yes, you can make it official. Tell Ingeborg who you need to set up the machinery and I will issue the instructions today. If what you fear is correct, then there is no time to waste."

In the outer office, Kondratieff paused to wipe the sweat from his hands, and took a drink of water from the cooler. The hubbub of half-whispered conversations among the usual crowd of visitors, with and without appointments but all eagerly seeking an audience with the Secretary, died at first as he became the temporary focus of their attention, then rose again as he was ignored. To them, he was part of the furniture. David Kondratieff, the science man. Probably talking to Ustinov about the bad harvest in southeast Asia; no wonder he looked nervous, poor chap. They envied his easy access to the inner sanctum, but knew the responsibility, and the visibility, that went with it. Better to be one of the pack, even if it did mean a long wait, if easy access to the Secretary left you looking that wrung out.

Kondratieff tried to keep calm, act as if his visit had indeed been routine. Forty-seven years old, science adviser to the RN, the man the scientific community, what was left of it, regarded as God, and still that man in there could leave him feeling like a nervous PhD student facing up to his oral examination. Well, he'd done it. Pulled the wool over the old man's eyes, for sure. All he had to do now was get the astronauts behind him, and solve a few minor, routine problems – like getting half a dozen or so antiquated space shuttles all set to fly at the same time.

He turned to the calm, green-eyed woman who guarded the Secretary's outer lair.

"Well, Greta, the old man likes me today. He approves my plans."

Greta Ingeborg inclined her head. She knew what that meant. More work for her.

"And you just happen to have a directive that you would like me to put on top of the pile for signature."

"Greta, you're a mind reader." Kondratieff smiled. "And while we're waiting for the old man to get around to making it official, I'm sure you can get Frances Reese pulled off

21

routine duties and assigned to me to help plan a certain mission."

Greta smiled back. Kondratieff felt good. Things were going his way.

# 2.

The East African sun beat down upon the village. A road, once made up but now reverting to the track it had been for hundreds of years before the arrival of the white man's civilization, snaked past dusty fields in which the unharvested coffee crop had been left to die. An abandoned lorry, its wheels long since vanished, stood alongside a half-heartedly stripped down tractor, left with its gearbox missing and dust blowing into the engine. Overhead, the sails of a modern, aerodynamic windmill turned lazily in the fitful breeze, pumping water from the deep well – the one lasting benefit of technology for these villagers. In one cool hut, traditionally designed with open walls to allow the same breeze to blow through, a group of women were deep in discussion.

"What use is Nairobi to us anyway, I ask you?" The speaker, a tall woman with a commanding presence, dared with her eyes anyone to contradict what she was saying.

"Nairobi government is men's government, and we all know what men are good for. Sitting in the shade and drinking beer." There was a ripple of uneasy laughter. But not all were yet convinced.

"How can we buy food for our children? We've got no roads, no lorries, no market anymore. We grow the coffee, but nobody buys it. How can we buy food?" The plaint came from a tired looking woman at the back of the group. In London, New York or Moscow, even today, her appearance would have indicated someone well into middle age. But she held a baby to her breast, and another small child, less than two years old, sat, wide-eyed, by her skirts, sucking his thumb.

"Sarah Mandela, sometimes I think you just don't listen. The worst thing that ever happened here was the road, the lorries and the market. Who is it works in the fields all day to grow coffee? We do." There was a murmur of assent from the group. "And who is it takes coffee to market and gets money? Men do. And what do men spend money on? Not food. Beer. Whisky. Transistor radio. TV. No baby can eat transistor radios. Remember the old ways. If we grow food instead of coffee then we all have plenty to eat – even the men. Sure, we've got no beer, and we've got no TV. We don't need a road, because we've got no lorries. Women work in the fields all day, but we're used to that. And what we grow we keep. For our own village. For our own children. Money is just no use to us."

Once again she glared fiercely at first one woman, then another, willing them to understand. Nobody held her eye. The muttering began again, as the women talked among themselves, wondering about the possibilities.

**Dragontamers**
**Reuters, Reykjavik**

RN Secretary General Yevgeny Ustinov announced today that the New Aeronautical and Space Administration is being asked to draw up plans for a possible mission to the comet known as the Dragon. Such a mission would be the most ambitious space effort for more than forty years, and would involve most of the six shuttle spacecraft now serviceable. A team of astronauts would be in space for more than a year. Their objective, to ascertain whether raw materials from comets and asteroids in space could be used to help redevelop a space colony, without the need for reliance on resources from Earth.

The Dragon is officially named Osaki-Mori, after its two Japanese discoverers. Astronomers believe that it is a ball of frozen material that has been orbiting our Solar System, far from the Sun, ever since it formed, four and a half billion years ago. They predict that when the Dragon passes through the inner Solar System next year it will produce the most spectacular heavenly display since medieval times. Although it will pass by the Earth only about ten times as far from us, at its closest, as the distance to the Moon, there is no danger, an RN spokesman told Reuters today, of a collision or harmful effects on our planet.

"The exciting thing about this comet," science adviser David Kondratieff told a news conference in Reykjavik this morning, "is that it is being captured into a close orbit around the Sun. Jupiter's gravity has pulled on it in such a way that it is entering a stable orbit stretching more or less over the region of space between ourselves and Mars. And that means we can make a rendezvous with it and investigate the prospect of mining the comet's head for raw materials. Normally, a comet rushes into our part of space, past the Sun and off into space again in a matter of weeks, and there'd be no hope of our spacecraft matching orbits with it in the time available."

The comet provides the first opportunity this century to witness a sight that many astronomers now believe was responsible for the dragon legends of antiquity. The long tail of the comet will resemble the appearance of a "cosmic serpent", while it is possible that outlying fragments of dust, no bigger than grains of sand, associated with the Dragon itself will fall through the Earth's atmosphere, burning up as shooting stars and making it seem as if the Dragon is breathing fire . . .

Ustinov smiled as he laid the hardcopy printout on his desk. If there was one thing you could rely on the bureaucrats for, it was an effective smokescreen. Ask them to organize the construction of a new irrigation scheme in Mexico, and all you'd end up with would be committees proliferating like flies, money and time being wasted, and the hungry being lucky if any relief came their way this decade. There were too many administrators with too little to administrate. But tell them to plant a nice little story with the media, a judicious deception here and the occasional downright lie there, and they were in their element. But he owed his present position to the system; he was, ostensibly, a system man. Much as he'd like to, he daren't try to dismantle it, or even make major reforms. Use the system; make it work the way it was set up to work, but more so. That was how he'd got to the top, and that was how he'd stay there, for a good while yet.

Wheels within wheels. Of course, only a handpicked few had any idea of the real reason for the comet mission. The rest believed that this was a grand effort in the tradition of the Roman circuses. A diversion to take the minds of the people off their empty stomachs. There was no chance of the truth leaking out. Even someone with the astronomical knowhow – and there were precious few of those about since the troubles – would need a major computer installation in order to calculate the perturbed orbit of the Dragon accurately enough to realize what was going on. And the few major computers in the world today were the most precious assets of the Reunited Nations, securely guarded and with access allowed only under a rigid system of priority and security classifications. Of course, there were still some small machines, home computers, unlawfully in private hands. But nobody with access to such a machine would have the data, or the computing power, required to plot the orbit precisely.

The Secretary smiled again. His administrators really were excelling themselves on this one. It was almost worth the whole business just to get them out of his hair for a while. Why, if he could keep the red tape specialists occupied with this for the next five years, perhaps there'd be a real prospect of using the really competent people – and he knew who they were – to get some real work done. He leaned forward, purposefully, and thumbed the intercom button on his desk.

". . . and following up the news from Reykjavik of the first deep space mission for half a century, Liz Mackay has been talking to Dr Nigel Cooper, the Director of the RN Observatory in the Canary Islands."

The image on the wall screen cut away from the seated figure in the studio to a stock shot of the observatory from the air, zooming into the big dome then cutting again to an interior. Cooper sat behind a desk in a book-lined study, talking to an off-camera Liz Mackay.

"Fake." Jenny Garcia's quiet comment was heard only by her two companions – the bar was never busy at that time in the late afternoon.

"Huh?" Jonathan Feinberg's attention was concentrated on the tube; he only half heard her remark.

"Fake, Jon. Illusion. Tricks of the trade. What do you expect of the tube? There's no study like that on top of the mountain. It's all you can do to breathe up there. The offices are halfway back down to sea level."

"I suppose you've been there?" The gentle chiding came from a tall, tanned man, slightly older than the other two. Frank Ellison was perhaps in his late twenties, the others not long out of their teens. His bantering tone made it clear that he knew full well that Jenny had never been to the Canaries.

"Ah, come on, Frank. Do I have to be a lumberjack to know that bears shit in the woods? I know astronomy; I know guys who've been over there. It's a great observatory, nice tele-

27

scopes, but you need an oxygen mask if you're going to chatter away like him," pointing at the screen.

"Hey listen." This from Jonathan, still absorbed in the interview. They both turned back to the screen.

". . . so the new comet should provide a much more spectacular display than Halley. And then it will come back again every two years, more or less, until it's burnt out. Of course, we don't have details of the final orbit yet. We'll need to observe its first pass by the Sun before we can calculate that."

"Is that at all dangerous, Dr Cooper? We probably all remember the people who panicked, especially in California . . ." a chorus of boos and scattered applause rose briefly from the occupants of the bar ". . . when Halley came close by a few years back. Of course, nothing happened. But if a fragment of comet did hit the Earth, how much damage would it do?"

Cooper had been nodding sagely throughout the long question. He was as primed to answer it as Liz had been to ask it. The network toed the RN line when it was told to (after all, the RN controlled the satellites, and without the satellites there'd be no network), and Cooper was as eager as Ustinov to avoid any panic.

"There's absolutely no danger at all. From our point of view, it's rather convenient that Halley came by within living memory, because that showed everyone how harmless these encounters are.

"Of course, there have been impacts in the remote past. Some astronomers believe that the Earth got its original atmosphere that way, from cometary impacts when the Solar System was young. And there'll almost certainly be showers of meteorites associated with this one – shooting stars, that burn up high in the atmosphere. It'll be pretty spectacular, no doubt about that. But I'll be very surprised if anything at all gets through to the ground."

That ought to be firm enough, he thought. Kondratieff had been clear – none of your scientific ifs and buts, no talk of probabilities and odds against, be absolutely firm on the lack of any danger, and I'll get the Council to agree the mission. Cooper didn't know how it had been done, what favours Kondratieff had called in, or what arms he had twisted, and he didn't want to know. They were getting a real scientific space mission at last, for an opportunity that came not once in a human lifetime but once in the lifetime of a civilization. If David wanted a quid pro quo, that was fine by him. Besides, the odds on a collision were indeed very small. In the unlikely event the comet did hit the Earth there'd be nothing anyone could do about it, he rationalized, so there wouldn't be any point in panicking anyway.

"I guess you kids were too young to remember Halley's Comet." Ellison had seen enough of the show. It was obviously degenerating into the usual official line. Everything was fine with the world, the RN was doing a great job, nobody ever had to worry about anything. He needed a drink. At his gesture, the barman refilled his glass. "Everything fine with you, Bill? Not panicking about a giant comet wiping out your bar?"

"Well, I tell you frankly, Frank," the barman, who had been paying no attention to the broadcast, caught the bantering tone and replied in kind, "the only time you have to worry about anything is once it's been officially denied." And he moved on to attend to the needs of his other customers.

Jenny was less inclined to go along with Frank's mood.

"I may be younger than you, but I still remember Halley all right. It was one of the things that turned me on to astronomy. I wish I could be on that expedition. But I guess I'll have to make do with my trusty reflector."

"Have you seen it yet?" Jonathan was back fully in the conversation as the tube turned its attention to ice hockey, a sport he detested.

"Are you kidding? Two-metre mirrors, that's what they've got, on top of a damn great mountain. I'm stuck down here practically at sea level, with a 15-centimetre. I won't see it for months yet. Well, certainly not for a few weeks."

"Pity."

"Why?"

"Well, we could track it. I've got an orbital software package. Copied it from a hacker in Berkeley. He uses it for playing space war games, but it could be fun to try it out on the real thing."

"Would your machine be good enough?" Frank was intrigued. "They've got some pretty fancy equipment up in Reykjavik and you heard the guy saying they can't tell exactly where the comet's going to end up."

"Oh, sure. They need the big machines to do the detailed work. I'm not in their league." He glanced around, checking that nobody outside their group was in earshot. "But the 479's well up to hacking out a halfway decent orbit. If I had a bit more memory, it'd be almost as good as the computers they've got in those shuttles. But you can't get memory at any price these days. Even so, I reckon we'd beat any hacker in California on a simulation like this, if we had the data."

"Don't look at me." Jenny was attracted by the idea, in spite of herself. Jonathan's illegal computer setup wasn't exactly the crime of the century. He probably wouldn't even get arrested if the authorities found out about it, just have the gear confiscated – punishment enough for a dedicated freak like him. But it gave a certain frisson to their relationship, especially when he used the machine to calculate astronomical data for her. Would they confiscate her telescope too, for aiding and abetting the misdemeanour? It didn't bear thinking about. "You can get data somewhere else. Try your friend in Berkeley; they must know someone at Santa Cruz, and there's still an observing program running at Lick."

"Nah. Too risky – too many people. I just need one person, someone I can trust, with a neat little telescope and a rare talent for observation.

"Bill!" His sudden shout turned a few heads in the gathering early evening throng. "Another drink for the lady."

Frances Reese was a short, chunky woman with the square shoulders of a one-time swimmer. She was thirty-eight years old, and she was the most experienced shuttle pilot in the entire New Aeronautical and Space Administration. Which meant that she had a few more hours in space than any of the other eight qualified astronaut pilots still on the payroll. At the moment, she was extending her lead over the rest, floating in the *Sir Fred Hoyle* with the Earth two hundred miles above her, while a battery of instruments in the hold monitored the grainlands of the Ukraine. Anything had to be better than this, she told herself for the hundredth time. It hardly counted as spaceflight at all. Here she sat – well, floated – in a vehicle capable of travel beyond Mars orbit, provided she didn't want to land it anywhere. And all it was ever used for was near-Earth orbital work, monitoring crops for rust disease, or tsetse fly, or whatever was the agricultural flavour of the month. Sure it was important work. It helped keep people fed. But one of the original American shuttles could have done the job as well, back in the 1980s. Hell, the old FH itself had been as far as the Moon in its time, servicing Lagrange One. If those idiots hadn't been so careless, she'd be there now. That's what she was training for when the accident happened, reducing her career prospects to those of a glorified bus driver.

Now Kondratieff had come up with this crazy scheme, and somehow pulled the wool over the Council's eyes sufficiently to get them to agree – in principle. All they needed were the volunteers to fly their lunatic mission, and faith in the worn out machinery they were supposed to fly it in. But Kondratieff was a sly old fox. He knew he'd get his volunteers all right. Even if it was the last flight any of them made. Even if it finished off the fleet and left them with no more buses to drive. No human being had ever gone out beyond Mars, and the way things were going nobody else would ever have the chance. Ustinov and the Council probably meant well. They weren't evil people, just mindless bureaucrats. Anyone with half a brain could see that things were slowly coming apart, with each food crisis bringing the ultimate collapse a little closer. People had no spirit any more. They didn't even make the best use of what they had. What they needed was a fresh start, new incentives. She was sure of that. And she would have volunteered to fly the mission to Comet Osaki-Mori just for the hell of it. But now Kondratieff was pulling her into his web of intrigue. Everything had to be so complicated and underhand, and people were going to die as a result. It wasn't in her nature, and she didn't know if she could pull it off without arousing the suspicions of the other astronauts. *They weren't mindless bureaucrats, after all . . .*

It proved every bit as tough as she had expected. The surprise was how easily she had been able to persuade Bill Noyes, her acknowledged number two in the space pilot hierarchy – number one in the eyes of some of the male chauvinists still to be found in the Corps. Poor Bill; he knew something was up, but still trusted her enough to follow her lead. Always the English gentleman, he had been her friend and confidant, sometimes a shoulder to cry on, for more than ten years. He made no secret of the way he felt about her, yet he had never, since that night in '74, tried to persuade her to change the basis of their relationship. Sometimes she almost wished he had; she knew he'd wait forever, and that put her under no pressure to make a decision that might spoil what they already had. Or might lead to something better. But she hadn't really expected him to be so ready to fall in with her and

Kondratieff on the Dragon proposal. Maybe he really couldn't bear to have her so far away. One thing was sure. Without him, she might have been hard pushed to get the mission off the ground.

Jim Russell was the other big surprise, refusing point blank to contemplate the scheme, and recruiting a vociferous opposition to Kondratieff's plan.

"Sure, I'm a bus driver," he'd responded to her jibes. "What's wrong with that? The pay is good, the hours aren't too bad, and people look up to you. I didn't join the Corps to spread mankind's mission to the stars, or even Mars. I want to eat good and have a nice apartment. Look what happened to Lagrange. Too ambitious, and now nothing's left."

"So what happens when the comet hits, Jim?" Bill's quiet interjection had met with short shrift.

"Come on, Bill, you don't believe that crap any more than I do. The chance of a disaster must be less than one in a thousand. But whatever happens to the comet, if you go out there, we lose the shuttle fleet. Even if we all live to tell the tale, which I very much doubt, we end up with no buses to drive. And what does the RN do then? Gives us each a nice medal and sends us packing to join the benefit queues."

The debate raged for hours. Trained to be independent, selected for the ability to make their own decisions, the Astronaut Corps – all nine of them – were well able to descend into a glorified debating society if they so wished. The outcome was close. She'd wanted all nine on the mission; she got five, plus herself. That would have been only one pilot for each shuttle, if *Aries I* had been spaceworthy. But they were down to five shuttles anyway – one pilot each, and the Commander in reserve. Bill Noyes had the *Hoyle*; Mary Xu *Aries II*. The two Russians, Valentina Romanova and Mikhail Savchenko, were still arguing about who got *Discovery* and who got to drive a bus with a Russian name, *Predpriyatie*, since Chuck Wenzel refused to give up his beloved *Tsiolkovski*.

But with only five ships, it had been easy to find enough volunteers to fill up the few available places, once the pilots had selected themselves. Only a small proportion of the mission observers and scientists Reese and Kondratieff approached were willing to join the mission, but there were plenty for them to approach, and there was only accommodation for two of them, plus the pilot, in each shuttle on such a long journey. That made it all the more galling that Ustinov had wished this woman Blixen on them. Room for only fifteen people in all, and one of them had to be a useless parasite. The fact that Blixen was nominally in command of the expedition was so obviously a joke that it didn't rankle at all; Reese knew who the astronauts would turn to for orders, if they were willing to take orders from anyone at all.

Of course, Jan Du Toit, the big South African geologist, really counted as two people, in a Corps where to be small was usually an advantage. Maybe he'd make up for the presence of Blixen. The rest were just people, colleagues she'd worked with occasionally, or scientists she'd never really met before, but who came with Kondratieff's blessing. Bertorelli and Yuri Finnegan (whose name still caused mirth even in a society where, for the élite at least, marriages across national boundaries were far from rare); Perez and Wolf, strangers to her; Jackson, so quiet and self-effacing that she hardly knew him even though they had worked together many times; the astronomer Saha; and Anna Cherneva. Fourteen people, a political commissar, and five broken down shuttles to change the course of humanity. Sometimes, she thought, Jim Russell might have a point, after all.

# 3.

"Well, comrades, what do we make of this?" The grey haired woman at the head of the table waved a hardcopy printout of the Reuters "Dragontamers" newsflash. They all had copies before them, together with other data concerning the planned expedition.

"Has old Ironfist begun to crack up? Or is there some method in his madness?"

She looked directly at each of her companions in turn. This room was secure – this whole building was secure – but Susmann still licked his lips and glanced nervously about him, as if expecting a tap on the shoulder. She made a mental note. Whatever was happening to Ustinov, Susmann seemed to be unable to stand the pressure. He'd have to be watched – perhaps even eliminated. They'd come too far now to risk everything through sentimental attachment to even a founder member of the group.

"Of course there must be more to this story than we have been told." The silence was broken by a younger man, confident, self-assured even in the presence of his seniors. "Ustinov never plays less than a double hand at anything. The trick is to find out his real game, and turn it against him. This could be our great opportunity."

By which, she thought, Vassili clearly means his great opportunity. The opportunity to replace one *de facto* dictator by another wasn't exactly what she had in mind, nor, she hoped, what her colleagues in the Soviet had in mind. They were a small group, mostly Russians, all professing the original ideals of communism, including collective leadership. Of course, someone had to chair their meetings. It was natural that it should be her – she was older, more experienced than them. She knew the mistakes that had been made in the past, and how to avoid them. But Vassili had the impetuosity of youth. He was only forty-six after all. How much of his undoubtedly valuable contribution did they owe to his communist idealism, and how much to his desire for self-advancement? That was how the world had got into this mess, in the first place.

The leaders of the old Soviet Union had certainly been wise to agree to the constitution of the RN. At that time, they could never have defeated the capitalists. The Incident showed only too well what the results of military attempts to achieve world domination would be; and that was quite apart from the risks of nuclear winter, the prospect that even the victors in such a conflict would perish. No, the great successes of communism in the past had come from working within the system. You only had to look back to the way Lenin had achieved control of the party itself, and then to the way the party had taken over the government in old Russia following the revolutionary events of 1917. Now, there was a world government, in all but name, and with a little subtle manoeuvring they could take control of that too.

But Ustinov was no fool. He played the system with a mastery Lenin would have admired, and he limited his dabblings with democracy to levels of government well below his own. What did it really matter if the Georgians, or the English, or the Californians had elections from time to time? His real fondness was for power, in his own hands. By playing off factions within the Council against one another, he had achieved more power than any of them. None dared move against him, unless he made a mistake. Was this comet expedition the mistake they needed? If so, they had to be ready to seize the opportunity when it arose, before any of the other groups on the Council could organize themselves. A distraction would help . . .

"Vassili may well be correct. Ironfist may be overplaying his hand this time, whatever his motives. With so many resources devoted to this comet expedition, and so much publicity, any outcome that can be presented in a bad light will be a disaster for him, personally. Mikhail – " she pronounced the name Russian style, although the man she addressed had been born in Chicago, and actually christened, in a church, with the name Michael. He looked at her steadily.

"Yes, Comrade Chairman?"

"I would suggest to the committee that some attempt be made to encourage opposition to this expedition by extremist groups. Mikhail is our expert in such matters. Perhaps he has some ideas?"

"The Green Army? Of course, they're quite mad. But useful?"

"That's not enough." The red-haired woman sitting alongside Vassili broke in. " I don't say it isn't worth trying, but the Kouru base is sewn up tighter than a drum skin, and getting news out of that part of the world is always difficult. We need to make waves in North America, the old United States. That is where publicity can still hurt the old man. The Third World hardly counts, except for Kouru, and Europe will always do what it is told to do by Reykjavik. The only way to worry Ustinov is to make trouble in North America – somewhere like Washington, or California."

"There is a group – but no, it wouldn't be any use." Susmann had forgotten himself enough to begin to volunteer information, but quickly stopped, with an apologetic shrug.

"Come, Comrade, let us hear it. We will decide what is useful, together." He could be so infuriating. Frightened of a mouse these days, a real risk to all of them, and yet the information carried in his old head was worth preserving as long as possible – as long as he could be persuaded to part with it, of course.

"Well, my information is not so up to date as that of Comrade Mikhail. I no longer have such a position of eminence in the Bureau. But in California, and in Washington State, not the old capital, you understand, there are groups of people who carry the ideas of rugged individualism to extremes. At least, there were such groups, when last I heard. They are called 'survivalists.' I think they want civilization to collapse, and are just waiting until they can play their games for real. They were very disappointed when the Incident was contained and the RN removed the threat of nuclear war. But whether such groups are still active, well . . ." He gave the apologetic shrug again, smiled weakly, and looked down at his papers.

"There are still such people." Mikhail let his irritation with Susmann's bumbling show, annoyed with himself for letting the old man get in first with something he should have thought of himself. "They were involved in the local panic about Halley's Comet on the American West Coast. We had detailed reports on it; some even got on to the news. Laura is right, it is impossible to keep things out of the news in North America.

"Somehow they spread a story that the comet would strike the Earth. It's as Comrade Kiril says," he smiled at Susmann as he used his name, combining the implied friendship of the familiarity of the given name with the formality of the 'comrade', "they seemed to welcome the idea, and took no notice of the official predictions of the comet's orbit. They looked pretty silly after it had gone by, though, and I think they lost a lot of members. Only the hard core are left, and they've used up much of their resources, as well as their credibility. Hardly a force to be reckoned with."

"But, comrades." The woman at the head of the table was clearly in charge, whatever the lip service paid to collective responsibility. "Surely we are agreed that force is the least of our requirements. We need activity, activity that will embarrass Ustinov. A hard core of fanatics could be very useful to us, whatever the basis for their fanaticism. And the comet is coming back, even closer than before.

"You say these people have weapons?"

Mikhail nodded. "Old fashioned guns, rifles, pistols and so on. Simple mechanical items, that they expect to need when more complex technology breaks down. Not just for hunting, either. Their philosophy seems to be that they will need self-defence against marauding bands of starving city folk who try to follow them into the hills."

"Even better." Her mind was made up. "Armed gangs threatening to shoot innocent civilians. Hardly something the RN could ignore, and very embarrassing to the Secretary. Laura, you must find out just how close this comet will come next time, and perhaps adjust the figures slightly to suggest a genuine threat." It was noticeable that she dropped the formal 'comrade' when giving orders to her supposed equals. "If we feed these people a little information, perhaps some misinformation, we can get them more worked up than before. Ustinov is trying to make sure his name is associated with this damned comet, so we have to make sure the comet's name is associated with catastrophe. Then his name will stink by association. And since the comet isn't going to collide with the Earth, the catastrophe will have to be man-made." And preferably in North America, although there was no need to put that into words for her audience.

"Are we agreed?" She scarcely waited for the formal nods of assent. "Then we all have work to do. It would be unwise for all of us to meet together too often. I propose that each of you keeps in touch with me, and that I should coordinate our efforts to ensure that we do not miss the opportunity when Ironfist Ustinov stumbles." Once again, the nods were a formality. She sat back in her chair, satisfied, as they took their leave. It was not, of course, that she sought this burden of responsibility. But who else among the group was competent to act as coordinator?

The heat and humidity that brought the tropical jungle pressing up against the perimeter fence of Kouru Base played havoc with sensitive electronic equipment, while fungus grew in the fuel lines and bacteria munched away happily at plastics and at the fuel itself. Something had also been chewing away at the innards of Carl Hammond's infra-red nightsight, judging by the blurred image he was getting from his vantage point on the perimeter, squeezed between the jungle and the fence itself. In a way, that was a comfort. Ramon Torres had assured him that the surveillance equipment was more often out of action than it was effective, and that a temporary failure of this part of the circuit would neither arouse suspicion nor bring heavily armed guards rushing to the spot.

Ramon, of course, was always right, and he knew it. His supercilious air, immaculate dress and perfect command of what used to be called the Queen's English could have been calculated to make insignificant junior members of the team aware of their disposability. There are dozens like you, his whole attitude seemed to say, but only one of me. Go out on your mission, play your part in the forcible persuasion of the world bureaucracy that it must change its ways, and don't worry if you are caught and martyred. I can always find another peasant to do the dirty work. It only made it worse that the arrogant, impeccably dressed director of field operations, with his BBC holo presenter's voice, was, in fact, a peasant himself, while the field workers as often as not came, like Hammond, from privileged European or North American stock, equipped with degrees from prestigious universities. The bastard, thought Carl, rubbing the lens of his nightsight yet again and vainly trying to adjust the controls for a clear image of the launch site.

Abruptly, the buzzer sounded in his left ear. Three short notes. At least something was working properly. Returning the nightsight to the pouch on his belt, Carl swiftly cut through the lower strands of the fence, imagining his three compatriots doing the same at carefully spaced intervals on either side – assuming their receivers were working. Rain sleeting across from left to right helped to provide additional cover as he hefted the weighty pack and set off at a steady trot towards his objective, the fuel dump for the booster rockets used to hurl the shuttles into space. Fuel that ought to be used to drive tractors, or converted into fertilizers, being wasted on ego-boosting spectacular ventures into space, no good for anything except the self-glorying publicity of the Council. Fuel which, following the unique logic of Torres' group, would now be destroyed and used for no purpose at all.

The lights which suddenly blazed across the base were blinding to dark-adapted eyes. Hammond dived to the ground, burying his face in his arms. On either side of him, two other identical black clad figures did the same – the fourth member of the party was nowhere in sight, perhaps a victim of the equipment failures that had plagued the small team. A voice spoke in their ears, breaking in on their private communication link.

"Okay, the show's over. Get up and walk slowly forward, keeping your hands in plain sight and empty."

Obey, or run? Torres' instructions were clear. If caught, Hammond was to trigger the detonator in his backpack, going out in a blaze of glory and perhaps doing some damage to the base along the way. Well, Torres knew where he could stick his suicide switches. Carl was quite prepared to die for the cause, but he wanted to die fighting, or running, not by his own hand. He slipped the pack from his back, still undecided on his course of action. But the decision was taken for him, over the same communications link that had brought the soft buzzing of Torres' order to advance. Three closely spaced explosions inside the base were echoed by a lonely blast out on the perimeter fence, where the lagging member of the team met the same fate as his colleagues.

"I'm not sure I can go through with this, David."

"For God's sake, Frances, it's too late to back out now. We've been through everything a hundred times. It's all set up."

Kondratieff moved the glass in front of him to one side, and leaned forward, his elbows on the table, bringing his face as close as possible to Frances Reese in the small booth. The bar was neither overcrowded nor quiet; a carefully chosen time and place so that they would be inconspicuous, an anonymous part of the crowd, and not overheard. But, of course, if anyone they knew should happen to drop in, what could be more natural than to find the planner of the Dragon mission having a quiet drink, after a hard day in his office, with the Commander who would be in charge once the mission left the ground.

If the mission left the ground.

"Look. Everything's going really well. The old man doesn't suspect a thing, you've got your crews – okay, you didn't get everyone you wanted, but they're all competent astronauts – and three of the ships are ready in Earth orbit. A quick ferry job with the others, you'll be in space in a week, and after that nothing can touch you."

"What about Blixen?" Reese's hazel eyes frowned back at him across the table. Absently, she traced a pattern on its plastic surface with a finger dipped in the weak beer. "When you talked me into this, you never mentioned I'd have her on my back. And Roy, going off like that to the Cape Town job. I wanted him to pilot *Aries II*. Mary's OK, but she's no Roy. There's nobody I can talk to, apart from you, and once we're on our way . . ." Her voice trailed off and she sat, frowning at the beery doodle before her.

"It's only for a few days, Frances. Pick your moment to tell them, present it the way we planned, and they'll all be with you. These are all intelligent people. They're used to thinking for themselves. They're not dummies to jump when Ustinov shouts 'frog'. Let alone when Blixen gets on her high horse. Let's face it, you're just about the typical astronaut, only more successful than most."

"Because I'm better than most."

"Okay. I'm not denying it. Why do you think I got you into this? Because you're the best. But also because you're typical. If you see the logic behind the Dragon mission, so will the others. The only reason we can't tell them before you leave the ground is to make sure nobody outside the inner circle gets a whisper of what's going on."

"I'm still not sure. Everything made sense at the beginning, but the further down the line we get the less clear it seems. Ustinov's no fool, he must know you are hiding something. Yet he's poured an enormous effort into this project. Much more than we expected originally – you have to admit it."

Kondratieff nodded, and sipped his own drink.

Reese continued. "So what's in it for him? I mean, what does he see in it for him?"

"Publicity. Bread and bloody circuses. Don't you see, all the time you and the Dragon are on the holo screens there's no news about Africa, or the trouble in Greece, or anything else, for that matter. This whole system is falling apart about our ears. The old man thinks he can use you as a smokescreen while he patches up the damage and feathers his own nest. What he doesn't know is that we're going to shake the whole bloody system to bits. If this thing comes off, the world will never be the same again. And you've got to admit, anything will be a change for the better."

"'If', David? I thought it was 'when' this thing comes off." She smiled, faintly. Kondratieff reached across the table and took her hand.

"Sure, Frances, 'when'. And you'll be a hero long after they've forgotten all about me and the man up there." He nodded towards the back wall of the bar, in roughly the direction where, less than a mile away, First Secretary Ustinov was still in his own office, high in the RN building, even at this hour.

"Oh no, David." The smile was broader now. "No heroes; no heroics. If you understand us astronauts so well, you'd know better. We'll carry out your crazy scheme, if all goes well, but we won't be risking our own necks. Safety first, that's our code.

'I guess it's just pre-launch tension. I don't like the secrecy, and I don't understand all the politics, but after all that is your job, and you've never let me down yet. I don't even know that much about the situation in Greece and Africa, if the news is as heavily censored as you say it is. But I do know that the way things are going in NASA there'll be no space corps in another ten years, and that fits in with what you tell me about the rest. So, one big gamble for a better future for the world. If the team buy it. There's no way I could coerce them, you know, and no way that I'd try to. But either way, win or lose, we'll all be coming back. Whatever else falls out of the sky, you can be sure there'll be at least three shuttles and a full crew of astronauts, alive and well. There are no heroes in space, only careful astronauts and dead fools."

Kondratieff smiled back. For a minute he'd thought she might really be going to renege on him, even try to tell Ustinov what he had in mind. "What about Lagrange?"

"Especially Lagrange. They were all fools. You don't build a habitat on hope and a shoestring. You don't fly shuttles on hope and a shoestring. You do it properly or not at all. And that's why, I guess, I'm in this with you." She raised her glass, still with an inch or so of the beer she had been sipping for nearly twenty minutes. "Here's to us, David; and to the Dragon."

# 4.

## Dragon heads for rendezvous in space
## Reuters,
## Reykjavik

The comet is leaving us after a closest approach (perigee) to just within two million kilometres from Earth, RN Science Bureau announced today. Although never closer than five times the distance from the Earth to the Moon, this represents the closest encounter of our planet with another heavenly body ever recorded. Science adviser Dr David Kondratieff confirmed that the orbit had followed the path predicted by RN astronomers at La Palma, in the Canary Islands, to within five per cent. "We had every confidence in the calculations," he said, "but it's still a relief to have our confidence confirmed. Now everything is set for the rendezvous next spring."

That rendezvous will be with the spacecraft of the NASA Dragon team, named in honour of the comet, due to be launched in December on a month's long mission which will take them to a point in space near Mars orbit at the same time the comet arrives there, before beginning its fall back into the inner part of the Solar System. The object of the mission is both scientific and practical, Dr Kondratieff told reporters at a conference in Reykjavik. As well as seeking information about the origin of comets and the Solar System, the team headed by astronaut Frances Reese will be investigating the possibility of mining the comet for raw materials.

There was more, but Ellison didn't bother reading it. "See, lunkhead," he cried, stabbing a forefinger at the first paragraph, "two million kilometres. Call yourself a programmer? What did you tell us to expect? One and a half million, that's what you said. Had us all worried sick, Jenny packed and ready to head for the hills, and now we find you're half a million kilometres out. Useless, that's what you are." And he tossed the printout on the table.

"Hey, wait a minute." Feinberg's broad grin was in no way diminished by the assault. He took a sip from his beer, and stabbed a forefinger back at his friend. "I only said *no closer* than one and a half kilometres. Two million's bigger than one and a half million, right? Besides, what's half a million kilometres between friends, huh? I reckon we did a great job – best we could with the lousy data we had to work with."

"Lousy data!" Jenny threw a cushion at him. "I picked that thing up when it was scarcely past Jupiter, I track it for night after night, freezing my butt off when I could have been going to wild all-night parties in Burbank, and that's all the thanks I get. Lousy data, indeed!"

They were all delighted with the success of their amateur efforts. Frank Ellison seemed especially pleased, and had contributed the beer for the impromptu party.

"I knew you guys were good. But I have to say it, I didn't know you were that good. What do you do for an encore?"

Jonathan shrugged. "Find another problem. Dig up some memory, if I can. There's a guy over in Pasadena, who says he knows where I can get it. But I'd have to trade in the bike to cover it."

"It's easy for you." Some of the euphoria was fading from Jenny's expression. "Where do I find another problem half as much fun as that? Comets don't come by every year."

"That one does," Frank reminded her, "or at least, every couple of years. Until it runs out of steam."

"Yeah, but now we know where it's going. It runs to a timetable, and it'll be visible most of the time with the naked eye. Not much skill involved in predicting its path or seeing it."

"So what is the timetable?" Frank scrabbled among the papers for the story again. "Mars next May, right? Then back here six or seven months after that?"

"Not Mars, Frank. Mars orbit. Mars won't be there at the time, it's off round the other side of the Sun."

"No chance of a collision with Mars, then?" His jibe restored some of the humour of the occasion.

"Definitely no closer than one and a half million kilometres – if Jenny's data is any good." Jonathan smiled, and rolled off the couch on which he had been lounging. "I can soon tell you, if you really want to know. Put the latest distance from our friends the RN Science Bureau in, plus our own pathetic efforts from the last couple of nights," Jenny aimed a swift kick at him as he passed, "and we'll get Jenny's timetable printed up for her, so she won't have to go seeking the Dragon any more."

He walked over to what seemed to be the standard console of a holo projector, but which actually housed his pirate 479. The deception wouldn't fool anyone looking for the computer, but it stopped casual visitors asking too many questions.

"C'mon, Jenny, feed us the figures while Frank gets some more beers out of the fridge."

Frank took his time in the small kitchen, drinking his own beer and gazing out of the window while listening to the quiet voices and occasional muffled laughter from the other room. They were great kids. Jonathan seemed able to make almost anything electronic out of a bent pin and a piece of string – skills which enabled him to earn a fair living as an itinerant holo repair man, or Jack of any electrical trade, in spite of his unusual working schedule and fondness for long hours playing with computers. Jenny was much more conventional, a science teacher at the high school, but they seemed good for each other. He brought her out of herself, she helped to brake his wilder flights of fancy. And where did he come in? Nudging thirty and still acting like a student, hanging out with a crowd five or six years younger than himself, working when he had to but not if he didn't have to – and he'd have to find something soon, for the winter, to fund his backpacking plans for next spring.

If only he had the skills Jenny and Jonathan brought together. He'd never seen anything like the way they bounced ideas around, the precision of her painstaking observations, the almost casual way Jonathan took the data and chewed it up in that machine to produce a forecast the RN could only just better, with all their computing power. No wonder the government tried to keep toys like that to themselves. Jonathan could go far if he could manage to curb his wild streak, or if Jenny could do it for him. If there was some legal way to harness their combined talents, he ought to be able to make the three of them rich.

A louder peal of laughter brought him out of his reverie.

"Hey, where's the beer?"

He returned carrying three fresh, ice cold brews, but held them out of reach. "Not until I get the timetable. You've gotta work for a living round here."

"No use, then," Jenny giggled, lounging backwards, sitting on the floor with her hands behind her to support her upper body. "Whizz kid here can't hack it. Says he needs more data."

"Sad, but true." Jonathan reached for the beer, and Frank relented, letting him take one. "The beast goes too close to Venus, then we aren't quite sure how close it passes the Sun, and by the time we've followed the projection out to Mars – Mars *orbit* – " he corrected himself and Jenny smiled, "the errors have built up. It's downhill from there on in, but we don't know exactly where we're starting from."

"So you've still got a problem to solve. Can't take you off the case yet. That's cause for celebration." He handed Jenny her beer, and they toasted each other, silently. "So why the hysterics?"

Jenny carefully set her glass down on the floor. "It's this guy.

He ran the projection anyway. Said he was going to frighten you with it, but I talked some sense into him."

"Frighten me? How?"

Jonathan put on a serious air. "Well, Frank, I guess you really should be the first to know. It's much worse than last time. We've got a projected closest approach of within a half a million kilometres. It could be bad, very bad." He shook his head, and took another swig at his drink.

Jenny, equally mock solemn, spoke up again. "But tell him about the error margins, Jon."

"Oh yes." Jonathan's smile stretched across his face. "There is what we in the forecasting trade call a certain margin or error in that prediction. A little matter of plus or minus five million kilometres. You thought my last guess was bad, and it was. Thirty per cent error. I ought to be shot. But this time we've got a potential error of one thousand per cent. Don't even know which side of the Earth it's gonna pass, only that it comes by somewhere in a volume of space about a hundred times bigger than the Sun itself. Oh, lackaday!" And he buried his head in his hands.

"There, there." Jenny patted his shoulder. "You can always go back to mending holos." He groaned, pitifully, and covered his head entirely with his hands. "Or maybe we could keep tabs on the beast and try to do better next time." Jonathan raised his head, and nodded, eagerly.

Frank smiled. The game wasn't over yet, after all. If only there were some practical way he could get involved, instead of just sitting back and admiring it all.

From halfway to Mars orbit the Earth-Moon system made one of the most striking features of the Solar System – a double star with one component far brighter than Venus seen from Earth. And Frances Reese had all the time she wanted to admire the beauty of the view.

The tether connecting her to the *Hoyle* was just two hundred metres long, and it was fully extended. The shuttle itself looked like a child's toy, floating against the star-jewelled backdrop of the Universe. Half-hypnotized in her meditations, when she looked that way she felt as if she could reach out and grasp the spaceship, cradle it in her hands and carry it on personally to their destination. The comet itself, racing towards their rendezvous out past Mars, was invisible, lost in the glare of the Sun, where the automatic filters in her helmet would cut in and reduce visibility so that the stars vanished entirely, if she turned her head that way. But she could just pick out the sparks of light that represented the other craft in her tiny flotilla, spread out enough to minimize the risk of more than one of them being damaged in the unlikely event of a meteor strike, but comfortably within visual contact. A tiny flash of additional light, gone as quickly as it had started, showed where Valentina had briefly fired the attitude jets on the *Discovery*, undoubtedly changing its orientation in space to point the communications antenna more directly at one of the other craft.

They tended to "talk" to each other in pairs, one spacecraft to another, for hours at a time, playing chess or other games, swapping musical and holo recordings, or just chewing the fat. Then, when one pair of crews had run out of things to say to each other, there would be a mutual readjustment, with antennas being directed at new partners for a while. It helped to break up the boredom, and give them the illusion that something was changing in this eternal void.

After the hassles and hurly-burly of the weeks before launch, they had all welcomed the peace of space, at first. But now it was becoming too much of a good thing. Three people in each small shuttle, however carefully matched up to avoid known personality clashes, still drove each other to distraction at times. The privilege of being allowed to suit up and leave the shelter of the craft for a few minutes every "day" (the ships kept Reykjavik Standard Time) was one jealously guarded. Even though they all knew the risks from cosmic radiation, which limited their visits outside, any of the other fourteen members of the expedition would have gladly swapped their most treasured possessions – Valentina her flute, Yuri his collection of 1990s rock revival tapes, Jackson whatever it was he kept locked from view in his cubby (she suspected pornography, but didn't give a damn as long as it kept him happy) – for the Commander's prerogative of additional time on her own to think about her plans. Nobody begrudged her the additional solitude; they all knew how much they would need it if they carried the burden of command; but it was the one thing, out here, which almost made that burden look attractive. If only they knew just how big a burden she carried. Flying off as heroes to save the world – even as unsung heroes, since the world couldn't be told of the risk – was all very well. Playing political games and subterfuge, maintaining a facade twenty-four hours a day, was quite another. Without her solo time out here, she simply wouldn't be able to pretend much longer.

She held her hand up, occulting the double planet of the Earth-Moon system with her fingers. A line from one of Yuri's tapes ran through her head – something about a child's balloon, eclipsing both the Sun and Moon. Just like that, she thought, only it's my hand that's eclipsing both the Earth and Moon, and then it's as if the Earth doesn't exist at all. From out here, you can see just how vulnerable it is, just how much our home is at the mercy of astrophysical forces that could brush it aside the way a man might idly brush aside an annoying insect. Well, they were on their way, and nothing between here and Mars orbit was going to stop them. They'd got away in time, and if all went well at the rendezvous they'd have the fusion engines up and running in time to push the beast off its track.

All they needed, apart from the equipment they carried with them, was the regularly updated information from the computers on Earth about the orbit of the comet itself – information that would be absolutely crucial once they were pushing the comet sideways, changing its trajectory minutely with every hour that passed. The data link with Earth had to be maintained, and so she had to maintain this pretence, keeping to Kondratieff's cover story all the time.

It had to be worse for him, of course, stuck in Reykjavik and seeing Ustinov regularly on other business. He knew that all his plans would crumble if Ustinov got wind of the truth and cut off the supply of information to the Dragon team. But he would have to make sure Frances got the real figures, while pulling the wool over Ustinov's eyes with cooked up data, showing what the Secretary expected to see, for as long as he could. Poor old David. But still, he'd made his bed, and ought to be used to it by now. She doubted if she could ever get used to all these machinations – which was why, of course, she was an astronaut, not a politician. And certainly no hero. At least there was no personal risk to herself. The worst that could happen would be if Ustinov aborted the mission and she had to come home, chastened, to be grounded. David had made that clear – she could hear his voice echoing in her brain even now.

"So what if he does find out? I know what the consequences will be for me, and I'm prepared to take them. But he can't take any action against the heroic astronauts. There'll be too much personal prestige wrapped up in this venture. Whatever the outcome, Ustinov must present it as a personal triumph. And to do that he needs his heroes, especially the commander of the team, alive and well, smiling out of the cube at all the people. If the mision fails publicly, there are plenty of people on the Council ready to put the political knife into Ustinov's back. And old Ironfist is too clever by half to let that happen."

"No, Frances, you don't have to worry about yourself, or your team. Just take care of the job, and come home safely. Whatever the outcome, you're assured of a hero's welcome."

A hero's welcome. It was all so meaningless, from out here. What did she care whether Ustinov or Kondratieff won this little game of bluff? What did it really matter whether or not the comet, or part of it, struck the Earth? In a million years, would the Solar System, let alone the Universe, be any different as a result? Well, she was committed. She wouldn't change anything – she didn't really see how she could change anything now. And it might, it just might, all lead to an improved prospect for mankind. In which case, perhaps the Solar System really would show a difference in a million years from now.

Cheered by this line of thought, which she almost convinced herself was true, she chinned the send button on the small panel below her faceplate.

"Bill?" She knew Bill Noyes would be at the controls all the time she was out of the ship. "I'm coming in. Open the front door, will you?"

John Jackson, on watch in the control room of the *Predpriyatie*, monitored the brief message from Reese to her ship. There wasn't much else for him to do, since being on watch simply meant floating in the control room, observing the play of lights across the panels, ready to respond if any of them flashed red – and knowing full well that if any of them flashed red he'd probably be dead before he *could* respond. In this situation, either everything worked perfectly, or there was complete and utter disaster. Of course, a disaster was highly unlikely. Almost impossible, except for deliberate sabotage. But they went through the motions of watch keeping. Good for morale; good for discipline. Jackson actually quite approved of this. Discipline was important to him, always had been.

He didn't really approve of Commander Reese in other ways, though. He didn't approve of her being a woman, for a start. In his book, although women might make very good subordinates, and should certainly be allowed to do any work men did, they didn't make very good commanders. History bore him out. Look at the mess Sri Lanka, India and Britain had got into when they'd been foolish enough to elect women as their leaders, in the previous century. Women in command were too prone to think, when they should be acting on instinct; too careful about weighing up both sides to every question for so long that the answer was useless by the time they came out with it. At least the pilot of his own ship was a man – Mikhail Savchenko, still delighted at his petty triumph over Valentina Romanova, who had to make do with *Discovery*. Jackson wasn't sure that he approved of Mikhail's obvious delight at getting to drive the "bus" he wanted – but he certainly preferred having him as captain to a woman. Ironically, although neither Jackson nor Savchenko knew it, that was *exactly* why they were together now.

Reese knew Jackson's prejudices only too well, and had taken care to keep him away from both herself, Valentina and Mary Xu, for the long voyage across the Solar System. Jackson always followed orders, but somehow he did so more willingly, and with more obvious willingness, if they came from a man. The permutations she had been left with weren't much to choose from. *Tsiolkovski*, commanded by Chuck Wenzel, already had Jan Du Toit on board, and the big man had to be part of a three-member crew together with the tiny Perez, simply on grounds of his bulk. Mary Xu, Gerry Wolf and Bertorelli made a happy team on *Aries II*, and had worked together before; Bill and herself had to put up with Maria Blixen, or, Frances was sure, someone would murder her. So there wasn't much choice left. Jackson went to *Predpriyatie*, and Mikhail went with him, along with Saha. And Valentina at least had two other Russian speakers with her, Anna Cherneva and

Yuri Finnegan, to make up for the English name of her ship, *Discovery*.

Frances Reese had not wanted any trouble, and she had known the risks they would face during the boring phase of their journey, risks from within themselves, rather than from outside agencies; the Devil making work for idle hands. She wasn't worried about after the rendezvous. They'd all be working together then, too busy to bother with petty personality clashes, and free to mix off duty with whoever they chose. No, it was the coasting phase of the journey that posed the real risks of that kind.

Jackson extended his right hand and punched a button on the display.

"Log Commander Reese returning to *Hoyle* at," he glanced at the digital display flicking by on the main board, "17:47, RST."

A sure sign of female weakness, he thought to himself. Indulging herself with additional spacewalks. Thirty minutes each, in each twenty-four hour period. That was what the regulations said. But she went out twice a day, and sometimes stayed for forty or fifty minutes. Sure, he knew about the responsibilities and privileges of command. But if he was in charge, he'd play it by the book, let everyone see that he was one of the team, not someone who indulged himself. Well, they were halfway. He'd be interested to see how her leadership stood up to a real test, when they got to the comet and had some real work to do, against a tough deadline.

"So, Mikhail, just the two of us, together, eh?"

She was stating the obvious, but wanted to leave him in no doubt that it was her idea that they should meet face to face, with no other members of the group present. In truth, it made sense.

It was simply too dangerous to bring them all together too often, with Ironfist so watchful, and there was no need for everyone to be burdened with information that only she required. Of course, if would be easier if they could meet a little more readily . . . she squashed the errant thought, firmly. Best not even to think in such defeatist fashion; and essential not to let Mikhail, or any of the others, begin to think she wasn't completely in control of their plans. This business with the comet was going to be decisive, one way or another. It had to be her way.

Mikhail, ignorant of the turmoil in her brain, began to reply. "Yes, Comrade Chair – "

"Just 'comrade'," she smiled, "I think that will be sufficient. Now, what have you got for me?"

"Mixed news." He closed his eyes briefly in thought, obviously summoning all his facts in orderly fashion before speaking. She approved. Haste was seldom wise. Progress came through cautious, careful planning and small steps forward on to tried and tested ground.

"Old Susmann has been dreaming of the past, I fear. There is no organized group in California, just a rabble. But I have established contact, through a third party, with a band of these survivalists near Los Angeles. They have been informed – of course, you do not want the details, but they seem to be eager to believe the information, whatever its source – they have been informed that there is a real risk of this comet striking the Earth. In exchange for a promise of protection when the time comes, my agent has agreed to supply them with some modern equipment, for 'self-defence'."

He shrugged. "The agent does not believe they would keep to their bargain. Their idea of self-defence seems to have a lot in common with Adolf Hitler's. They will certainly cause some trouble with their new toys, perhaps they'll rob a bank or something, but I doubt if it will fit your needs. Even so, we have a useful channel for feeding information to these people, and influencing the sub-culture through them. As long as our man is feeding them equipment, they will find him valuable, and the more they find him valuable the more likely they are to believe his words and act on his advice."

"And *your* man?" The slight emphasis distanced herself from the operation. "What does he believe?"

Mikhail smiled. "But of course, comrade, he is acting under the direct orders of the full Council. His instructions come from the office of Ironfist himself – or so he believes."

"Well, it's not all bad news then."

"Far from it, comrade. The rest is better. More dangerous, perhaps, but better." He paused once more, marshalling his thoughts.

"There is a useful group of Green Army bandits in place near Kouru. The leader, Ramon Torres, is efficient, and dangerous. We can use him, but afterwards . . ."

She nodded, signifying understanding of the implication. Once Torres had outlived his usefulness, he would have to be liquidated.

"Torres is eager to carry out an attack on the shuttle craft at Kouru, the one being readied for the Moon mission. He lost several men in an attack on the Dragon team, and insists that this last shuttle must be hit. It is a pointless exercise, but there are ways in which he could he helped. The security systems are good, but not so effective if they are switched off from the inside. So, if I can help Torres in this small way, he would lend us his support for another mission.

"He even has an outline plan. According to Torres, the deep space tracking station in Australia is unprotected. The Green Army has not been active there. If we provide transport, he will do the rest. And without that link, the Dragon mission will be cut off from Earth for half of every day."

"Useful." It was her turn to sit for a moment, deep in thought. "Not a major blow, but useful. Embarrassing to Ironfist, even if there is no more to this Dragon mission than meets the eye. More than embarrassing, perhaps, if there is some deeper plan. He will have to make alternative arrangements, change his plans in a hurry. And when plans are changed in a hurry, new opportunities arise. Yes, useful. I approve."

The meeting was at an end.

# 5.

Ben Kingston was big, black and a man. He was used to women – especially tribal women – doing what he told them. But this tall, calm woman was different. Hell, she wasn't the village chief – she wasn't even the daughter of the chief. Her name, Hadel Bukumbi, wasn't even on the list of important people that Nairobi had given him, people he had to sweeten up to ensure that the resettlement project went smoothly. Yet here she was, the biggest fly in the ointment, not only refusing to move but seemingly in complete authority over the other villagers, who backed her to the hilt. The men were useless – the village elders that had supposedly been fixed up with all the right bribes to make them bend to any suggestion from the aid headquarters simply sat back, with a shrug, and let her get on with it. It wasn't natural. Yet, he had to admit, she carried her authority well, like a real chief, not like the Nairobi lackeys he dealt with in most of the villages.

Damn the woman! Damn Nairobi! Why couldn't they give him better information? He leaned against the side of the All Terrain Vehicle, took the broad-brimmed hat from his head and wiped the sweat from his face with a large handkerchief.

"Are you hot, Mr Kingston?" There was no trace of sweat on her elegant body, wrapped in a traditional length of printed cotton. "Perhaps you would like to sit in the shade of my hut, where we can offer you some cool refreshment?"

She was playing with him, demonstrating her superiority.

"Thank you, uh, Miss, Mizz," he stumbled over the form of address. She couldn't be married, no village man would let his wife behave like this; her manners and language suggested that he treat her like a European, but her clothes and appearance suggested she was just a village woman. He stumbled on. "Uh, Bukumbi. I would like to, but I'll have to report back to Nairobi in person. The ATV will get me there, but it isn't the quickest way to travel. I'll have to start soon."

"I'm so sorry that we have caused you so much personal inconvenience, Mr Kingston." Were the cool eyes mocking him? "But as you see, we are quite happy here. We have no wish to move to the south."

"But you don't understand." He tried again, desperately, to make the position clear. "Everyone from this region has to move. The scientists in Nairobi and in Reykjavik," she seemed unimpressed, but he continued, "tell us that the change in the rainfall is permanent. It will not be possible to grow the crops we need here any more."

"Maybe there is no prospect of growing the crops Nairobi needs, Mr Kingston. I'm sure the scientists are right," a slight movement of her right hand stifled his attempts to break in, "I met many scientists during my time at the University of Cambridge." Damn and double damn! She was not only mocking him, but also probably better educated than anyone in his department. "No doubt they are correct in their assessment of the climatic shift. But, as you see, we seem to be able to manage well enough to grow our own food, even in these troubled times. I have already explained to you. We do not wish to participate in the present cash economy which you people from Nairobi find so desirable, for your own good reasons. We ask nothing from you, except that you leave us alone, to live in the way of our ancestors. And I think you will find that there are other villages nearby that feel much the same."

That was all he needed. A revolution, with a prophetess already spreading her sedition far and wide. Maybe he could get her arrested – but no, the thought dismissed itself as soon as it appeared in his mind. Even if they found some trumped up charge, it would only make a martyr out of her. Well, he'd tried to talk sense to her. They'd all just have to take the consequences. If necessary, he was sure, Nairobi would authorize forcible resettlement, and stifle this nonsense about giving up money and going back to self-sufficiency in the bud. They'd never allow such independence among the villages, not as long as the full weight of the RN was in place to back them up.

"This is what you oughta go for, Frank." The big, blond bearded man reached into the case, like a conjuror pulling a rabbit from a hat, and hefted a short, business-like weapon with a stubby magazine jutting out in front of his fist. It had obviously been looked after – it looked new, in mint condition. It wasn't what Frank was interested in, but he obligingly rose to the bait.

"What is it?"

"AP 31. Two kay plastic slivers in there," he patted the magazine, "and it'll spit them all out in a minute."

Even allowing for Rick's tendency to exaggerate, that sounded pretty impressive – and lethal. No wonder his group kept the gear hidden away in this cave in the mountains. Frank had enjoyed the hike, but suddenly he felt a cold sweat down his spine. Christ. He hoped they hadn't been followed. If the authorities knew about this, he'd be inside with Rick and the others for a long, long time.

Rick laughed. "C'mon, feel how light it is. It won't bite. And there's no cops lurking in the woods to see you."

Cautiously, Frank took the proferred weapon. With the strap over his right shoulder, it nestled easily against his side, snub nose pointing out. You could wipe out an army with a couple of these, he thought. Unless they were equally well equipped, of course.

He smiled at Rick. Better keep in with these guys. "Pretty neat, Rick. But a bit hyper for hunting."

Rick beamed back, and reached for the gun. "Depends what you're hunting, Frank. When the crunch comes, the most dangerous animal around is gonna be the two-legged kind – and I don't mean bear. Know what I mean? Hunting rifle's okay for getting meat; we've got plenty of those. But this is a pretty nice valley here; gonna be plenty of folk eager to push us out, and we're not gonna let them.

"Think about it. The offer's still open. We'll be glad to have you on board. Few enough people around with your survival skills, God knows. But the rest – they can go to Hell. Except for the girls, of course." He laughed again, and Frank responded, thinking, these guys are even crazier than I gave them credit. But he had to keep them sweet. If they thought for one minute he wasn't on their side, after they'd taken him this far into their confidence . . .

"Thanks, but no thanks. I wouldn't know what to do with one of those. All I want is some computer gear, for the kids. Hell, I bet you never get a chance to use that stuff, anyway."

Rick shrugged. "Suit yourself, ol' buddy. There's a metal box full of computer stuff in back of the cave. Take your pick – no charge."

Frank looked up, startled. He'd come prepared to bargain hard.

"No charge. Just a promise. An understanding. You'd better make the most of this gear while you can, 'cos I reckon time may be shorter'n you think. When it happens, well, just remember who your buddies are, that's all. I ain't one to ask favours, but I could use you, up here. With a hunting rifle if you like, one of these," he patted the AP 31 affectionately, "if it comes to it.

"This computer stuff's just junk, anyhow. No use in the real world. You use it to sweeten up that kid Feinberg, and while he's busy see if you can't make a little time with that girl Jenny." He laughed again, unpleasantly. "Some of the guys think you're crazy, running errands for the wimp. But I say crazy like a fox, huh?" Rick tapped the side of his nose with his index finger. "Get it on if you can, buddy. She'd be welcome up here, too – but not him." The smile was now more of a leer.

Frank was too startled to protest at the innuendo. Hell, it was obvious to any right-thinking person that he didn't feel that way about Jenny. Even if he did, he wouldn't act like that. But the other stuff. What was Rick getting at?

"But why do you think . . ." he trailed off.

"I've got my contacts. This stuff," he waved the AP 31 round, indicating several other cases similar to the one the gun had been pulled from, "it don't grow on trees, you know. The word's out. Few months, year maybe, there's gonna be some big changes around here. You got survival skills, a young chick in tow, you'll be welcome in the valley. But no computer-hacking wimps and pansy office boys. You hear?"

Jesus Christ, thought Frank. The man's serious. What the Hell is going on? Better get the gear and head back on down the trail, as soon as I can get away without making these crazies think I'm a police informer . . .

Feinberg rubbed his red, itching eyes in his hands and leaned back in his swivel chair. There was an ache in the small of his back, and across his shoulders, from the hours he had spent bent over the console of the 479, lost in his, and the computer's, private world. His left leg was numb. With both hands cupped behind his head, he leaned back as far as he could, trying to stretch the kinks out of his muscles. What time was it?

His left forefinger stabbed at the panel before him, touching an icon which carried the image of an hour glass. Obediently, in the top left corner of the cube a digital display appeared, flicking off the seconds. It was 3:47 am. Time, Feinberg told himself, for a beer.

Standing and turning towards the kitchen, he stumbled as the weight came on to his numb left leg, and pins and needles sensations shot through it. Leaning against the wall for support, he noticed for the first time that the room was dark. He'd been hacking since dusk the previous evening; no wonder his muscles were cramped. But it was worth it, getting the improved system on line and testing it out.

His loud command "Lights!" was followed by a sudden brightening of the room, and an even louder shout of "Dim!" as his eyes reacted to the glare. After images flashing before him, he made his way to the kitchen and the beer.

Who would have thought Frank, of all people, could have located the extra memory for him. He'd never regarded Frank as one of life's achievers. A nice guy, sure, good for a laugh, a drinking companion; and always a good audience, willing to listen to him explaining his latest toys. But he never seemed to work at anything, except his hiking expeditions in the hills. Ironic, really, but logical when you thought it through. Some of those weekend backwoodsmen were far more serious than Frank about the business, and went in for their hobby in a big way. Jonathan had known, vaguely, about the survivalists. He remembered from his childhood, and the stories his father told him later, about the crazies who made for the mountains when Halley had come around, convinced that civilization was going to end in a major disaster, and that they would rule the roost, what was left of it, afterwards. They even had their own bible, a work of twentieth-century science fiction, which described a post-holocaust world, and which they took as their gospel. What was it, *On The Beach*? *The Hammer of God*? Something like that. He couldn't remember now, he was too tired. But he'd never been a great one for reading fiction, himself.

You needed plenty of equipment to survive the fall of civilization. Food, clothing, weapons – all the groups had caches of those all right. Even AVRs. But only the smarter, and wealthier, of the original ones had gone in for technological toys that might still be useful in a post-technological era. Solar powered satellite communications gear, in case some of the comsats were still functioning when the smoke cleared; and even computer equipment, old pre-Incident stuff, never registered and never picked up by the authorities, but still useful. Some of it was beautiful quality, for its age – portable military equipment. It had been tucked away in a bunker in the mountains, shielded from the electromagnetic pulse, of course, in sealed metal containers, perfect protection against the EMP, but only practicable for a computer in storage, not being used. Anything up and running had to be unshielded, by definition, so information could get in and out. So it was all the working computers, and the home installations standing unshielded on desk tops around the technological world, that had been wiped out.

According to Frank, there was a lot of stuff around. The weekend survival freaks wouldn't part with a gun, or even a decent hunting knife, for love nor money; but it seemed they didn't think an old portable computer was much good for anything.

Not much good – hah! He'd show them this time, all right. Just wait until Jenny and Frank got a load of this. Beer in hand, Feinberg made his way back to the console. It had been the Devil's own job getting the obsolete units matched up to the 479, and as usual whenever you changed the configuration of a computer you had trouble with the programs that used the new systems to the full. It ought to be okay now, though. He'd get that uncertainty down below five per cent before the night was out, especially now that the comet was round the Sun and heading back out to Mars – "Mars orbit," he heard Jenny's imagined voice chiding, and raised his beer in salutation.

He had the parameters set up, with Jenny's latest data. The display still showed the digital clock, flicking seconds away steadily, in one corner of the cube. Through the middle ran a curving bar of solid white, the Earth's orbit, with a fainter red line, marking the orbit of Mars, high and to the right. Between the two, a blue line reached out from stage left, the direction to the Sun, and curved out to Mars orbit before bending sharply back in to cross the white bar. Figures – dates and distances – glowed at intervals along all three lines when Feinberg prodded another of the icons on his display board. He doubted if Secretary Ustinov himself had a better display, although he knew that the figures coming out of the RN computers would still be that tantalizing bit better than his own. But it was going to be bloody close.

He swigged the beer, and sat down, hunched forward and staring at the display with widening eyes. For more than seven hours he'd been working on the system, deep in an abstract problem combining his electronic and programming skills. Now everything was working, and it was only as he came out of his coccoon that he began to realize the implications. At first, all he'd cared about was getting the thing to work; then, to beat the efficiency of his previous orbital projections. Pride in the beauty of the display also made possible by the additional memory followed quickly on the heels of pride that the new combined system worked at all. But now he was beginning to realize, with the part of his brain that worked like those of most human beings, just what it was the display was telling him.

Holy shit. It really was close. His best projection gave the comet passing within a third of a million kilometres from the Earth – scarcely any further away than the Moon. And his margin for error was just under a million kilometres, assuming he had hacked the thing properly. The width of the blue line varied to represent the uncertainty in the calculations, a trick he was especially proud of. It was a thin line out at Mars orbit, growing discernibly fatter as it neared the projected position of the Earth. Just fat enough, indeed, to swallow up the planet. Christ. It really could be on a collision course. The news bulletins hadn't said anything about that. In fact, come to think of it, they hadn't said much about the comet at all these past few weeks. But it was definitely coming back closer than before. He leaned back in the chair, feeling the tiredness creep over him as the beer helped him come down off his programming high. Closer than before. That *would* be spectacular. Wonder what Frank's freaky survivalist friends would make of that! Have to call him, and Linda, first thing in the morning.

His head was dropping to his chest, and his eyelids drooping. With an effort, Feinberg roused himself enough to make it to the couch, where, not for the first time after such a session, he fell into a dreamless sleep. While he slept, the soft glow of the red, white and blue lines continued to trace the intercepting orbits, while the flicking figures in the corner of the display marked the steady march of time.

# 6.

She floated into the gloom of the control room and found Bill Noyes at the console. *Still* at the console! Six and a half hours before, when Reese had headed for the seclusion of her own cabin, he had occupied precisely the same position. Had he left the room to eat, drink or perform any of the other bodily functions most people found necessary? How many sleep shifts had he foregone, she wondered idly, while he played with that damned radar echo-sounder. Well, he'd fought so hard to get the thing installed on the *Hoyle*; no doubt he felt he had to justify it, somehow.

*Science*, she thought despairingly. It was the last thing she wanted any of her crew preoccupied with now, of all times. So close to the first crucial test of the mission, the rendezvous phase, she felt the weight of command heavy on her shoulders. Reese was suffering from a plague of what-ifs: What if the dust bombardment close to the comet proved so intense they couldn't "land"? What if the comet turned out to be so fragile they couldn't de-spin it without the ice breaking up? What if the crust was too soft for the shuttles to anchor? What if . . . She peered over Noyes' shoulder, not really interested in what he was up to.

"Bill!" she exclaimed. "Computer time's at a premium right now."

His head jerked in surprise. "Hey! Don't creep up on me like that!"

She ignored his protest. "That fancy graphics stuff uses a lot of memory, Bill. And it's hardly essential to the mission."

"I know, I know." He pushed at the control panel, swivelling the seat he was strapped into in the zero-G, and rubbed at his puffy, sleep-starved eyes. "I'm only using spare capacity," he assured her, shrugging his shoulders rhythmically to ease the stiffness in his neck. "I promise I won't interrupt any of the ship's programs. Check for yourself."

"I believe you." At least she had his attention. "Okay," she settled into the seat beside him, and secured herself loosely with a lap strap, "what've you got there?"

The holo display portrayed what looked like a 3-D colour image of a lopsided onion. At least, the central region looked like an onion. Further out, the image lost definition and trailed off to one side.

"It's the halo – the coma, viewed through radio eyes." Bill's pride showed in his voice, in spite of his tiredness. "We're inside the coma, of course, so you don't see it all. The image covers about – oh, a hundred thousand klicks."

"And it all comes from echo data?"

"That's right." The pride showed signs of turning to smugness. Nobody in the Dragon team, except Noyes, had ever expected the thing to work. He obviously expected praise, but Reese wasn't feeling charitable today. She kept tight-lipped. Noyes, scarcely chastened, continued.

"It's all around ten megs. So we get a resonance even in this thin stuff. The colours represent different ion densities. Close in," he gestured, "where it's high density, white; further out, the red . . ."

"Yes, low density. I've got the picture. Hardly a world-shattering discovery though, is it?"

"You did ask."

"Sorry." Perhaps she *was* riding him too hard. "Go on."

"So, we're inside the coma, and coming up from behind. See the knots and streamers." He fiddled with the controls, and a portion of the image enlarged, blurrily. She noticed the irregularities for the first time.

"Small density inhomogeneities, caused by interactions with the solar wind. Lucky to resolve anything that small, with this crude instrument. But this stuff," he shifted the focus again, "this is really interesting, up the front . . ."

"The bright line?"

"Yeah. It's the bow shock – where the solar wind slams into the coma."

"So?"

"Ah, it doesn't look much in real time. But watch this – a little movie I've made up."

"A movie? I thought you didn't use much computer time?"

"Ah, hell, it's only a *little* movie. Twelve hours compressed into a minute."

She frowned, but the image had already changed. The bow shock was moving, waving rhythmically in and out.

"See how the changes in the solar wind press the coma down towards the comet and then let it out again. I can get minute by minute data out of this – the astronomers back in Iceland'll wet themselves when I send it all back!"

"And what use is it?"

"C'mon, boss." He smiled. "What use is a new-born baby? Damned if I know what they'll do with it, but that's the beauty of pure research. You just do it, then somebody does something with it – something unexpected. Okay, we're here for a practical reason. But the opportunity may never come again. We've got to get *some* science out of the mission."

If only you knew, she thought. Even Bill, if he knew her real plans, would have trouble thinking about anything else, let alone abstract science. She held up a hand, defensively. "Skip the sales pitch. It succeeded, you got the echo-sounder. I'll let you play with it. Within reason. But I just can't afford distractions. We've all got to be single-minded about the main objectives of this mission. No point in getting the scientific research done if this thing," she gestured at the display, "drops in the wrong place. Have your fun, within reason. But get your rest, and keep your mind on the proper job. Understood?"

"Understood. The minute my ... hobby ... begins to interfere with my duties, you can eject me from the airlock, in my underwear ..."

"Don't think I wouldn't!" She smiled. How important he was to her, she thought, and to the mission. If she didn't have just one person she could talk with, comfortably, as an equal, she'd crack up. That was the real trouble with the bloody echo-sounder; it gobbled up his spare time and left her without a shoulder to cry on. Oh well. If she showed a bit more interest, maybe he'd be more approachable.

"Where's the nucleus?"

He shook his head. "We're still too far out to see it. Wait till we're close in."

"Which means?"

"A thousand klicks. Maybe two."

"So even with your toy we're blind till then?"

"Well, of course, we know where it is."

"But I'd like to catch a glimpse of it, just to see what we're up against."

"Sure, Frances."

Was he humouring her? Oh well.

"What a sight. The nucleus itself, waiting since the Solar System formed, and us the first ever to set eyes on it."

"Don't get carried away, Bill. It's just a snowball. I don't care where it came from. What I need is information – mass, angular momentum, trajectory. Enough to kill its spin and shift it sideways. Then home."

She released the strap, and pushed herself out of the seat.

"Look, I'm off to the galley. Breakfast. Want some?"

"No, thanks."

"Then make sure you're in your cabin, asleep, when I get back."

"Aye, aye, cap'n."

But he wasn't. Half an hour later, when she returned, fed and refreshed, he was still there. Mary Xu had joined him.

"For God's sake, Bill!" Her good humour began to evaporate.

"Listen to this!" Ignoring her tone, he whipped off the headphones he was wearing and pushed them her way. Like a big kid, she thought. Well, enthusiasm was good for morale.

She grabbed the floating headphones and pushed one earpiece against her ear. A faint crackle was all she could hear.

"Put it on the speakers."

He did. The crackle filled the control room, getting louder as he fiddled with the controls.

"Rain!" said Mary.

"Sounds more like an automatic gun to me. What is it, Bill?"

"Dust! Comet dust hitting the detector."

"How big?"

"Oh, anything up to a thousandth the mass of a sand grain."

"That small?"

"Mary, that's big! Huge! If one of those little buggers hits us at fifty kps it'll go clean through the outer hull."

"And the inner?"

"Probably. But don't worry. We're matching velocities, not making a flyby. But that's not the point. What do you think of it?" He waved at the speakers.

"What?"

"Actually 'hearing' it. Cosmic rain. I mean, it's one thing getting all the data on readouts and stuff, but this is real – well, sort of. More romantic."

"Romance, Bill?"

"Well, you know. Who cares if a light flashes on an array, or the computer tells us what's going on? Sometimes I envy astronomers from the old days, before they had computers and CCDs and all the rest. Actually looking through telescopes with their own eyes – even making drawings of what they could

73

see, not photographs. The electronics kind of gets in the way, sometimes."

"I see what you mean." Mary looked thoughtful, struggling with the concept. Frances smiled. Bill would never get the concept across to Mary Xu, the pragmatist. Bill, Bill, she thought. You dreamer. I know you better than you think. That damned radar echo-sounder is no use to man nor beast, but I know why you fought so hard for it.

How many people can you know in a lifetime? Really know? One, two . . . maybe half a dozen, if you're really lucky. The thought suddenly struck home to her, with an almost painful clarity. Bill Noyes, she told herself, I know just what makes you tick.

"Ingeborg."

"Sir?"

"No calls for the next hour. I've cancelled the meeting with the Kenyan delegation. Tell Security I want no one to enter this wing for the time being."

"Yes, sir."

Secretary Ustinov sat at the holo console, his fingers flicking expertly over the controls in a well-rehearsed pattern. The thin red line of the comet's projected orbit pierced through the entwined green and blue strands of the Earth-Moon double orbit, just as Kondratieff had set up the simulation. But everyone in the civilized world knew, of course, how to adjust a holo program to show different variations on the programmed theme. A standard holo wasn't a proper computer, just a display unit for pre-recorded, or broadcast data; Ustinov's display was different in that it connected directly to the mainframe machine in the basement of the RN headquarters building. But the controls were essentially the same as those he, like everyone else, had grown up with. It was easier to make the consoles suit the user's habits than to train every user in the ways of each new piece of computer gimmickry, whether hardware or software. Especially when nobody got their hands on such computing power without a high security clearance, something only achieved after a lifetime of forming habits, of one kind or another.

Always explore the alternative options; never commit yourself irrevocably to one line of action. Ustinov had his own habits, and a dozen times in his long career he had confounded his opponents by means of a carefully secured line of retreat; this comet business was too big to leave to chance, or to the plans of others. He had to check out possibilities that Kondratieff had neglected to tell him about, perhaps even possibilities that Kondratieff had not yet perceived for himself.

A tiny adjustment to the orbit, and the simulated comet passed by outside the entwined blue and green strands. A tiny adjustment the other way, and the red line precisely met the Earth's twisting green line. Once the fusion engines from the shuttles were in place, using the comet's own raw material as reaction mass, it would be as easy for the astronauts to deflect the orbit one way as it would to shift it the other – or, Ustinov corrected himself, not easy, just no more difficult to do one than the other. What had Kondratieff said? "A few minutes later, and the sliver of comet that caused the Tunguska explosion would have destroyed Leningrad." He'd looked it up. Lenin himself had been in St Petersburg, as it then was, in 1906. Who could guess how world history might have been changed if such an impact had taken place? How big a sliver of comet would it take to destroy Iceland? Would Kondratieff be crazy enough to plan assassination by remote control, not only killing the First Secretary himself but wiping out the seat of World Government at a stroke? The thought was ludicrous. The result would be anarchy; chaos. The astronauts would never agree to that; their whole lives revolved around government patronage, high technology and their secure roles as members of an élite. If they dropped a sliver of comet on Iceland, all that would vanish overnight.

He knew the woman, Frances Reese, vaguely. And of course, he had had a thorough check carried out since he gave the mission the go ahead. She was totally apolitical. A career astronaut, reliable, neither for nor against the system, as long as it kept her flying in space from time to time. Whatever Kondratieff had planned, he was staying here on the ground – in Iceland, Ustinov decided; he would see to that. Reese was in charge of the expedition, and she would never endanger her career. After all, the atomic engines of the spacecraft, essential to do the job of pushing the dirty snowball around, could always be adjusted to a rather different task. It never failed to amaze and delight Ustinov how easy it was to find would-be martyrs, ready and eager to give their lives for a cause. Most of them didn't much care which cause, but after the RN's psychology section had finished with them they were almost indecently eager to immolate themselves at his behest.

Of course, Reese and Kondratieff had had a completely free hand in choosing all the crew members, except Maria Blixen, from the pool of qualified personnel. But, given the limited number of volunteers and the balance of skills required, their final choice had been largely predictable. Some of the waverers, who might have volunteered and thus made the choice slightly less predictable, had all, curiously enough, recently, and separately, been given incentives to stay on Earth. One had been offered a promotion into a ground job he had been after for some time; another had a son who was suddenly taken ill, so that she was rushed to his bedside. It is easy to arrange such things when you have absolute control of an efficient bureaucracy, and there was no common thread by which even the most suspicious observer might link these events, and several others that happened about the same time.

As First Secretary Ustinov knew well, there are two ways to establish an agent in place, openly or otherwise. He had told Kondratieff that Blixen would be his representative on the mission, and he had left the rest of the choice up to him; but, as it happened, without any direct pressure being applied, one of those chosen owed loyalty not to the Corps, or to the New ASA, but to the First Secretary himself. How convenient – for Ustinov.

Maybe he'd be better off without a space corps, anyway. The thought was a new one, and the First Secretary examined it carefully. One less drain on limited resources; a dozen or so newly martyred heroes to inspire the workers of the world to greater efforts.

But, of course, Kondratieff might be telling the truth. The astronomers all agreed that the scenario he described was possible, although they disagreed on how probable it was. Scientists never seemed to agree on anything that really mattered. "We deal only in probabilities, First Secretary. Nothing is certain in the world of science." Hah! Ask them if the Sun was going to rise in the East tomorrow and they'd probably tell you that there was a finite chance that it would explode overnight and burn the Earth to a cinder. Probabilities were all right for them, but a politician needed a racing certainty, or at least to hedge his bets. He couldn't afford to simply hope for the best, as Kondratieff well knew. But at least he could keep his options open. Reese was the key. Control her, and you had control of the mission, whatever happened to Blixen and her colleague. Judging from her record, she'd probably simply obey orders. But he wanted a backup. Some means of applying pressure.

Ustinov found what he was looking for, or rather what he had hoped to find, at the foot of page thirty-seven of Frances Reese's file. The name Roger Bryant. It rang a bell. As yet it was only intuition, a sixth sense operating below the level of his conscious mind. But intuition had served him well in his steady

John Gribbin and Marcus Chown

climb up through the RN ranks to the post of Secretary General, and he had learned to let his subconscious lead him where it would.

For weeks he had worried about the comet mission. He *must* retain control over it. He trusted neither Kondratieff nor Reese – he trusted nobody – and soon Reese would be halfway across the Solar System pursuing the comet. Where was the leash with which he could force her to obey him, even across a hundred million kilometres?

He read the paragraph that had caught his eye: ". . . Edward's Air Force Base, California. Astronaut training exercise went badly wrong. Diving for quoits on the bed of the 15-metre pool, Reese was trapped when an extruded Y-beam, part of an old underwater mockup of a space station, broke from its support and trapped her at the bottom of the pool. Trainee Roger Bryant dived in promptly, and it was chiefly thanks to his quick reaction that Reese did not drown. Bryant received a commendation from NASA and the USAF . . ."

Roger Bryant. That name had crossed his desk, and recently. Ustinov prided himself on his powers of recall. Now, where had he seen that name? He leaned back on the hard seat of his chair and closed his eyes meditatively. In a moment he had it. He leaned forward and rapped the intercom button on his desk.

"Ingeborg, get me a hardcopy file on Roger Bryant. I believe he has submitted one, possibly two, proposals to the RN to reopen Hipparchus."

"Won't take a moment, sir."

Ustinov rose and strolled to the scenic window. From the nineteenth floor of the RN building he could see way beyond the outskirts of Reykjavik to the brown, treeless hills of the dismal island's interior. It was an unreal, almost alien panorama, with plumes of steam from hot springs billowing up to meet an angry, reddened sky. The new volcano, Falster, which had risen out of the Atlantic a century after Surtsey, was responsible for the terrible hue of the sunset. It had already pumped half a cubic kilometre of debris into the stratosphere. At least, that was what the geophysicists claimed. Ustinov continued to stare out of the window, his eyes unfocused as his thoughts turned back to Roger Bryant.

Bryant and Reese. What had he got? What could he use? Reese had a reputation for extreme loyalty to her friends, and Bryant had saved her life. As far as he could tell, the debt had never been repaid. Here was a weapon he could wield, if need be, against the Commander of the comet mission. But to use it effectively he needed to have some inkling of what Kondratieff and Reese were up to. So far, he had nothing.

For days he had poured over the computer animated projections of the comet's orbit, playing and replaying the collision sequence. He had varied endlessly the initial orbital parameters and watched the comet intersect the Earth-Moon system. Sure, if the orbit was known as accurately as Kondratieff claimed – and Ustinov doubted that – the comet would come down somewhere in Earth's northern hemisphere. But, if the error envelope were expanded just a touch, the Earth would escape catastrophe by half a million kilometres. Why, the comet might even strike the Moon.

The thought lingered, briefly, in Ustinov's mind. It had never occurred to him consciously before. Perhaps it was important; perhaps not. Either way, it was now filed away with all the other interesting, but probably useless, snippets that his subconscious used as the basis of his "intuition".

Ustinov's secretary entered the office with a yellow file. He took it and smiled before gesturing for her to depart. The file held a fresh biog printout and copies of two recent funding proposals. He didn't bother to return to his desk, but flipped through the file standing by the window. He took out the most recent proposal and scanned the title page: SALVAGE OF MICROCIRCUITS FROM HIPPARCHUS. Yes, he vaguely remembered the proposal now. He had given it a cursory glance six months before. Sure enough, at the bottom of the title page was his own semi-legible scrawl. *File*, it said; in other words, *ignore*. The scheme was harebrained, he recalled.

Hipparchus had been abandoned some forty years before. In its heyday it had grown from the former American base to be crewed by over a thousand technicians; the first permanent, self-supporting settlement on the Moon, equipped with a mass driver, chemox plant, laboratories and hydroponics greenhouses. The first human beings to owe allegiance to a world other than Earth had been born there in the euphoric days following the establishment of the World Government. Now Hipparchus was abandoned, its sunken corridors depressurized and its machinery and vehicles idle. The Lagrange disaster had made space a dirty word, and Hipparchus had suffered in the backlash. Ustinov could remember, though he could only have been twelve or thirteen, the videocasts of the last ships to leave. It had touched him, even at that early age, for he knew, deep down, that mankind, after three million years of expansion, was turning its back on the last frontier, perhaps forever.

On the second page a segment of text gave the rationale of Bryant's proposal. ". . . The Solar System is littered with expensive hardware going to waste. The space junk of a century of manned and unmanned exploration orbits in space or lies on the lunar maria. I propose the systematic collection of microcircuits constructed from scarce strategic metals. A five-man shuttle mission to Hipparchus, the greatest concentration of such materials, would be profitable and would benefit the whole human race . . ."

The whole human race! What rubbish. The human race was past needing molecular memories and muon microprobes. What it needed was the low-tech of robot ploughs and drone harvesters . . .

Ustinov appreciated, of course, that Bryant's "rationale" for the proposed mission was no more than a pretext. But what was the real reason behind this ridiculous scheme? He pulled out the biog. It was short, but gave him the answer. On the third page of four, after detailing Bryant's research career and short spell in the dwindling astronaut corps, it was stated plainly and unambiguously. It wasn't a reason that Ustinov would have guessed in a thousand years. "Bryant is obsessed with the notion of returning to the Moon. The obsession stems from his grandfather, Commander James Edus Bryant, fourteen years chief engineer on the Hipparchus mass driver. Roger Bryant first showed his desire to follow in his grandfather's footsteps at the early age of nine. In a school essay written in . . ."

Ustinov smiled again. Someone in intelligence had been doing their homework, he mused. He closed the file abruptly and stared out at the darkening landscape. The Sun had gone, but its sickly light still reflected off the dust-laden clouds, where flickers of lightning could now be seen, adding to the atmosphere of Armageddon. The Secretary General's intuition was working overtime. Put all the ingredients into the pot, stir vigorously, and see what came out of his subconscious. Reese's debt to Bryant. Bryant's foolhardy scheme to reopen Hipparchus. And the random thought, filed away only minutes before, that the comet could strike the Moon as easily as the Earth. Why would anyone want it to strike the Moon? *Did* anyone want it to strike the Moon? It wouldn't hurt to play safe. Ustinov owed his present position to, among other things, a natural caution that made it instinctive to hedge his bets and cover all options. To his delight, a plan for covering this particular option was already crystallizing. There was little logic behind it, and he would have had difficulty explaining his actions to anyone. But that was one of the perks of being Secretary General. He didn't have to explain his actions to anyone. He crossed to the desk and thumbed the intercom.

"Ingeborg?"

"Sir?"

"I want Bryant informed that his proposal to reopen Hipparchus has been approved by the RN. And check with NASA how long it will take to fit out the spare shuttle for a five-man mission to the Moon. Got that?"

"Right away, sir."

"Good. Now get me Ralph Conway in Shuttle Support."

The intercom was silent for the best part of a minute. Then a deep Texan drawl boomed out at him.

"Secretary General?"

"Sorry to disturb you at this time of night, Ralph. Just a quick question. What's the chance of the spare shuttle left by the Dragon mission making a return trip to the Moon?"

"*Aries I*? Well, without a substantial overhaul – a really major overhaul – I'd say fifty-fifty. I mean, it was only left because it's hardly spaceworthy."

"I know, I know. Thanks, that's all I need to know. You can go to bed now."

"Before I go, sir – I don't know what you have in mind – but let me put it this way. If you asked me to fly such a mission, I'd refuse."

"OK, Ralph. Don't worry; I'm not asking."

Ustinov walked back to the window. The shroud of darkness had completely fallen and the lights of Reykjavik twinkled below him. Now, all that remained was to pick the optimum time to inform Reese that Bryant was on the Moon. That could be done when the *Hoyle* and the other shuttles were well on their way. There was just one worry still bugging Ustinov as he gazed at the lights. Would a fifty per cent chance of Bryant getting off the Moon be low enough for what he had in mind?

The Secretary hated to take chances.

# 7.

"Hey, Pappi! Look – I got an A in maths!"

The crashing door and joyful shouting burst in upon Kondratieff's reverie, even as his wife tried to stop the whirlwind.

"Hush, hush, Davidovitch. Your father is busy."

But the door was open, and the damage done.

"Oh, Mutti," the pet name was an echo of the time when little David was a baby, and they had been stationed in Cologne. Kondratieff smiled at the memory of happier days.

"He isn't busy, Mutti, I can see him, just sitting in the chair. And, look, I got an A, in *maths*!"

Somebody, after all, still had things in proper perspective, thought Kondratieff. Worrying himself sick wouldn't do any good now, even if Ustinov was going round like the cat that got the cream. What *was* he up to? Why had he authorized this bizarre lunar mission? Surely he didn't believe Bryant's mad scheme to salvage high-tech materials from the Moon? Even *Bryant* doesn't believe that, he just wants to get up there, using any excuse. But, try though he might – and he'd been worrying at the problem for well over an hour – Kondratieff couldn't see any connection between this sudden enthusiasm for lunar activity and the Dragon mission. Well, Bryant and his crew would be up and back long before the Dragon mission reached its climax.

He sighed, and stretched out his legs, knowing that

Davidovitch would take this as an encouraging signal. There was nothing to be done today. Soon, the Dragon team would have to start altering the course of the comet *towards* the Earth. Then, he would have his part to play, ensuring that Ustinov saw only the doctored data. Tomorrow, he had to fly down to the Canaries to let Cooper in on the secret. Cooper would play ball. But the more people that knew the truth, the more chance there was of the secret getting out.

This time next year – this time next *week*, if Ustinov got wind of it – they might all be dead. Well, so be it. The plan was unfolding as it must, and he could only follow it. But meanwhile, something truly momentous had happened.

He stretched out his arms, and pretended to yawn.

"I must have been dreaming, Larissa. I could have sworn I heard Davidovitch, running into the house and shouting something about getting an A in maths!"

He turned towards the door, in time to catch the broad smile of relief on her face. She knew something was up, but she also knew better than to interfere. And if her David was ready for an evening of more domestic matters, that could only be a good thing.

Little David was already by his father's chair, struggling to pull a battered exercise book from his bag.

"I *did*, Pappi. I did *too* get an A, look . . ."

Lara Kondratieff, framed in the doorway, continued to smile, softly, as father and son bent their heads together over the book.

"Come on Anna, give us workers a hand." The voice of Mary Xu jolted Cherneva out of her reverie. Damn her, she thought irritably. The first time outside that tin can of a spaceship in three months, and someone has to spoil the opportunity for quiet reflection.

"What do you think you're up to, anyway – sunbathing?" Bertorelli's laugh distorted in the small speaker of the suit radio. Ha, Ha, thought Cherneva, very funny. She made no attempt to move, but remained where she was lying, flat on her back, barely aware of the tiny pull of the comet holding her in place on its surface. She was a hundred metres away from where her two companions fussed over the drilling rig, staring upward and outward into space. For a fleeting moment, before the interruption, she had convinced herself that she was adrift, floating free in space, away from all interruptions.

"Give me a break, Mary, I'm tired."

"Come off it, Anna, we've hardly started. There are still five more cores to do after this one, and you can't be tired already."

"Okay, I'm fit. But why spoil my fun? You don't need me yet. I've done my duty humping the gear over here with you, but it only takes two to operate the rig. Let me sit this one out and I'll do the same for you at site six."

"But with three of us . . ."

"No buts. With three of us we'll get in each other's way and take twice as long. I'm taking a break. Regulations, you know. No spacegoing personnel shall be on duty for more than four hours without a rest period of at least twenty minutes."

With this, totally fictitious, parting shot, Cherneva cut the radio. Strictly against orders, but she was annoyed at the disturbance to her reverie, and the other two were close enough to see her with their own eyes. There wasn't any danger, except for stray micrometeorites, and there wasn't much anyone could do about that, if it happened. With no atmosphere to speak of, an errant dust particle winging its way around the Solar System wouldn't burn up and advertise itself in the black, jewel bespattered sky. The first anyone would know would be a hiss of air escaping from the suit and a fog of ice crystals forming as the pressure dropped – Christ! What was she thinking of? It was all Mary's fault, for breaking into her meditation. Take a deep breath, and start again.

She closed her eyes. Clearing her mind, she concentrated on breathing, slowly, in and out. Gently does it. She felt her pulse rate drop, and, with composure regained, slowly opened her eyes once more. It worked. She was floating in space again, alone among the stars. The more she looked, the more she saw. Watching one patch of sky, straight ahead, she could see stars in between the stars, and stars between those stars, and . . .

And they were moving gently across her field of view. She had aligned herself along the spin axis of the comet, so that if she twisted her head she could see stars detaching themselves from the ragged, seemingly distant horizon, and rising high above her. A twist the other way, and she could see stars being extinguished, one by one. The Universe being born and dying, only to be reborn again, solely for her pleasure.

She focussed on the zenith once more. Stay here long enough, and she would see the same stars coming round again. But in a day or so all that would change. The length of the comet's "day" would increase as they spun down the icy mountain, until the stars themselves froze in the sky and ceased to move. With a few judicious blasts of the fusion engines, they would have stopped the entire Universe from spinning, thought Anna.

The white band of the Milky Way was overhead, bisecting the night sky. It was so much brighter than she had ever seen it before. She fancied she could pick out individual stars, but in the back of her mind a detached part of her reasoning ability whispered that it must be an illusion. The bright stars of the Southern Cross shone against the white mist. The Magellanic Clouds, easy to spot; and – wait a moment – the Coal Sack! A great bite taken out of the Milky Way. On Earth, the dark cloud of the Coal Sack nebula was visible only because of its contrast with the white of the Milky Way behind it; out here, though, it looked black even against the space between the stars. Because, she reminded herself, there were stars in the space between the stars in the space between . . .

Staring into the Coal Sack, Anna caught a glimpse of infinity and had to close her eyes to stop her mind being sucked in. A bottomless pit. *Could* you lose your mind out here, if you stayed too long? She puzzled lazily at the notion, the image of a strange wandering spacefarer, found on Ceres or Vesta, or one of the moons of Jupiter, his body intact but his mind gone, lost in the bottomless pit of space. Maybe. But not her. She opened her eyes again, slowly, slowly, and allowed her brain to slip completely into neutral while she gazed at the white band of the Milky Way, her private mandala.

Something had happened to the Milky Way, the tiny voice in the back of her head pointed out, quietly. A piece had broken off and was falling towards her. She watched, fascinated, as the blob of star stuff approached, slowly getting larger and spinning as it came, obscuring first a few stars and then a few more.

Suddenly alarm bells began jangling deep inside her skull. My God! Another comet on a collision course! Get out of the way!

She dug fingers and the claws of a boot into the ice and tried desperately to roll to one side, out of the impact zone of the incoming giant iceberg. She knew it would be useless. Why hadn't they been warned? What had happened to the radar watch? As she spun, she saw the thing again, suddenly shrunken to its true size as her eyes took in the perspective. It impacted where she had been lying, in a puff of snow. In the same instant, she saw Mary Xu and Bertorelli, the starry reflections on their visors unable to conceal the laughter on their faces. She had been the victim of one of their jokes again. To hell with them.

She clicked on her suit radio and gave vent to her feelings.

"Come on, Anna, it was just a snowball. Can't you take a joke?"

Just a snowball! Her heart was still in overdrive. The shock could have killed her. But what was the use in protesting? Two against one, and she *had* been a bit standoffish, from their point of view. The sooner this drilling operation was over the better. She rose to her feet, and lurched unsteadily, the clawed boots biting at the ice, towards the drilling rig. Pack horse time again, she thought, her mind once again focused on the mundane, scarcely noticing the burst of glory as the Sun rose above the equipment and the polarizers on her visor automatically cut in to reduce the glare. It was going to be a long day . . .

"How stupid can you get!"

"Who, me?"

Jonathan, startled at the noisy interruption, looked up as Jenny crashed into the room.

"No." She threw a shoulder bag into one chair and slumped in the other herself, kicking off her shoes. "Them. Idiots."

"I guess Frank was right, huh?"

Jonathan looked only mildly concerned. She wanted to take hold of him by the shoulders and shake some sense into his head. Maybe he was an idiot too. This wasn't just some stupid hacker's game they were involved in.

"I thought you agreed with me – Frank wouldn't have gone along if you hadn't . . ."

"Oh, sure. I agree, in principle. If a bloody great snowball's going to hit the Earth, we ought to try to tell someone. It's just that I didn't really think you'd get very far."

"Jonathan, I didn't get anywhere. It's official. 'Nothing to worry about, no need for panic.' Those robots down at the cube won't blow their noses without permission. No scaremongering about comets hitting the Earth, or else."

"Or else what?"

She seemed to have his full attention at last.

"Or else – I don't know what else. But you know Leroy, the guy who did the interview with me about the astronomy group?"

He nodded.

"Well, I got through to him. We had a coffee together. He warned me off personally, as if he was doing me a favour. Wouldn't go into details, but lots of heavy hints about something he's dug up but can't go public with. He says, after what happened when Halley came by the RN's got some trick up its sleeve. Gonna round up the survivalists for their own good. And anyone who tries to spread disaster rumours gets some unspecified, but probably highly unpleasant, special attention.

"Jonathan, what are we going to do?"

"Don't believe anything until it's officially denied."

"What?"

"You remember. I could've been wrong, you know. I mean, I know I'm pretty good, but this rig," he waved a hand at the equipment beside him, "isn't in the same league as the stuff they've got in Reykjavik. But if they're rounding people up and putting such a tight lid on even reasonable speculation. Well, it adds up."

"How many people did you talk to?"

"I tried everybody on the list. Didn't actually talk to anyone except Leroy."

"Too many."

He stood, and looked around.

"Better get hold of Frank. No choice, now. We either go along with him and head for the hills, or we sit here and wait for the RN heavies to knock down the door."

"You really think?"

"I told you, I could be wrong." He smiled. "But I could even be right. And if they're dishing out hard labour just for even thinking about the unthinkable, I know where I'd rather be. Frank'll look after us."

"Yeah, Frank." She smiled back, weakly. "Better start packing, huh?"

"What in God's name was that?" Reese supported herself against the rec room wall as the groggy sleepers assembled. While they slept, she had been on watch, working, as always, at her desk console. Blood seeped from her nose where she had hit a support stanchion when the first big shock had struck. She pawed at the leaking droplets, but it did no good, only staining the sleeve of her tunic. As the myriad tiny droplets slowly settled and were dispersed by the air currents, she spoke through an incongruous pink haze.

Bertorelli proffered the tiny vacuum cleaner they used to clear up such messes, but she waved him aside, turning from one crew member to another as she sought an explanation of what had happened. Nobody had one. Then Finnegan, white from shock, blurted out "Du Toit!" and Reese felt a sickness inside. He was out there, somewhere, a human needle in a landscape they hardly knew in the first place and which had now been twisted out of all recognition by – something. By forces they had failed to recognize or anticipate. By the unexpected – and the unexpected could mean the end for the whole mission, not just Du Toit.

"Mary, get an all round scan working, at once. Bertorelli, see if *Aries* can be got ready to fly. We may have to go out and find him."

*

As Du Toit gazed down the seemingly endless cliff, his brain suddenly adjusted and shifted the perspective. The "cliff" became a flat floor; and it no longer seemed endless. In fact, it was only a few metres across. He stood once again and "walked" across to the other side. Looking over the edge, he saw the same scene repeated. He was on a small chunk of ice, a faceted, irregular lump. Secured by his clawed boots, he could roam at will over the surface, but there was virtually no gravity at all to hold him in place or give a sense of direction. In that case, he told his brain firmly, anywhere I am standing the ground is straight down beneath my feet. And don't you forget it.

A sudden flash of light caught his eye, and he turned (slowly! carefully! this lump of ice may not be very big, but he preferred to stay on it rather than float off on his own) to look. What was it? Then another flash, slightly to one side, and he realized what was happening. The icebergs surrounding him were rotating, and like faceted jewels they were catching the light of the Sun as they did so. It was beautiful. But admiring the beauty of his surroundings wasn't going to get him back to the safety of Dragon base. There was no reply to his Mayday, which meant that either his transmitter or his receiver were useless. Or both. He'd soon know; if Reese had heard the electronic cry for help she'd have the *Aries* off and running after him in a matter of minutes. After all, he couldn't walk home.

Du Toit continued to stand quietly, watching the shifting display of glinting icebergs around him, conserving energy and oxygen. His own miniature world was also rotating, he noticed, so that the Sun had now "risen" completely to the zenith and was dropping away behind him. Think! he commanded his still dazed brain. There's no reply to my signal, and no sign of *Aries*. They haven't heard me. He took a small drink of water from the tube next to his mouth, and chinned the bar to release a stimtab. He'd have to pay the price of increased heart rate and higher oxygen consumption in order to clear his head. Maybe Mary Xu was right after all. He wouldn't get out of this hole by physical effort. What he needed was a bright idea, some intelligent scheme to signal his whereabouts to the others. C'mon, Jan, he subvocalized, show Mary you're not just a big physical ape.

He began to feel better, physically and mentally, as the stimulants got to work. The Sun set behind him, and Du Toit saw the comet itself, the Dragon, rising high in the sky of his tiny world. So near, and yet so far. He felt colder in the dark, and, although his brain was clearing and he knew this was purely a psychological reaction, began to walk towards the horizon so that he could see the Sun again. Dig one boot in, and thrust backwards; unhook without pulling yourself to a halt; dig the other boot in, and twist; repeat indefinitely. The rhythm flowed back. And then he had an idea.

"He must be out of oxygen by now." Bertorelli and Mary Xu were together in the *Aries II*, floating free amongst the debris of the cometary convulsion. There was little doubt that Du Toit was out there somewhere, but where? Hopefully, they'd nosed among the fragments looking for a spacesuited figure, but to no avail. It was far worse than the proverbial needle in a haystack. He might be no more than a hundred metres away, but with no means of signalling his presence they'd never know, unless they struck very lucky indeed.

Xu thumbed the talkback button and spoke to Reese at Dragon base. "We'll stay out here until we run out of air if you like. But I'd rather be carrying out an intelligent search pattern than just drifting at random."

"There is no intelligent search pattern, Mary. He could be anywhere in the shoal of ice. It's up to him to signal to us, anyway he can, and then I want you out there ready to grab him. I'll give it another hour, then we'll admit defeat."

Reese turned away from the console wearily. Things could

have been worse. Their main work was done, the fusion engines were mounted to shift the orbit of the comet as required, and the installation had only suffered minor damage in the quake. They could complete the mission without Du Toit. And they'd all known someone might get killed along the way. But somehow the idea of losing him on a sightseeing trip, on his day off, seemed much worse than if he had suffered an accident while working on the engine installation.

Wenzel's head came through the hatch, followed by the rest of his long, thin body. Politely, he adjusted his attitude to match the "up" of his commander.

"Boss, I've got something weird. I don't know what it is, but it doesn't make sense, and you said to watch out for anything unusual at all."

"What is it, Chuck?" Wenzel had been monitoring the search program set up by Mary Xu. It was their last hope of detecting any signal Du Toit might try to make.

"Well, it's like this. All these chunks of ice out there are rotating, and I've had the computer work out all their rotation rates and velocities. It's easy to monitor them from the way they flash in the sunlight. I had a half-baked idea that I could extrapolate back to the ground zero of the break up, and work out a search based on the probability of an object with Du Toit's mass moving at a typical velocity having travelled a certain distance by now. But it's no use – the search volume is still far too big."

"So what have you found?"

"It's one of those little icebergs. Its rotation is speeding up. At first I thought it might be Du Toit, using his jetpack to increase the spin of the thing, or trying to steer it back to us. But there's no trace of his exhaust plume in the spectrum of the thing, and anyway if he had a working jetpack he could fly right in the front door. Besides, the change is tiny – I'd never have noticed if the computer hadn't flagged it as an anomaly. But it just isn't natural. How can a lump of ice in space start to rotate faster all on its own?"

"I've no idea, Chuck, but we're sure gonna find out. In this universe, if something doesn't seem to be obeying the laws of physics, chances are there's intelligence at work. I only hope it's Du Toit."

She turned back to the board, and flipped the toggle for *Aries II*.

When Xu pulled the fogged helmet off Du Toit's shoulders, he was nearly unconscious. The suit's air conditioning, damaged during the quake, hadn't been able to cope adequately with his recent exertions, and his face was running with sweat. He breathed deeply, opened his eyes and smiled weakly.

"Hi, Mary. I'm glad it's you. But I could've done with you getting the message sooner."

"You big ox, Jan. You had us all worried to death, you know. But we should have guessed that superman was indestructible."

"Indestructible, but crazy." Bertorelli, his smile equally broad, interjected. "Who else would have tried to walk home on a piece of ice floating in space, like some demented logger floating on a Canadian river? When Reese told us that iceberg was spinning up and we drifted over to take a look, I don't know what I expected to see. But it sure wasn't the sight of you running over the horizon like the Seventh Cavalry charging to the rescue."

"Just took a little intellectual effort to work it out." Du Toit, though exhausted, was recovering fast in the oxygen rich atmosphere of the *Aries II*. "Action and reaction, equal and opposite. Law of conservation of angular momentum. If I push one way to walk round the ice, the ice has to spin the other way to compensate. Faster I walk, more the ice spins. Knew you big brains would understand icebergs don't spin faster by magic, and the shiny surface made a great mirror to signal with. Mary's right – intelligence is the key to survival."

"But not just intelligence," she acknowledged. "If I'd been in your shoes I might have had the idea, but that lump of ice would never have noticed my body mass trying to make it spin up. Survival of the fittest needs brain and brawn, and I'm glad it was you out there, not me.

"C'mon Jan, we're taking you home."

# 8.

She scrambled higher, through the thick bushes, ignoring the branches that whipped across her face and scratched her hands. Behind, she could hear sounds of pursuit. But were they any closer than before? She paused for breath, lying quietly, trying to control her rapid breathing, listening intently. They certainly weren't any closer. But then, why should they hurry? They knew she must be on one of the peaks of the ridge; all they had to do was check out each one in turn and she'd be caught.

"Frank'll look after us." Jonathan's confident words echoed, mockingly, in her head. Frank had looked after them, all right – led them straight into the arms of that crazy, Rick. She shuddered at the memory, left hand automatically rising to touch her bruised lip. Bastard. The sounds of pursuit were no closer; her breathing was easier. For the first time, she had a chance to take stock of the situation, and try to plan some effective evasive action.

Jonathan – how was Jonathan going to get out of this? Poor Jonathan had been convinced there was somebody after them almost from the moment they reached the hills. But it couldn't have been. Rick's mob came down from higher up. Jonathan, lugging that case of computer gear all that way – well, no crazier than her, with her telescope mount, and the precious mirror secured in her lightweight backpack. She felt behind her. Still there – but no more telescope, of course. Better off without it, really. But what the hell.

Frank had done his best, after all. After he'd been so stupid as to lead them up here, that is. The warning shot, smashing into Jonathan's precious packages; Rick stepping out, covered by his companions. That sneering expression. What had he said? She still wasn't clear exactly what had happened. Something about leaving the wimp behind, about Frank breaking the rules. That maybe he'd forgive him if he shared the chick.

Her hand touched the bruise again. Time to be moving on. At least Frank had bought her a little time, gave her the chance to make the break, when that ape grabbed her, and she'd tried to fight back. Then she was sprawling on the ground, tasting blood. And Frank, swinging that old rifle he was so proud of. And the zipping noise, and Frank seeming to explode, and she was in the bushes and gone. And Jonathan? She had no idea. Just hope he had enough sense to go down hill instead of up, she thought grimly. I'm going to get a splendid view from here, but I won't have long to enjoy it. But still, some instinct forced her back into motion, upward, away from the intermittent sounds of her pursuers.

The ground seemed to be levelling out, and it was lighter up ahead. The trees were thinning. Jenny paused and wiped sweat from her face. She couldn't understand why it was so quiet behind. They were certainly taking their time chasing her. But she'd make the most of it, even if she was heading in the wrong direction, up hill instead of down. Maybe they were chasing Jonathan instead – she bit back the thought, refusing to allow herself to hope that he might be distracting attention from her.

The trees were definitely thinning out. Was that good, or bad? Open country ahead; she'd be easier to spot, but she'd be able to move faster – if her strength held out, which didn't seem too likely. Time to ditch the mirror, after all?

She moved forward again, more slowly, picking her way between the last few trees towards the open sky she could see beyond. She stopped. Open sky, but no open rolling plains.

She felt sick as she realized why her pursuers were taking so much time. A few more steps confirmed it. She was on the edge of a steep canyon, falling away precipitously to the glint of a river below. No way forward. Just sideways, or back. And by now, the grinning Rick undoubtedly had his men spread in a semicircle around her.

Slumping against a tree, she gazed out across the canyon. Probably better to jump rather than let that mob get their hands on her. Now, she allowed the suppressed thought to surface, but turned around to comfort her. With any luck, Jonathan had got away while they were concentrating on her. After all, why would they want to bother with him?

She watched the glinting water far below, tracing the course of the river westward where the canyon broadened out, listening carefully for sounds of pursuit. Go for it, river, she thought. That's the way to go. Wish I was going with you.

There was something going on over there. A flash of light on the rotor blades of vehicle. Had to be the cops. Maybe Jonathan was right when he thought they were being tracked.

What was it Leroy had said? RN planning to round up the survivalists? Hope flickered briefly, then died. If the chopper was part of an RN patrol, it would still be hours before the ground forces got up here. If she had a radio, she could call in for help and be gone before Rick knew it. She shivered again. Interrogation by the RN and a lockup downtown were beginning to seem preferable to life in the mountains, even if downtown was about to be destroyed by a comet.

She pulled off the backpack, and leaned back more comfortably against the tree, still watching the chopper as it beat backwards and forwards. Must be over the ground force. Couldn't be dust she was seeing below it, must be her imagination. Looking west, with the Sun beginning to drop towards the horizon, she could only keep track of the chopper because of the way the light glinted on it.

There was something else moving, too. Another flash of

light, down on the ground. There. In the middle of the to and fro beating of the chopper. Yeah, for sure. Must be RN patrol in vehicles. Not interested in hiding, of course. They knew they'd have the measure of anyone up here. Probably looking right at her, if only they knew it. But not much chance anyone down there was using a telescope big enough to see her plight.

A telescope! She leaned forward, suddenly, kneeling and reaching for the backpack with hands that were trembling slightly. Oh God. If only there's time. If only someone down there is awake. Feverishly, she fumbled with the fastening of the pack.

"Camera Five!" Roger Bryant put his seat into a spin, deftly scooped up a squeeze-tube from the provisions crate on the floor and swivelled full circle until he was facing the wall screen once more. After just three days at Hipparchus he was feeling serenely confident in one-sixth G. Grandpa would have been proud of him, Bryant felt sure.

He fumbled blindly with the pull-loop as he adjusted his eyes to the grey, crater-strewn desolation twenty metres above the Bunker. Camera Five looked out from its elevated stalk on to an unremarkable flat plain, truncated by the claustrophobically close horizon. The battered wall of the plain, seen so clearly from space, was way over the rim of the world. Bryant still had difficulty accepting that a three-kilometre high mountain range, so close by, could be so completely hidden. Well, maybe it'll take a few more days, he thought, for my Earth-bred brain to come to terms with the curvature of the lunar surface.

The only signs of man were in the foreground. An intricate network of balloon-tyre tracks, fifty years old but as fresh as the day they were laid down. Bryant knew that it was likely they'd persist for another fifty thousand years, now that mankind had come and gone. Until, that is, they were finally washed away by the meteorite rain from space.

"Camera Six!" Bryant enjoyed the obedient, but mindless, way in which the scanning system jumped to his commands. But as the wall screen blinked, a sharp pain shot from his fingertips and he dropped the squeeze-tube on to the console before him. "Jeezus!" He'd forgotten to hold the self-heating sachet by its insulating band. Why in God's name did they have to get so hot? He shook his scalded fingers and swatted at the little cloud of droplets drifting towards the control panel. The tube, of course, had sealed itself as soon as his fingers had released their grip. Just as well. The last thing they needed was moisture in the works. But he needed moisture himself.

When he was satisfied that the mist of droplets had dispersed, Bryant picked up the tube and gingerly put it to his mouth. It tasted awful, but he drank it anyway. Dehydration was a problem in the Bunker, with pressure only just over half of the pressure at sea level on Earth. Bryant had imposed the limit to avoid straining the fifty year old seals, and he had also had to keep the mix of oxygen in the atmosphere low while Abel fixed the chemox plant. But the worst of their discomfort would be temporary; in twenty-four hours the headaches and sluggish thinking would be behind them. Abel, after a day of tinkering, had declared the chemox plant operational and was now out with a crawler and hopper mining oxygen-rich ilmenite from the open-cast site ten klicks to the north.

But Bryant planned to keep the pressure low, and put up with the need to drink litres of coffeesub to replace moisture sucked out of the body by the thin atmosphere. He'd increase the proportion of oxygen, but there was no point in building up a big pressure of nitrogen if it blew out a hatch and let the oxygen leak away. Anyway, Abel ought to have plenty of fresh – freshly made – water for them once he got a few tonnes of rock to attack with his chemical plant.

They had toyed with the idea of pressurizing a whole floor of Hipparchus Base once oxygen production was underway. Abel thought it might be possible, after building up a supply of ilmenite. It would certainly make the task of salvaging equipment from abandoned labs easier if their domain could be extended out beyond the bulkheads of the Bunker into the base proper. At present, the Bunker was a tiny, warm, oxygenated nest in the midst of a maze of unpressurized corridors, labs, and living quarters. It contained the bare necessities for five men; a shirt-sleeve environment amid a warren of eerily deserted tunnels where the vacuum was as lethal as space itself and a wrong move could kill a man as surely as a holed suit topside.

Still sucking at his squeeze-tube, Bryant peered at the view from Camera Six. In marked contrast to the previous scene, this one was cluttered by human artifacts. It showed the view out over the southern extension of Hipparchus Base. Lift shafts, capped by pressure domes, broke the surface in half a dozen places, connecting the sunken world of the base to the topside world of the Moon. Clustered about several of the domes were abandoned crawlers, and one balloon-tyred bus, flipped on to its back like a helpless centipede. The final abandonment of Hipparchus half a century ago had not, clearly, proceeded with anything like the calm dignity of the history books. It had been a hasty and ignominious retreat back to the cradle, back to Earth.

That world now reigned supreme in the lunar sky, a steely blue crescent hanging always near the mid point of the heavens, but slowly going through the cycle of its phases every twenty eight days. Perhaps it was for this sight that Bryant had striven all his life. Perhaps now he could stop his restless search and accept the quiet life, his Everest climbed. Or perhaps there was more.

"Camera Ten." Softly, more of a request than a command. The view shifted to show the Earth hanging in space, just as it would always be there in his imagination. When he looked upon that indescribable beauty, he dared to believe that humanity might have a second chance. The euphoric days of Apollo and

Neil Armstrong hadn't returned for a generation, until Mackenzie and Wright had returned to the Moon. Now he was there, but only briefly. It might be another generation before it happened, but perhaps the great days would come again in another century. After all, the appearance of the Earth from its sister planet had scarcely changed in the century and more since Armstrong. If you didn't look closely, you couldn't tell the haze of photochemicals stretching out from northern hemisphere cities from normal cloud; there was no way to tell that the desert over Hopeh Province was itself a creation of the atomic age. The damage mankind had done – was doing – to his home could still, surely, be halted and reversed.

Bryant's musings were shortlived. There was a sudden, silent flare of light at the bottom of the screen, on the knife-edge boundary between planet and space. The image of Earth dimmed as filters cut in automatically to compensate for the glare. A new light had been born, challenging the pre-eminence of the Earth. But this was a manmade brightness. And even as Bryant watched, the fierce light peaked in brilliance, flickered, and died.

"Landing Strip!" The image shifted again. "Zoom!" The dust-shrouded form of *Aries I* appeared on the screen and grew bigger. "Stop!" The bare rock behind the main fusion engine was glowing orange and rapidly shifting down the spectrum to dull red. As the dust dispersed, Bryant looked for Higuchi and Templeton, and caught the two space-suited figures emerging from an underground shelter two hundred metres from the test site. When the rock had cooled sufficiently, they would make their way back to the lander and check out the external fuel lines, cooling loops, and, from a safe distance, the exhaust nozzle itself. Then they would report to Russell in the cabin of the *Aries*.

"Patch me to *Aries*."

"Roger?" Jim Russell's voice crackled over the air. Bryant took a last suck of the squeeze-tube and tossed it in the general direction of an empty crate to his left. He leaned forward, as if trying to get close to Russell.

"How did it go, Jim?"

"You saw the burn?"

"Yes, I saw it. Lasted about three seconds, then died."

"That was programmed as a ten-second burn, Roger. The main engine cut less than a third of the way into the program."

"Serious?"

"I don't know yet. I'm running the diagnostic programs on *Aries'* computers. But you know we got a third-rate shuttle here. The space-fit vehicles are all off chasing that damn comet. I'm beginning to think we were lucky not to end up as vapour when we came into Hipparchus."

Russell's words brought back the memory of those last stages of the approach, when *Aries I* had dropped from orbit and skimmed across the walled plain of Hipparchus. Bryant had been so enthralled by the sight of craters rushing beneath that he had hardly noticed the main engine falter. What had chilled him to the bone was the sight of Russell's face when he had glanced sideways to see if anything was amiss. Panic was something he had never expected to see in those calm, competent eyes. But Russell had known that if the engine cut out completely on that final orbital burn his twenty years as a pilot would count for nothing. The laws of orbital dynamics would take over, and the powerless vehicle would be committed to a landing wherever gravity chose, and not on the smooth strip at Hipparchus next to the base they were depending on for food and oxygen.

But the falter had been no more than a hiccup. A brief additional burst of power, and *Aries* was set on its landing orbit, circling the Moon just one more time before it touched down – powerless, indeed, but a deliberate powerlessness with placed it in the right place at the right time.

Jim Russell was speaking again. "Roger? Had any more thoughts on why Ustinov suddenly okayed this salvage operation and gave us the last shuttle? That man never blows his nose without a computer forecast of the implications."

"I know, Jim, I know. But I still can't see it. Back home, I thought – well, we all thought – that he'd want to use us for something when we got back. And we reckoned that whatever he wanted in return it was worth it for the trip. Now, I really don't know. That glitch coming down brought it home to me. We're so vulnerable with any possible rescue vehicles out beyond Mars. We might not have made it down at all. What can he want so bad that he's willing to gamble on us pulling through this mission?"

"At least we're here, Roger. And we've got life support for an indefinite stay. Hell, if it came down to it, we can wait for the others to get back.

"Anyway, we'll be finished here in about twenty minutes, and I'll come right in with the diagnosis."

"OK, Jim. Fingers crossed."

Bryant watched the three small figures pile into the crawler and the dust envelope as it lurched forward. It skirted the lander and headed for lift shaft one, the one that led down to the Bunker. He ordered the screens blank, and gathered up four of the food bags, pulled all four rings, and waited. A few minutes later the vibration of the elevator shaft reached him; there was the clank of boots conducted through the metal flooring; then the hiss of air filling the small lock.

Jim Russell emerged carrying his helmet under one arm and a tool box in the other hand. The airlock, hastily welded in place three days before, was only large enough for one man to use at a time.

"Well?" said Bryant expectantly. The other's weary expression worried him. For the second time in three days Bryant had caught the shadow of uncertainty behind Russell's professional mask. As the airlock began to cycle again, Russell put down his helmet and tool box, took the drink Bryant preferred, and collapsed unceremoniously into a seat. A snail-like trail of fine talcum dust led from his boots back to the airlock.

Well? Bryant wanted to say it again, but he knew better than to press his chief pilot. In his own time . . .

Russell looked up and forced a smile on his tired features.

"I'm afraid we are stranded, Roger. I can't fix the main engine. They did a thorough job."

"They? Who?"

"How the hell do I know? The Green Army bastards, I would've guessed. Who else is crazy enough? But the equipment's damn good; as good as any I've seen. If they've got that kind of gear, it's a miracle we survived takeoff.

"Whoever it was, they wanted us to stay on the Moon. And they made damn sure we wouldn't have any choice in the matter. Two of the coolant lines have been damaged, and we found this on the third."

Russell held out for inspection, a limpet timer, as thin as a thumbnail and not much bigger. Bryant took it and peered at it.

"Set to trigger a small explosive charge during our final burn. Without coolant, the engine won't run for more than a couple of seconds at a time."

Bryant turned the tiny device over and over in his hand. "Definitely set to trigger on our approach burn? Or was that just luck?"

"I don't know. What difference does it make?"

He shrugged.

"Maybe you're right about the Greens. They'd want a nice big explosion just before we went into Earth orbit, where everyone can see it. Now, if they set this, and got their timing wrong, it would've shut down until the main engines restarted on our lunar approach. It isn't just a timer; it's a remote monitor designed to measure the flow of fluids in the system and trigger a servo somewhere else after a certain amount has gone past. I've used them myself, during my groundhog days with the nuclear facility up in the Lakes. They are supposed to be safety devices, but it all depends, I guess, what kind of slave mechanism they're hooked up to. But it isn't the kind of thing I'd expect the Greens to carry in their backpacks.

"One bomb didn't go off at all, which doesn't say much for their organization. The other one could have been late. Which fits their track record, but not the use of a sophisticated device like this. Well, it makes no difference. I think we're in for a long stay at Hipparchus. At least until the Dragon team returns."

Hyashi Higuchi had emerged from the airlock, listening intently to their conversation. But Bryant hadn't noticed. It didn't make sense. Why had they been sabotaged? So they would be at Hipparchus for a long time? That would be no big deal. He wanted to be at Hipparchus for as long as possible, and the base could support the five of them indefinitely.

Higuchi spoke.

"Well, Jim. This puts things in a different light, doesn't it? When the RN says we mustn't come to the Moon, then I want to come – so much, that I come even when the RN gives permission. But now somebody wants us to stay here. If someone wants us to stay here so bad that they destroy our shuttle, then I think I want very much to go home."

Bryant hardly registered Higuchi's remarks. They ought to be safe while they waited for Frances Reese and her team. Funny that his path should cross hers in such a way, after all this time . . .

# 9.

"Where's Finnegan?" Reese's question was snapped out, expressing her irritation. This was serious, and she wanted everyone present.

"As far as I know, he came over from *Tsiolkovski* with Anna. He's probably still in the lock. Anna? What's happened to Yuri?" But, before Anna Cherneva could answer, Finnegan's head and torso wriggled out of an access hatch.

"Someone want me?" he panted. He propelled himself into the throng, caught hold of a deck support stanchion, and righted himself – all rather skilfully. "Sorry if I'm late for the party, Commander. I was admiring the view outside the ship. Has anyone taken a look at the Milky Way lately? I mean, wow, it's like . . ."

"Okay Yuri, tell us later." Reese interrupted impatiently. She cleared her throat, a familiar signal that she wanted silence.

"Just a few words before you down too much of this." She held up a squeeze-tube filled with liquor and grinned mischievously. Contraband booze, but in moderation, and if the Commander didn't take it in good part, well, she wouldn't have been the Commander. Someone let out a cheer, and laughter spread cross the room.

"As you know, I planned this celebration to mark the end of the first phase of our work here. We've cancelled the spin of the comet, and now the fusion engines are in position for the big burn. I've never seen a group of people work so hard. Thanks, all of you. We're actually ahead of schedule; you've done a fantastic job."

Smiles broke out on weary faces all around. They were responding, as Reese knew they would, to a pat on the back. Elementary psychology; raise the morale of the troops; let them have a fling to celebrate. But there was more to it than that, she thought. They really had done a fantastic job, and she was proud of them.

"As I said, this gathering was supposed to celebrate the completion of Phase One. That's the good news. But I'm afraid there's bad news as well."

The mood of the meeting changed noticeably, smiles fading from faces as they all turned towards her. The crew caught the tone of Reese's voice; they knew she was concerned about something, in spite of their success so far.

"Okay," Reese relented, "here it is.

"The last time we were in contact with Earth was eight hours ago."

There was a hubbub of conversation as they took in the message and made quick calculations in their heads.

"We spoke with Shuttle command through the American link at 13:45 RST, right on schedule. Gave them the good news, and they sent their congratulations. But when we tried to raise Canberra at 20 hours, we got nothing. It may be a minor malfunction somewhere down there – Bill says it definitely isn't our equipment. But we don't know for sure until we raise the Greenbelt dish again in five hours from now. *If* we raise the Greenbelt dish again.

"You all know how much the next phase of this mission depends on getting accurate data up from Earth to enable us to adjust the orbit of this thing accurately. As of now, we're dependent on a single communications station for that data, always assuming that whatever happened to Canberra is something local.

"That's not all bad news." She smiled, trying to relieve the tension. "I don't mind being out of earshot of the RN for thirteen hours in every twenty-four. But if anything happens to the Greenbelt link, we'll have the Devil's own job calculating the burn ourselves, and we just might get it wrong.

"Well, you've still earned a little celebration. We all need a break. But I thought you ought to know the worst, while we're all awake at the same time, for once. Go to it!"

It took a while for the party to get going. At first, the astronauts were too busy discussing what might have happened in Australia. But with the aid of a little contraband booze, brewed up strictly against regs, but to which Frances turned a blind eye, they soon began to relax, and celebrate properly. Hell, whatever foulups the guys in Canberra had made, at least *they* had done their work properly.

Some time later, when the party was in full swing, fuelled as much by returning high spirits as the modest alcohol content of the liquor in the squeeze-tubes, Reese suddenly remembered something Bill had started to tell her. What had he said about Maria Blixen? She looked about to find him, but he was sharing a joke with Bertorelli – a hysterically funny one, to judge from the frequent bursts of laughter emanating from the pair.

Then she spotted Maria – alone, detached as ever, sipping at a squeeze-tube, taking no part in the frivolity all around her. Yes, Reese thought, there was definitely something worrying about her. Even at the best of times she seemed to be lost in her own schemes, behind a cultivated smile. Today, in spite of the party, she wasn't even faking the smile. And she was rolling something in the fingers of her free hand, unconsciously, clearly unaware of the action. What was it? But then Anna Cherneva drifted across her field of view and, in a moment, Reese had become embroiled in a conversation with Mary Xu and Chuck Wenzel about whether being ahead of schedule meant that there was now time to undertake a serious search for biological molecules in the ice of the comet.

The next time Reese became aware of her, Maria's voice pierced the din and all heads turned in surprise to see her perched on a stanchion at one end of the room.

"Can I have your attention, please?" The noise level fell as several heated exchanges spluttered to a premature halt. "I've got something to show you all!" Blixen brushed a strand of dark hair from her forehead.

"Let it wait!" shouted one reveller, but Reese didn't notice who. She was too busy wondering what Blixen was playing at.

"Hear me out," Blixen demanded. "I guarantee you will all be interested." She shot a glance at Reese, a glance which was intercepted and understood immediately by the Commander. Reese saw in a flash what Maria was up to, and realized what she had been rolling between her fingers – the holo sphere of the Dragon's true trajectory. Reese had left her cabin open several times lately; she'd been busy, they were far from home, and it wouldn't be long anyway before she revealed Kondratieff's plan to the crew. She had no doubt they would go along with it. But it would have been easy for an experienced operator like Blixen to search it. Oh well, no real harm done. It would have been nice to choose her own time to reveal Kondratieff's scheme, but perhaps this was as good a time as any, while everyone was on an emotional high after the rescue of Du Toit. She crossed her arms and waited patiently for Blixen to get her introduction over. Reese's explanation had been prepared for months. She'd been worried about the initial reaction of the crew – nobody likes being deceived, however worthy the motive – but maybe Blixen would draw their fire and give her time to plan her entrance.

"I want to show you all," this time Blixen avoided the Commander's eyes, pointedly, "I want to show you a holo simulation your Commander has spent many hours replaying lately."

Someone gasped at the implication. Confidential material taken without Reese's permission or approval. Heads turned to Reese, now at the back of the throng, expecting a reaction. But her face was impassive, revealing not a flicker of anger. Confused, they turned back to Blixen.

She held up a small, silvery sphere between her thumb and forefinger for all to see. It was no more than a centimetre across, smooth and featureless. Reese had the sudden, ridiculous thought that Blixen was about to launch into a magic trick – now you see it, now you don't – but, abruptly, she twisted to face the holo panel recessed on the wall. Magnetic fingers jerked the sphere from her hand, suspended it above the read head.

"I have been considering the implications of this find, and intend to report to Secretary Ustinov as soon as communications are restored. *If* they are restored." She echoed the phrase Reese had used earlier.

"In view of what I have just learned, however, I cannot rule out the possibility of sabotage at the Australian tracking site, and therefore we must expect that Greenbelt too may be off the air, if only temporarily."

A buzz ran round the group; some heads turned towards Reese, others stayed fixed on Blixen's performance.

"In view of this change in the situation, I need your help immediately in removing Frances Reese from her position. I have no doubt that you will give me that assistance, once you see what I have to show you.

"Read!" Blixen ordered, and the silver ball began spinning rapidly. A second or so later it stopped dead. She plucked it from the air and addressed the unit once more: "Play!"

The overhead lights dimmed obediently and a ball of hazy light appeared a few feet from the holo panel, in clear view of everyone. Two balls coalesced out of the fog, one four times the diameter of the other. They were separated by a distance greater than the diameter of either; it was obvious to everyone that they were seeing a representation of the Earth and its Moon, suspended in space. For a moment, nothing happened to the image. Someone sucked noisily at a squeeze-tube.

"Wait!" Blixen ordered sharply, brushing that same recalcitrent strand of hair back from her eyes yet again. "Watch the comet's projected orbit." As she spoke, a tiny green sphere appeared at the edge of the picture, trailing a luminous green thread behind it. The green sphere swept in on a slow, graceful arc. The Earth spun rapidly on its axis; the Moon and the Earth danced lazily around each other in their orbit. Closer, the green thread extended towards the double planet.

The image expanded as the comet neared its destination. The observation point changed. Now they were looking almost along the comet's trajectory, so that the curvature of its path was exaggerated.

Without warning, the comet veered sharply in the gravity field. There was a gasp from those assembled as realization dawned; the comet was dipping around the Earth, losing speed as the gravity of the planet tugged it back in its orbit, and swerving, travelling ever more slowly, towards the Moon!

"Hey, that's not right!" Mary Xu protested, but there was uncertainty in her voice. Like the others present, she had the disconcerting feeling that she was standing on very soft sand indeed. She turned to her Commander, hoping for a sign that her fears were groundless, that she had not misplaced her trust. "Frances?" Nobody ever used the Commander's first name. But Reese didn't seem to notice the personal appeal; she seemed bound up in her own thoughts.

By now the Earth-Moon display had vanished, to be replaced by a page of text and numbers, hanging in mid-air. There were the names of shuttles against numbers: orientation of fusion engines in celestial coordinates, burn durations . . . Everyone assembled knew those numbers by heart. After all, hadn't they spent the past week setting up the fusion engines on the surface of the comet, matching those very specifications? There was no doubt now that they had been misled, and by someone they had trusted to the hilt. They were helping to nudge the comet towards the Moon. But why? And why hadn't they been told?

From the front of the room came Blixen's cocksure, accusing voice. "Okay, Frances, suppose you tell *your* crew," the emphasis was slight but noticeable, "just what you're playing at – you and Kondratieff."

All heads turned as Reese pushed through the throng to join Blixen. Maria moved to one side. Reese took a deep breath.

"Right Maria, thanks for the show. You gave it more impact than I ever could." She flashed a smile at Blixen, but it met only granite. She turned to her crew. "Yes, it's true. We're going to drop this comet on the Moon."

Reese looked around the group. Almost weightless, she had one arm hooked around the stanchion to maintain her position. Relaxed, happy that the secret could now be shared, she felt a natural smile spread across her face as she watched the others wrestling with what she had said, and what they had seen.

"The Moon? What on Earth for?" A babble of voices rose around her.

"Do you really want to know why?" she asked quietly. Slowly, the noise died down, as they turned back to her, wondering.

"Can't you make a couple of intelligent guesses between you? Take a deep breath and think hard."

Bertorelli saw it first. "Deep breath – air – it's the oxygen! You want to put an atmosphere on the Moon! But will it work?"

"Of course not." Bill Noyes was checking through a calculation on his computer. "To keep an atmosphere a planet has to have an escape speed at least six times the mean velocity of the molecules in the atmosphere. For oxygen at about zero Celsius the Moon couldn't keep an atmosphere for more than a few hundred years. Molecular weight's too low – only thirty-two. Right boss?"

"Up to a point, Bill. The one-sixth rule works for keeping an atmosphere for a *very* long time – billions of years. But as long as the atmospheric molecules have a mean velocity less than about one-fifth of escape, it still takes hundreds of millions of

113

years for more than half of them to leak away. Jeans worked it all out, back in the 1920s. Still no good for oxygen, but even at about a hundred Celsius the Moon could keep a respectable atmosphere of carbon dioxide for as long as any of us are likely to be interested. The extra mass from the carbon means the molecules move just that much slower at the same temperature. The trick is to get the $CO_2$ there in the first place, which is where we come in."

"So who wants a $CO_2$ atmosphere?"

"Come on, Mary, you know better than that. The Earth started out with a $CO_2$ atmosphere, and the odds are it got it from a comet, or several comets. Why do you think I chose this ship to lead the expedition? I knew the RN weren't bright enough to make the connection, but after all Hoyle was the guy who made the theory respectable. All the Earth's atmosphere, all the water – all the volatiles – came in from space after the planet was formed. The first volatiles had to come from at least one hard landing, but once *any* atmosphere formed it would act as a brake and slow down any other cometary chunks coming in from the outer Solar System. We're going to provide the Moon's hard landing – only we're making it as soft as possible by using the Earth's gravity to slow the Dragon down as we come in. Once we've done that, we can lob any odd bits of ice and snow in from the asteroid belt, or from short-period comets, and they'll stick. We can add material faster than it evaporates, and if we want oxygen to breathe we can keep it in domes or underground. We're riding $10^{18}$ tons of carbon dioxide and water. It won't exactly make a thick atmosphere, but it's a start. Add that to soil and sunlight and you've got a pretty good basis for growing plants."

"And you've got a perfect meteorite shield."

"Right. And the temperature will stabilize out. Don't you all see? We'll be offering the world a second planet. The RN will have to go for it."

"But why didn't you let us in on this from the start? It's dynamite. Any astronaut would give his right arm to be involved." For once Jackson, so quiet and thoughtful that you scarcely noticed his existence, was moved to make a contribution.

"Jack, I couldn't. You know the trouble we had getting permission for a mission to save the world. If David Kondratieff had told Ustinov that there was no threat to the Earth, but he'd like to borrow all the shuttles to try out a crazy scheme to make the Moon bloom, you know what would have happened."

"Nothing!"

"Right, Chuck. Until now, only two people have known the full story. Kondratieff, back there in Reykjavik, and myself. And I'm mighty glad that I don't have to keep the secret any longer. I take it you approve?"

"If it will work." Jackson again.

"Well, we're going to find out. The problem is slowing the comet's speed in its orbit to drop it in nice and gently just behind the Moon in its orbit around the Sun. We want the softest possible impact, or all these lovely volatiles will simply splatter back out into space. Jupiter's done half the job for us; we have to do the rest, with the aid of a gravity assist from the Earth. That's why some of us, at least, have to stay on board this thing during the closest approach to the Earth, to make any final adjustments before we hop into the shuttles that still have engines and skip off home, to a hero's welcome."

"I don't think so, Frances." It was Maria Blixen, back at centre stage, hands on hips in a slightly ludicrous attitude of authority. No one moved. An expectant hush descended on the rec room. Most were still coming to terms with what they had heard. Now they were to witness the inevitable confrontation between Reese and Blixen. Loyalties were to be tested, and it was all too soon.

For the first time, Reese looked worried. She faced her

audience, rather than Blixen, watching to see the reaction in their faces to the words she expected to hear.

"You've deceived the RN Frances, you and the traitor Kondratieff. You've sacrificed the entire shuttle fleet on a crazy mission that wasn't even necessary. You want to feed your own ego. Create a new world? And risk all our lives in the process?" She indicated the group with a sweep of her arm. "You must be mad. Kondratieff has scaled new heights in megalomania, and you have followed him like an obedient puppy. This plan is so insane that, I admit, neither I nor Secretary Ustinov had any notion of what you were up to. If he had, he would have vetoed this madness. Your own figures show that the intended trajectory takes the comet much closer to Earth than if we left it alone. Even if you could use the Earth's gravity to swing the comet towards the Moon, the risks are enormous. The tiniest error could bring catastrophe.

"But, believe me, the First Secretary knows you are up to something, and that is why I am here. I cannot allow this insanity to continue. If the Earth is really safe, then we must remount the engines in the shuttles and return them all to Earth, in good condition, for future use. We must not, under any circumstances, increase the risk by shifting the comet towards the planet. Then, those of you that remain loyal can indeed expect their hero's welcome. The Council is generous to its supporters." She paused for a moment, to let the message sink in. Then she took a deep breath, and drew herself up to her full height, reciting a ritual formula in a sing-song voice: "By the power invested in me by Secretary Ustinov and the Council of the Reunited Nations, I hereby relieve you, Frances Reese, of your command of this ship and of this expedition, and I hereby assume full command and authority for myself. You are all witnesses." Blixen looked for support to the assembly.

Reese bowed her head and waited. It was inevitable that her political officer would make some move of this kind. The success or failure of the mission hung on the next few moments. But the power of speech seemed to have deserted everyone. The silence stretched uncomfortably.

"Frances, I am now Commander of this expedition. Disciplinary action will – "

There was a sudden movement among the crew. Blixen broke off and stared at the faces before her. "Has anyone got anything to say?" There had been an imperceptible drift of bodies, away from Blixen, towards Reese. No individual seemed to have made a move, but somehow there was a noticeable space in front of the newly self-proclaimed Commander. Like a shoal of fish, impelled by the will of a supra-organism, the group had coalesced, in uncanny fashion, around Reese. Now, it was Blixen's turn to look uncertain. "Well?"

"I'm afraid I have to back the Commander." Bill Noyes nodded towards Reese, to make it quite clear which Commander he meant.

"And me." Mary Xu, her expression grave.

"Me too." Bertorelli, biting his lip before he spoke.

That was it; in no more than a minute every member of the crew had pledged support to Reese and to Kondratieff's plan. She wanted to rush forward, to hug them all. They were risking their lives, their careers, everything, on her word. The gamble had paid off, as she had assured Kondratieff it would.

"Thank you," she said quietly, her eyes misting just a little. She pulled herself together with an effort of will. She was still their Commander. Blixen's knuckles were white as she balled her fists by her sides. Reese could see she was not used to being defied. A political animal, ingrained in the system, it really had never occurred to her, even after living with the mission for so many weeks, that any more than one or two ringleaders could possibly oppose the authority of a duly appointed official of the Council. For a moment Reese was shocked by the anger she saw contained behind Blixen's eyes.

It was the anger of a wild, injured animal. Reese had not expected such hatred; used to the logic of scientific argument and reasoning, she was just as unprepared for Blixen's continuing hostility in the face of the inevitable as Blixen was unprepared for the group's decision.

"I have to confine you to quarters, Maria. I'm sorry. And, of course, I cannot permit you to send a message to the RN. You're quite right. Ustinov would never agree to the risks involved in making use of the Earth's gravitational slingshot, even if he could understand the importance of dumping this mass of volatiles on the Moon. It's almost certain that some fragments of the comet will strike the Earth at perigee – but only small fragments. Without the data link from Earth, though, we can't fine tune the orbit enough to be sure of hitting the Moon just right, so we have to keep the truth from Ustinov as long as possible – and I don't want Kondratieff compromised until the last minute."

"It doesn't matter. Secretary Ustinov," pride in her role as an agent of the Secretary himself shone out in her audible use of capital letters, "is personally interested in this mission, and expects to see the status reports that I send every forty-eight hours. The next one is due in ten hours. You know that. When I fail to make the transmission – "

"We'll say you're indisposed – suffering an acute attack of space sickness."

"Don't be stupid, Frances. The Secretary is no fool. He'll guess."

"That's a chance we'll just have to take, Maria."

"For God's sake, Frances, do you realize what you are doing? This is *mutiny*!"

Yes, thought Reese, as Bertorelli shepherded Maria away to her cabin, I know what I'm doing. Now, when she returned to Earth her career would be just as surely finished as if she stayed up here. But that scenario was nothing new. She'd known all along what this mission meant, and expected to be made the scapegoat. Months ago, she had decided she could make that sacrifice, and for months she'd carried that knowledge inside her, alone.

Now, at least, she had the support of her crew.

# 10.

THE ATV bounced its way off another rock and over a small, but steep ridge. He glanced at the girl sitting beside him, securely strapped into her seat. She took no notice of the jostling and continued to stare straight ahead, even while her limbs were being shaken. Shock, he decided. Hardly surprising. But at least she'd told him enough to have them hurrying back down to the city, ahead of the column. Soon fix her up down there, and get the full story.

Pity they couldn't have spared the chopper, but air cover was essential with those bandits still at large in the woods. Nevertheless, his instructions from Reykjavik were clear; anyone seeming to have scientific evidence that the comet would strike was to be isolated, interrogated, and all transcripts sent to Reykjavik by secure messenger. The material was not to be trusted, even in code, to radio or other communications links. Secure messenger meant himself, with any luck. Maybe promotion, if this was what the Iron Man wanted. And if he could only break down her accomplice, the hacker. The medics said he'd live, and be able to talk in a few days.

He wondered, briefly, if her claims were true. She certainly believed it. No other way a city girl would have been up there in the hills with those crazies. But it didn't matter to him. Whatever the comet did to anyone else, for him it was a chance to be noticed, favourably. And if he got to Reykjavik, he'd have even less reason to worry. Stick close to the Iron Man; you can be sure *he'll* be in a safe spot!

Ustinov's bombshell came on the tight beam from Earth, forty-eight hours after Maria Blixen stopped sending her reports. They were close enough to Earth now for partial video, but only a wavery two dimensional image. That was enough to show them the Secretary's determination. The fact that he was addressing them directly, instead of through a routine intermediary, was enough to show his suspicions about their activities; but, always the political animal, he made no direct mention of them. The tight beam couldn't be intercepted on its way up through the Earth's atmosphere and out into space, but no doubt several dozen technicians and broadcast service personnel were listening in.

"We were all sorry to hear of the unfortunate disability of one of your number. I do hope that, although she is at present unable to speak, Maria Blixen can join you in viewing this message." There was no pause for a response; the time delay for round trip signals was still too great to make worthwhile conversation possible. The microphones in the rec room were closed. Blixen, allowed to view the broadcast on sufferance and under close supervision, glowered at Reese, but said nothing. "In view of the most urgent nature of your mission, we are all aware that nobody can be spared from their duty for long."

None of the assembled astronauts noticed the effect of this sentence on one of their number, "standing" quietly at the back, with eyes directed, like everyone else's eyes, to the screen before them. "Most urgent" and "duty"; the key words, spoken by the First Secretary himself, so that there could be no mistake. A slight pause in the rhythm of breathing, and a glance round the assembled group were all that might have betrayed a mounting sense of excitement, had anyone noticed. A lifetime of frustration and months of training were about to achieve fulfilment and release, making the ultimate sacrifice for the glory of the State, to assure the safety of Ustinov himself, and, of course, to create a martyr whose name would live for evermore.

But the Secretary was still speaking, obviously ensuring that his true message would be unnoticed by the others. What he was saying seemed to be causing consternation; more than enough to cover up the adrenalin rush brought about in one individual by his earlier words.

"I also have some slightly bad news to impart, especially for Commander Reese. In the wave of enthusiasm following your departure to rendezvous with the Dragon, I allowed myself, it now seems unwisely, to be persuaded to launch another expedition."

"*Another* exp . . ." Bill Noyes' stifled his exclamation as he realized Ustinov was continuing smoothly with his prepared exposition.

"I believe all of you know of Roger Bryant and his ambitions for reopening Hipparchus Base."

Bill looked sharply at Frances; he knew the debt she owed to Roger, and how disappointed she had been when he turned down the chance to join the Dragon mission.

"It seemed like an ideal opportunity to test out his ideas. We allowed a five-man mission under Bryant to depart in *Aries* . . ."

"Christ! That old heap."

"Shut up, Mikhail!"

". . . weeks ago. They arrived safely, but there has been some damage to their shuttle and it seems they are stranded – at least, until you return."

Ustinov's smile was like that of a cat that has just eaten a canary.

"Unfortunately, Bryant's team has been unable to restore the oxygen manufacturing plant at Hipparchus to working order. It seems there was more damage there than he had anticipated. So they are limited to the supplies they brought with them, and cannot wait for the successful completion of the comet's flight past Earth. One of your shuttles will have to divert to the Moon to rescue them, as soon as the comet's orbit is stabilized. That should not be too long now."

Ustinov told the lie convincingly, with an appropriate air of slight concern, but giving the impression that he knew deep down inside that all would be well, that there was no need to panic. It was convenient that there was no way for the Dragon crew to communicate directly with Hipparchus; let them think Bryant's danger was greater than it really was, and growing bigger by the hour. Then see where Reese's loyalties lay.

"As a military man myself, I understand that it is much easier to miss a moving target than to hit it, and we are computing the changes in the Dragon's orbit all the time. We can let you know as soon as it is safe to leave the beast and come home." And, thought Ustinov, I know how difficult it is to hit a moving target. Take one or two of the shuttles away, and Reese would have to abort her scheme – Kondratieff's scheme – whatever it was.

"I'll see that you get a copy of Bryant's report of the accident in the usual data link. We will both be interested in your response."

The Secretary's image faded and was replaced by that of a technician, who patched in a computer link to send updated information. Nobody paid any attention; it would all be recorded automatically.

"Well, the cat's out of the bag now Frances, for sure."

The speaker was Yuri Finnegan.

"How much do you reckon he knows?" Gerry Wolf chipped in.

"Everything, of course!" Maria Blixen was triumphant again. "You don't expect anyone to believe your stories about the Moon now, Frances; it's obvious the Secretary has uncovered your little plot. You won't get away with murder and sabotage now. Kondratieff will be in prison, not the next head of the Council!"

"Jan." As she spoke, Reese inclined her head towards the hatch leading to Blixen's quarters. The big geologist nodded, and reached out a hand to the tiny figure.

"Don't touch me! I'll go. Stew in your own juice for a while. When you're ready to listen to reason, I'll be there." She came as close to flouncing out as anyone could in minimal gravity. Reese shrugged. "Better lock her in, Jan, anyway."

"Quiet now, everyone. Let me think. Bertorelli, how accurately can they determine our orbit now?"

Bertorelli shrugged. "Of course, it's changing all the time as long as we've got thrust on the beast. But even though we haven't been thrusting long it would be easy for any competent astronomer to calculate that we're pushing it the wrong way, so that it will fly closer to the Earth than if we'd left it alone. Kondratieff's worked miracles in keeping the real figures away from Ustinov this long; it was inevitable there'd be a leak sometime soon."

"Damn! He's telling us to stop thrusting now and charge to the rescue of Bryant's group. That's clear enough."

"Why Bryant though? Why the Moon? Does he know what we're planning to do with the comet?" Saha's worried questions voiced many of their fears.

"No." Bill's quiet, authoritative voice caused all heads to turn in his direction. "If Ustinov knows that we are edging the Dragon towards the Earth, then he believes we are going to drop a chunk of it on him. Just like Maria said. Politicians worry about being assassinated and replaced. That's the way these people think. Sure it's crazy." He raised a hand to still the hubbub once more. "But it makes a kind of sense, from his point of view. From here on in, the orbital projections get more and more detailed. If Ustinov's seeing the real figures, he'll see us edging the Dragon closer and closer to the Earth, and he won't know for sure that we're on a grazing trajectory, using the Earth's gravity to slow the Dragon down and steer it at the Moon, until we skim past and head on out again."

"But Saha's got a point Bill. What about Bryant?" Reese's concern was apparent in her voice. Dropping lumps of ice on the Moon was one thing; dropping them on top of people – her friends – Roger Bryant – was quite another.

"I don't know." Bill rubbed his fingers through his hair in a tired gesture. "Look, try this for size. Ustinov sees us heading his way. So he persuades Roger to go the Moon . . ."

"That wouldn't be difficult!" They all laughed at Valentina's sally.

"Okay, he grudgingly accepts Roger's plea to go the Moon." Bill waited for a second wave of tension-relieving laughter to die down.

"Then, and this is what he must have anticipated."

"Or planned."

"Or planned, Frances, either way he's got Roger stuck on the Moon and only us around to help him. So, he reckons, we have to stop thrusting, let the comet go on its way, and hightail it to Luna."

"Only it doesn't make sense." Jan's deep, guttural voice held their attention while he ticked points off on his fingers. "First, Ustinov thinks we are going to wipe out millions of people just to get rid of him and his lousy government. Then, he thinks we'll stop doing all that just to rescue three people from the Moon. Meanwhile, we really are planning to drop this thing on the Moon, where these guys *just happen* to have been sent."

"There's more to it than just 'some guys' on the Moon, Jan. You're a geologist, you won't know this, but all the pilots do. I did something stupid in training once, long ago, and Roger got me out of it. He risked his life to save mine. It's all in the records. I guess Ustinov's spies could ferret that out easily enough. If there's one person I'd bust a gut to rescue it's Roger – present company excepted, of course." Reese smiled, at Bill in particular. "So our problem is worse than Ustinov anticipated. He thinks he's got a hostage to stop us, or to stop me, from destroying him. In fact, if we proceed as planned we destroy the hostage, and we can only hope that the rest of Kondratieff's plan works out and the world is changed for the better. For all we know, like Maria said, David could already be locked up. Or dead."

"For that matter, we don't even know for sure that Bryant's team is on the Moon. All the news we get comes from Earth on the tight beam." Du Toit seemed determined to raise objections. "We don't have a transmitter powerful enough to call Hipparchus, and they don't have anything to talk to us with, if they're there. Ustinov knows that. Maybe it's all a bluff."

"We could always do nothing." Chuck Wenzel was uncharacteristically subdued. "Leave the comet to its own devices. Rescue Bryant, be heroes, pretend we'd saved the world. The publicity would help the space programme. Wouldn't it?"

"Not if Ustinov's back in command of the situation." Bill Noyes exerted control again, aware that Frances could do nothing constructive. "Sure, we've got a problem. But we don't have to tackle it yet. Let's take a break, eat, sleep on it, and get back together when we've got some coherent thoughts. Meanwhile, we keep on as planned."

It was a dejected group that broke up and drifted through the various exits, a few to go about their duties, most to try to relax and puzzle over the change in their situation brought about by Ustinov's bombshell. But one departed purposefully, heading through the tunnel to the control room of what had been the *Discovery*, now largely cannibalized and serving as the nerve centre for controlling the thrust of the great fusion motors, dismantled from three of the ships and bedded securely into the surface of the Dragon.

In the long, white government building in Nairobi, the "aid executive" of the RN sat in his office in despair. In all but name, he was the Governor of a large part of East Africa; without RN aid, the economy would collapse. He was barely keeping his head above water as it was, struggling to produce crops that could be sold, or bartered with other countries and regions, to provide the raw materials for development and industrialization. It wouldn't take much to push the whole region back into a series of villages each looking out only for itself. Those idiots in Iceland had taken his only two competent lieutenants, to work on the insane Dragon project. How was he supposed to run a modern economy? And now this!

He flipped back to the first page of the report, and shook his head as he gazed at the photograph pinned to it. Bukumbi. Six villages following her lead, and not a damn thing he could do about it. Send in the troops? If he took them out of the city he'd have that falling apart about his ears. Bad enough that so many of his workforce were drifting away to the villages. Didn't they understand that they couldn't just grow food to eat themselves if they wanted to be part of the modern world? With no trade there'd be no economy, no help from the RN, nothing but isolated villages, like something out of Livingstone's Africa.

He reached a decision. Let them starve. No aid at all. Let them try to go back to the old ways, and see how it felt. One bad harvest and they'd be back, begging for help, ready to do what he said. No move, no food.

He slapped the folder shut.

He floated a couple of metres above the surface of the comet, drifting towards *Predpriyatie*. There was no need to worry about steering jets. Since Du Toit's accident, they had all been careful. The safety lines strung between the anchored ships made it easy. Just clip on to the wire, push with your legs, and away.

It was all most convenient. Steering jets, after all, ejected clouds of gas and might be spotted by Valentina, on duty in the *Hoyle*. This way, he was an almost invisible speck, moving slowly. If she did spot him, she would surely assume he was on some routine task. And in just a few minutes, it wouldn't matter if she did get suspicious.

The hull of the ship loomed up ahead of him, suddenly seeming to move rapidly towards him as his journey came to an end. Grunting with the effort, he swung his legs forward to meet the impact, cushioning his arrival like a parachutist landing.

There were no locks on the hatches. Simpletons, he thought. How can anybody be so naive?

Once inside, he removed his helmet. He wouldn't need that again, come what may. The outer hatch of the airlock was tight shut against the surface of the ship; the inner hatch gaped open, invitingly, leading into the interior. He squatted in the airlock, taking a stubby tool from his belt and probing at the exposed machinery of the hinge mechanism. There! With the switch disconnected, there was no way the inner door could close. And with the inner door open, there was no way that the

*Predpriyatie*'s computer would allow the outer door to be opened, releasing all the air from the ship. Only the explosive bolts, triggered manually in an emergency from inside the airlock, could ever open that hatch how. Nobody could get in while he was at work.

He pushed himself upright, overcompensating in the minuscule gravity and knocking against the helmet. On a sudden whim, he took the helmet and wedged that into the hinge end of the door, as well. Now, it was physically impossible to shut the door, whatever the computer said. Satisfied at this double precaution, he floated off, along the short corridor to the control room.

Being "on duty" in the *Hoyle* meant little more than monitoring the comm system, at this time of "day." With the bulk of their task completed, the group was too small to continue to bother with working shifts, and shared the same rest, work and food periods. Officially, it was now the middle of the night, and everyone was supposed to be tucked up in their bunks. Not, thought Valentina, that you would have thought so, from the activity going on in the past hour. Everyone was too fired up by Ustinov's ultimatum to sleep, and different small groups kept congregating in odd places, discussing the problem futilely, then drifting apart to try and get some rest.

She'd spotted the telltale light indicating the operation of the hatch, of course. That was really very naughty, especially after what had happened to Du Toit. But somebody obviously felt the need to be alone, and think.

She switched in the remote camera, and watched the anonymously suited figure clipping on to the line and sliding off towards *Predpriyatie*. Not Du Toit this time, she thought. Too small. Maybe one of the girls, or Yuri Finnegan, or Jackson. Whoever it was seemed to be obeying proper safety precautions, except for neglecting to tell her what was going on. Still, better keep tabs. The Commander wouldn't want anarchy to descend, no matter how bad the problem they faced.

"General call." The console winked an acknowledgement. "Hello out there. *Hoyle* base calling anybody who just happens to be halfway from here to *Predpriyatie*. Please acknowledge."

She frowned when there was no reply. The figure was already out of camera shot. Surely, whoever it was hadn't been so stupid as to turn the suit radio off? Well, she could always call again through *Predpriyatie*'s radio. But no point yet, since *Predpriyatie* was unmanned. Obviously whoever it was planned to go inside the other ship, now nothing more than a fusion engine anchored to the comet, for a quiet think.

Something in her thoughts brought her up short. She could feel the hair, cropped short to fit inside a space helmet, pricking all over her scalp. Something was wrong – badly wrong. Acting on some spacer's instinct, she hit the main alarm and was moving, suiting up fully, even as a babble of voices burst over the communication system.

She ignored them all, reporting by radio as she hurried to the hatch and waited, impatiently, for the lock to cycle.

"Commander, this is Valentina. Someone has left the ship and is heading for *Predpriyatie*. Won't answer my calls. I'm following."

The lock was open at last. She clipped on to the line, and pushed off, hard. She had no idea what anyone could do on their own out there – but that was what had triggered her into action. *Predpriyatie* was empty, ready to carry out its last task of pushing the comet in the required direction. If anything happened to that ship, the mission – the *real* mission – would be in trouble. Suddenly Valentina cared, a lot, about the mission. Maybe, she thought as she sped along, it's a wild goose chase. But if there *is* something wrong . . .

Reese's voice came over the comm as she was approaching *Predpriyatie*.

"Valentina, it must be Jackson. Everyone else accounted for. Saha, Wolf and Wenzel are right behind you, using jets." Damn! In her hurry, she'd not thought of that. They'd be here almost as soon as herself. "We're trying to contact Jackson by radio, but he won't answer. *Predpriyatie*'s computer is silent, too. He's got some sort of override on it. See what you can do."

As Valentina manoeuvred her legs into position for the landing, she looked downward, between them, towards the end of the ship. There was the slight glow of a discharge from the exhausts.

Oh shit, she thought. He's starting her. As the thought entered her mind, she noticed, for the first time, that the needle of the radiation counter in her helmet was sliding slowly towards the red. Can't worry about that now, she thought, as she keyed the radio.

"Commander. Valentina. He's running her up."

In the control room, Jackson looked carefully over his handiwork. How jolly decent of the Commander, he thought, to allow everyone their few kilos of personal possessions on such an arduous mission. No questions asked about the contents of those little bags – and if anyone had asked any questions, he was fully prepared to back up his story of a hobbyist's interest in computer knick knacks. Only now, in their proper place, those knick knacks gave him complete authority over the ship's computer, and enabled him to over-ride the safety interlocks on the fusion motor itself. With no safeties it was easy to arrange a modest little explosion, just fifty megatons or so, enough to wipe out this whole crazy expedi-tion, and to ensure his own place in the annals of the Party.

Just time, perhaps, to make sure that all those present knew who they had to thank.

He responded, at last, to the clamour of the radio.

"Thank you, Commander."

"Jackson! What the hell do you . . ."

"I think you had better listen to me, Commander."

The comm fell silent.

"Yes, this is Jackson. I have completed my mission, and there is no action you can take that will prevent the explosion of the fusion engines of this ship in about one minute from now."

Valentina heard the words even as she abandoned her attempts to open the hatch. There were more words, but she ignored them. The other three were just arriving. She switched her radio to local, as she began to move towards the rear of the ship.

"No use. Hatch jammed." No breath to waste on idle chatter. She was vaguely aware that they were trying, futilely, to get in to the ship. Where was it? Ah! The feature she'd been searching for swam into view. The servicing hatch, above the fusion engine itself. Pure vacuum behind that, no way to lock it shut from inside. Simply a mechanical hatch.

She turned the handle, and swung the hatch upwards. Headfirst, she pushed her way into the compartment. She could actually see the glow of components working up to powers beyond their designed tolerances; there could only be seconds left before the ship either took off or blew up.

There it was! The manual safety, the cutoff used by engineers when working on the drive, to ensure it couldn't be started in error. She reached for the override, twisting it into the safety zone. The glow faded as the engines died into inactivity.

Valentina shook her head, inside the helmet. Close! Very, very close. And all done by instinct. She laughed to herself, a little lightheaded. What was that buzzing in her ears? The laughter stopped. The buzzing continued, and drew her eyes towards the bright red, flashing panel of the radiation counter. Well, Valentina, you've really done it this time.

Suddenly tired, she turned and pushed her way back out through the hatch. Make the most of it, she thought. After all, it's the way you always wanted it to end. She drifted slowly down towards the surface of the comet, head back, watching the stars, ignoring the babble in her radio.

The little group of people around the main hatch turned and began to move towards her, asking questions she would never answer. And as they did so, the hatch itself blew open, triggered by the emergency release, and the figure of Jackson, suited up but helmetless, shot out, carried by the condensing vapours of the air from inside the ship. She watched as he drifted off into space, in a cloud of frozen vapours, like a miniature comet himself, his arms and legs slowly spread-eagling into a cross. Then, there was nothing to see but stars, and blackness.

# 11.

House arrest! Kondratieff had been prepared for many possibilities, but not for this. He was even ready to tell the truth, if he had to. The Dragon team must be pretty well safe by now, and they wouldn't need the data link much longer. Perhaps he might even have been able to persuade Ustinov to accept the *fait accompli*, and make it official. Or – imprisonment, and worse, if Iron Fist decided to display that side of his character. He had no illusions about what he was involved in. But this!

"Sir, I . . ." he hesitated, unsure of the best course to follow. "May I know the reason?"

Ustinov smiled. "It's just that I couldn't bear the thought of you travelling too far from my side, David. The Council will be in emergency session while the comet is passing. My place is here, with the Council. And, of course, I have invited the families of all the astronauts to be here, as well. It is, after all, the safest place on Earth. I am sure you have no intention of leaving in the near future. But I did want to make the position clear to you."

Safest place? Why was he bringing the families here? And what was the meaning of the emphasis on the Council? A light began to dawn in Kondratieff's mind. That report from California; Ustinov's agent hurrying off to the observatory. *He thought they were planning to drop a chunk of the comet on Reykjavik!*

"But, sir, it isn't what you think!"

"And what do I think, David? That you have been less than open with me? That there may be members of the Council who would be glad to see me out of Iceland at a time of crisis, when there is a need for a firm hand on the levers of power? And who might be equally glad to see me stay away?"

The Council! He thought Kondratieff was working for a dissident group on the Council! What tortuous scheme had the Secretary dreamed up in his convoluted mind? Maybe he thought Kondratieff was threatening to drop the comet on Iceland, so he'd brought the families here as hostages. But he didn't believe the threat, because he was staying here himself. He thought – he thought – suddenly, it clicked into place. Ustinov thought the threat was a bluff, to get him out of the Capital. The dissidents would stage a coup, revile Ustinov for running away from imagined danger, and see he never got back. It was brilliant. Kondratieff had to admit that. It might even have worked, if somebody had thought of it in the first place. Only, he for one doubted if a takeover by the Council would be any better than the old Devil of Ustinov himself. And the old Devil was up to something. He was giving the Council enough rope to hang itself, waiting for them to come out in the open and get snared.

This needed thinking about. He didn't want to get snared with them. But if he played his cards right, this could work out very well indeed. Ustinov ought to be pleased with the Dragon scheme for smoking out his opposition, even if it had happened by accident. Or, if there *was* a successful coup, the new powers in the land ought to be equally happy about the circumstances that gave them their opportunity. And it certainly meant Kondratieff needn't worry about the Dragon team now. Old Iron Fist was far too busy chasing shadows in the corridors of power to worry much about them – especially if he already believed the imagined threat was a bluff!

His mind was made up. Wait and see had served him well up

to now; a little more waiting could do no harm, and might help him decide which way to jump.

"Sir, I'm not sure that I understand your concern. But I assure you I've no intention of leaving Reykjavik. Unless you order me to, of course. And I assure you that I have had no dealings with any members of the Council that would not meet with your full approval."

There, let the old man chew on that for a while. Plenty of time yet to come clean about the Dragon mission.

Ustinov frowned. Perhaps he'd expected a different response?

"You may go. An escort will be waiting to take you to your quarters."

The Secretary rose and walked over to the large window, where he stood, hands clasped behind his back, gazing out as Kondratieff left the room.

In the *Hoyle*'s 50-centimetre telescope the Earth was just a tiny white crescent against the velvet of space. But that crescent was so dazzlingly bright that Frances Reese had to screw her eyes up to protect them from the glare. She could, of course, have cut in one of the instrument's dark filters – but Earth was not her quarry, just a reference point from which to offset the telescope.

She swung it across the sky. Another bright light jumped into view, but Reese overshot and it flashed away leaving only an evanescent streak, like a meteor trail in the night sky of Earth. In a moment she had compensated for her heavy-handedness and brought the light back to the centre of the field of view, where it gradually settled. It was another crescent, not nearly so bright as the Earth, nor so large. There was no mistaking it, of course; it was the Moon.

Her hand began to shake involuntarily and the image of the Moon, which she had so carefully steadied, began to shake too, flitting back and forth like a drunken firefly, before she cut in the automatics and left the computer to hold the telescope on target, feeding its image to the monitor screen alongside the instrument. She had not expected to feel such a strong emotion, but then she had underestimated the strength of the bonds which still tied her, after all these years, to Roger Bryant. Valentina, her friend, was gone. She could face that, and the uncertain future for all of them here on the Dragon. They had little chance, any of them, of getting home. She'd become reconciled to that, ties long since cut. But Roger had not entered into the equation. The thought which had reduced her to this unseemly state was that Roger was down there on the world she had earmarked for target practice, and there was nothing, absolutely nothing, she could do about it.

Reese leaned back from the telescope, slowly settling in a slump on the observer's couch as the tenuous gravity of the Dragon pulled at her. She felt so helpless she could scream. With Blixen, and the sabotage attempt, or even when Du Toit was lost in space, she had been faced with real problems that could be solved, and she had made damn sure that a serious attempt was made to solve them. But when there was nothing that could be done, what was the point in trying? She would have screamed had the observatory bubble been sound-proofed, but she was still the Commander of the mission. The most the Commander was permitted was a quiet sob, out of sight of her crew. Morale, you know, she told herself bitterly.

In the pitch darkness of the bubble Reese lunged for the torch and map she had laid down by the couch. Her hand struck a metal projection and she yelped as skin scraped cruelly from a knuckle. The sudden pain helped to calm her, though, and as she sucked at the wound she fumbled more carefully with her other hand until she found the torch. With its soft, red light she located the map and unfolded it on her lap.

Nearside and farside of the Moon. She ran her finger across the nearside portion – the side that always faces the Earth – until it rested on Hipparchus. Then she cranked up the magnification of the image.

Craters and mountain chains scarred a huge orange crescent which filled the screen. When her eyes adjusted, she compared the lunar terrain with the representation on her lap. Back and forth, back and forth she shifted her gaze, from map to screen, until she was quite certain; Hipparchus was not visible, it was hidden by the shadow. In a sudden fit of pique, she switched off the computer and swung the telescope away from her.

She had no idea what difference it could have made if she had succeeded in locating Bryant's rough position. She was operating on automatic pilot and could not speak for her subconscious. If asked, she would have found it difficult to say why she was in the observatory bubble at all. She had gravitated there, that was all, while her mind ran and re-ran the desperate events of the past forty-eight hours. It was a good thing she had come, though, she rationalized, because she needed solitude to think about Ustinov's bombshell – and where better to find solitude than the bubble?

Well then, *think*, Reese chided herself. She focused her gaze on the icy terrain of the comet out beyond the plasteel of the observing bubble. It stretched away until it was swallowed by shadows as black as space, and then the stars began. In the light reflected by the snow, knobs and irregularities on the skin of the Hoyle stood out as silhouettes: the comm dish – locked onto Earth; a cluster of reaction control jets – the means by which the *Hoyle* manoeuvred in space; and the radio echo-sounder – Bill's pride and joy.

The echo-sounder suddenly struck Frances as very comical. Under so much strain of late, her subconscious was looking for a relief valve and the spiky protuberances of the radio echo-sounder, looking for all the world like a set of reindeer's antlers sprouting from the skin of the *Hoyle*, provided it. For a moment she forgot Roger Bryant as she took in the unlikely piece of equipment. It looked an afterthought – principally, thought Reese, because it was. It was a scientific instrument on what was quite definitely not a scientific mission, for all the eagerness of the core-drilling team. Bill Noyes had been responsible for the echo-sounder; he had persuaded shuttle support, by various means – not all of them strictly according to regulations – to strap the aerial on to the *Hoyle*.

Frankly, Reese thought, the instrument was a white elephant. But then, she had no astrophysics training, as Bill never failed to remind her whenever she sniped at his elaborate toy.

She caught movement over by the cluster of shuttles. Two suited figures, impossible to tell who at such distance in the faint light. She followed their progress absently. Then they were eclipsed by the aerials of the echo-sounder. Damn that instrument – it was worse than useless! She had the irrational urge to get out there with a wrench and unbolt the thing. Trouble was, Bill would be heartbroken.

The two figures emerged into view once again. Another dozen strides and they'd disappear behind the comm dish. She still couldn't tell who they were, but one of the helmet's seemed to be green – Cherneva maybe, and also . . .

Then she forgot the figures in an instant. She dug fingernails into the arms of the couch, almost stopped breathing, galvanized by a sudden inspirational idea. The comm dish! Why the hell didn't she think of it before? She was up and out of the observatory bubble before the thought was even finished. For God's sake, they weren't completely helpless! They had the comm dish. They could warn Roger to get out of Hipparchus, to get to the mountains, or behind the mountains, someplace where there was at least a chance his team might survive. A slight chance, but better than nothing. Reese held on to it, mentally, as tightly as a shipwrecked sailor grasping at a piece of flotsam on the high seas. *Roger might still be saved*!

\*

"Where's the fire, boss?" Chuck Wenzel had been dozing in his seat by the comm panel when Reese burst through the hatch into the control room. For a split second, as he swam back to full consciousness, he had thought nightmare thoughts. An urgent message from Ustinov had come in and he had failed to log it; worse still, he had failed to relay it to the Commander, for hours (days?) while an unspecified cataclysm (a meteor storm?) loomed ever closer . . . A quick scan of the indicator board showed that no such message had arrived. Phew! A long drawn out sigh of relief was in order (he was innocent!) but he had to stifle it because Reese was breathing down his neck. Literally.

"Chuck, can we send a warning to Roger Bryant? Is it possible?"

"Sure, Commander." Trying to back away when wedged into a fixed seat was difficult, as Wenzel was discovering. What the hell had got into her now?

"No, Chuck. I don't mean through channels." Now she had clasped Wenzel's arms as if she was about to shake him. "No, I mean, can we send a message to Roger without it being picked up on Earth?"

"No way. Sorry." Reese let go of Wenzel and turned to see Mary Xu, entering through the same hatchway. "I wondered what all the noise was, so I came to see." Xu wriggled through, righting herself as she did so. "The answer is no. I already thought about it, and . . ."

"You thought about it? Why didn't you tell me?"

"Because it wouldn't work. You tell her, Chuck."

Wenzel, by now fully awake, was relieved that the heat was off him, and relaxed into his best lecture room manner.

"Well, Commander, I think what Mary appreciates is that the radio beam is too large. Right?" Mary nodded. "We've got a five-meter dish here, and we transmit at one centimetre. So our beam is spread by a tenth of a degree, which means we spray any radio message we send over an angle that big."

"That's what I reckoned," Mary Xu broke in. "And one tenth of a degree is much bigger than the separation of the Earth and Moon from this distance. Anything we broadcast to the Moon will be intercepted on Earth, and the other way round. We can't send a single bit which won't end up on Ustinov's desk."

"If that matters," grunted Chuck, irritated at having his spiel interrupted.

"Of course it does." Although deflated, Reese was back in command. "We've been through all that. Ustinov's tried three separate ways to stop this mission, and the least we let him know the better, until we've finished changing the orbit of this goddamned snowball and there's nothing he can do about it. We still need the orbital data from the Reykjavik computer. I want to warn Roger, but not at the risk of tipping Ustinov off. What about a coded message?"

"Yeah, great. If Roger knew what code we were using." Chuck wasn't yet mollified.

"Well . . ." Mary pursed her lips, the outward sign that she was deep in thought.

"Yes? Well what?" Reese prompted. Her face said it all. She was slipping off that piece of flotsam. Could Mary help her back on again?

"Unless you had some sort of personal code, something only you and Roger would understand. You know – shared experiences, private jokes, the sort of thing lovers understand."

"We weren't lovers, Mary."

"I know, but, well there might be something like that. Give it some thought, Commander."

"I will. I will. Thanks, Mary."

It was a disconsolate Frances Reese who left the control room, no more than ten minutes after her excited entry. Mary had certainly given her food for thought, though. Some sort of personal code; it was certainly an idea. But a code, any code, had its problems. There was always the risk Roger wouldn't decode the message, that he would remember things differently from her, even if she could dredge up something from their mutual past. Certainly nothing sprang to mind.

But then she thought of a more major objection, and her heart sank further. It wasn't sufficient that the RN should be unable to decode the message – they mustn't even suspect that there was a message! Officially, her response to Ustinov's news about the Moon expedition must give no hint that she had something to hide, least of all that she had secrets to share with Bryant. No matter what Ustinov suspected, or what he had found out from Kondratieff, she had to maintain her role for as long as possible if the mission were to succeed.

Reese propelled herself along the main corridor to her cabin. To bed, she thought, but not to sleep; to pull her hair out. All night if need be, because if she didn't think of something Roger would die for sure. She had had her hopes raised once, to no avail; but maybe there was a way. There just *had* to be.

# 12.

Somewhere around 3:00 am, shipboard time, Frances Reese managed to formulate the problem precisely. Not much for two hours of intense brainstorming, but at least it was progress. In the question lay the answer. The old adage that a problem well stated was a problem half solved had always stood up, in her experience. But, of course, that gem of distilled wisdom did rather presuppose that the problem actually had a solution. She still wasn't sure about this one.

She was perched awkwardly on the edge of her bunk, clutching her umpteenth squeeze-tube of coffee. At least that was one problem they didn't share with earlier space missions. No shortage of liquids here, since Yuri Finnegan and Gerry Wolf got the still going. Fusion power, and a world made of ice. They could have a swimming pool, if they wanted to. Irritably, she snapped her wandering mind back to the problem in hand. Sipping at the scalding liquid, she leaned forward so that her face was in the blast of air, set to cold, coming from the ventilator. Caffeine in her bloodstream, ice cold wind on her face, a maximum of discomfort to keep her tired body awake. She had to stay awake, for Roger.

Now. She set the tube down and ticked off points on her fingers, as if addressing an imaginary audience. It went like this. There was no way they could aim a radio broadcast at the Moon without it being detected on Earth. Mary and Chuck had convinced her of that. So that was a dead end. Logic dictated the nature of the problem – to find a signal detectable only on the Moon, not on the Earth. It was no good waiting until the Moon was in line with the Earth, shielding the radio signals, because the Moon was too small – most of the radio beam would go right past it, around the edges, and on to the bigger planet behind. Of course, it would be easy the other way round. Wait until the Moon was hidden behind the Earth, and you could easily send a signal to Earth without it reaching the Moon. Fat lot of help that was, though.

But the Moon was not the same as the Earth, even allowing for the size difference. That, after all, was why they were here, shepherding an iceberg halfway across the Solar System. The Moon had no atmosphere. And the Earth's atmosphere blocked a helluva lot of radiation from space – if it didn't, there'd be no life on Earth. What they needed was a signal that wouldn't penetrate the Earth's atmosphere, but would be detectable on the Moon. An ultraviolet comm laser might help, but they didn't have one. What they had was a transmitter designed to operate on precisely those frequencies that were best at penetrating the Earth's atmosphere and reaching the big dishes of the tracking network, down on the ground. Nobody had envisaged a need for any other kind of communication, so what they had was a radio system operating at centimetre wavelengths, and two lasers – an optical one and one running in the infra-red at 2.2 microns. All wavelengths chosen because they matched the windows in the Earth's atmosphere. And although she might be merely a glorified bus driver, she knew enough physics to realize that you couldn't jury-rig any of those systems to operate effectively at any very different wavelengths. The *Hoyle* and her sister ships simply didn't have the capacity to transmit in the ultraviolet, X-ray or gamma ray bands. She had refined the problem to its basic components, and logic told her that there was no solution.

*Roger, I'm sorry.* Even as she mouthed the words, silently, she knew that Bryant would never know that she had even tried to save him. That was the worst thing of all. Better to let him know that death was coming than do nothing at all. Better for her, that is, for her own conscience.

Suddenly, Reese wanted to sleep, to find peace in unconsciousness. But her brain buzzed with stimulants. It was physically impossible to descend into sleep until they wore off. Unless . . . She lurched out of her cabin into the access way. Two hatches along, on the left, was the *Hoyle*'s dispensary, but she managed to catch her shoulder twice in a cable duct before reaching it. It hurt, but there was nothing she could do. Her coordination was shot, and her body twitched like a galvanized frog's leg. She spilt a tub of endorphin capsules, watching them fall and scatter with lazy grace in the low G, before she found what she was looking for. The inhibitors went down with a mouthful of ice water from the faucet on the bulkhead.

Back in her cabin, Reese felt the drugs take effect. Chemical warfare was being conducted in her bloodstream. And then she slept. Only it wasn't a peaceful, relaxed sleep. It was an odd state between waking and sleeping, in which, periodically, she focused on the light in her cabin before being sucked back down into the world of half dreams and living nightmares. She was underwater, again, her legs trapped, floating but not free, unable to breathe, blackness descending upon her, until someone – Roger – was there, moving a tangle of beams and letting her float to the surface and life-giving air. Again she was floating, in space this time, looking down on the Earth-Moon system, with the Dragon rushing toward the Moon, trying to hold it back with her bare hands, but seeing it slip through her insubstantial fingers. She could see Roger, inside Hipparchus Base, oblivious to the onrushing doom, and she shouted to him; but, of course, with impeccable logic her dream-self realized that no sound could travel through the vacuum of space, so she was not surprised when he failed to heed her warning.

Then she was back on her bunk, scarcely aware of the tiny pull of the Dragon's gravity, floating, once again, and staring at the wall of the cabin, half awake – no, still asleep, but aware of her dreaming state, on her bunk but outside the *Hoyle*, looking at the outside bulkhead.

She had a set of tools laid out beside her on the bed. Nothing seemed wrong. She was outside the *Hoyle*, on the bed, with no spacesuit on, and a set of tools beside her. The dream logic had a grip on her, even though she knew she was dreaming. What were the tools for? She found that she could control the dream, up to a point. She picked up a wrench, and held it in her right hand. It felt good; it belonged there. The wrench was important. It felt right. She looked at the *Hoyle* again, seeing the ludicrous reindeer-horns of the echo-sounder in front of her. Ha! That was what the wrench was for. She would unbolt the stupid thing and throw it away, just as she had wanted to do yesterday.

She lifted the wrench to the bolts fixing the antenna to the skin of the *Hoyle*. There were eight bolts. Slowly, methodically, her dream-self applied the wrench to one of them and unscrewed it. Three turns and it began to spin freely, untwisting itself and popping out into the vacuum, spinning like a tiny gyroscope. Then the next. Three turns, and it was free. And another. And another. Until the last bolt, which broke loose and bounced up, as if pushed by a powerful spring. She followed its trajectory, staring up into the black sky spattered with diamond bright stars until she could see it no more.

When she turned back to the antenna, it was firmly in place, held by eight tightly screwed bolts. So, she applied the wrench again, carefully undoing each bolt, until the last one sprang out, as if on a spring. She knew she mustn't watch it, that it was a distraction, but she couldn't help herself. Once again she watched the bolt soar into the sky. And once again, when she turned back to the antenna, it was securely held in place by eight bolts.

And again. And again. Every time she unbolted the antenna, it fastened itself back to the skin of the *Hoyle*. And the worst of it was, she knew it was all a nightmare, but she couldn't break free from its grip. Suddenly, after how many unsuccessful attempts at unbolting the antenna she never knew, the cabin light loomed before her, and she fought her way towards consciousness, concentrating on the brightness, forcing her eyes open and her mind to clear. She fought, and she won.

As she overcame her disorientation, half sitting, half laying, her garments bathed in sweat, Reese was struck by the idea that something in the dream, the nightmare, was important. But she didn't know what, and already it was fading, dissolving in her memory. Quickly, she grabbed for the light pen and hit the "sketchpad" button on her console, and tried desperately to draw the scene she had pictured so vividly in her mind when she was asleep. The bed, herself, the tools, and the skin of the *Hoyle*, with its forest of antennas. She looked at the picture. It made no sense. Just a crazy dream, wish fulfillment about getting rid of the worse than useless antenna of the echo-sounder. Her mind only linked it with the drowning dream and the Moon dream because she was worried about Roger. Crazy dream logic.

She started to reach for the "erase" button. Then she stopped, left hand poised in mid movement, right still clutching the light pen, staring again at the white traces on the black screen. The echo-sounder! It was the answer. She sat, transfixed, for what seemed like minutes, but could only have been seconds. Then, even as she threw the light pen from her and leaped for the hatch, all thoughts of her dishevelled, sweaty state forgotten, she knew that she only had half the answer. She had seen the echo-sounder as the answer to her problems, but there was more to it than that.

Her momentum had carried her out into the access way by the time she realized her mistake. She felt like a skydiver who leaps confidently out of an aircraft, only to discover that her parachute is missing. She kicked angrily at the padded plasteel wall, bruising her foot and spinning awkwardly off balance, before heading determinedly for the galley. If she had half the answer, someone else could damn well come up with the other half, and quick. She was so close, it was such a good idea, there had to be a way to make it work.

All they had to do was use the radio echo-sounder to send a message to Roger. It operated at ten megahertz, well inside the range where the Earth's atmosphere was opaque to radio waves. It had to be possible to divert the power of the main comm system into the reindeer antlers and send a message to Roger, but even then it wouldn't be a tight beam like the one from the main comm dish. It would spread thin before it reached the Moon, only a weak whisper compared with the shout of the main comm beam. Maybe Roger Bryant wouldn't be able to pick up that faint whisper, anyway, just as he hadn't heard her shouting in the dream. But the worse thing was, *there was no reason why anyone on the Moon should be listening out at ten megs!*

"I was going to ask," said Mary Xu, picking her words carefully, "I was going to ask, whether you now think there's any way we can warn Bryant?"

Mary Xu, a full eight hours out of phase with Reese and at the end of her duty shift, paused between mouthfuls of her evening meal. The meal looked suspiciously like chicken curry but could have been almost anything.

The question hung in the air between them, but Reese made no attempt to answer it. Instead, in a weary and resigned voice, she asked for more coffee. Mary Xu, embarrassed, passed it and developed a sudden intense interest in her curry.

"The answer's no, Mary." Reese said suddenly. Xu looked up in surprise.

"Look, Commander. I'm sorry, I didn't mean to rub salt in. If you'd rather not . . ."

"There's no hope for Roger," Reese said, pushing her cereal, virtually untouched, to one side. "I went through all the possibilities, one by one. But it's hopeless, Mary. There's no way, not without giving everything away to the RN." Reese put her head in her hands. She was no longer making even a cosmetic attempt to conceal her defeat. "Roger's as good as dead," she said finally.

It unnerved Xu to see her Commander in such a state, and her relief was almost audible when there was a sudden commotion at the hatch and Bill Noyes wriggled through into the galley.

"Okay, what's going on here?" He opened breezily. Reese didn't even raise her head to acknowledge his presence.

"Bad as that is it, Frances?"

He sat down, reached across and tousled Frances' hair. She lifted her heavy head and looked at him with blank, red rimmed eyes.

"You look terrible."

"Thanks a lot."

"Don't tell me," he said, his face softening noticeably, "Roger Bryant."

"Right in one," Mary Xu replied, and went on to explain the reasons for Reese's state. Noyes bit his lip as he listened.

"All night, eh? And still nothing?" Reese shook her head.

"Right." He rapped the tabletop imperiously. "First off, stop feeling sorry for yourself. Next give us your ideas. All of them."

"It's no use Bill. They were all dead ends."

"We'll decide that, okay? Come on Commander," Xu noticed the emphasis and nodded. Bill was doing the right thing, reminding Reese of her responsibilities. "You know as well as I do that three heads are better than one."

"It makes no difference. There's no way to warn Roger. Don't you think if there was I would have thought of it by now?" Noyes ignored her.

"Could have overlooked something. Who knows? Now, stop being stubborn and lay your ideas on the table. Let's start with the most promising."

"I tell you, it's no good."

"Frances!"

"All right, all right. Well, I did think for a while – before I saw that it was ridiculous – I did think . . ."

"Yes?" said Noyes, impatiently. "If you've got even half an idea, share it. Let Mary and me be the judges."

"Okay, you're right, Bill. It was this: I thought that if we sent a signal at a frequency so low that it was screened out by the Earth's ionosphere . . ." She went on to explain her plan to use the radio echo-sounder. Before she had even finished, Mary Xu spotted the fundamental flaw in the idea.

"Signal's too weak, Commander," she said matter of factly.

"Exactly what I thought. That's why I didn't mention it . . ." Reese broke off. She would have derived a morbid pleasure from saying, I told you so, but she didn't, not out of any concern for Noyes' feelings, nothing as commendable as that; it was just that he was grinning from ear to ear.

"But that's it, Frances. You're brilliant!"

"Bill, the signal will be too weak. Mary just said it."

"It doesn't matter!" He was jubilant.

"Of course it matters. Bryant'll have no way of picking up such a weak signal on the Moon."

"But he will!"

"Look Bill. Do you mind not playing games with me?" Now it was Reese's turn to get impatient.

"Frances, didn't you think of the Hipparchus Array?"

"The Hipparchus Array?" At first it didn't click. Then Reese underwent a sudden and dramatic transformation. She let out a yell. She jumped to her feet and sprung across the table, scattering magnetic cutlery and bowls of food in her wake.

"Bill! That's . . . Oh, Bill why didn't I . . . ?" Her inertia sent them both flying in the low G. "And I nearly didn't tell anyone about the echo-sounder . . ."

"Will someone let me in on this please?" Mary Xu was looking puzzled.

"Sorry, Mary." By this time Reese had calmed down and Noyes had regained some of his dignity. "Frances, tell her."

"Well, I probably don't know any more than you, just snippets I've picked up in history books. The Hipparchus Array's a large radio telescope. Not a steerable dish, simply a network of dipole antennae strung together. Right, Bill?"

"That's about it."

"So?" said Mary.

"So it operates around a few megahertz! Astronomers used it for mapping the sky at frequencies so low that they were cut out of the Earth's ionosphere. They didn't even have to put it on Farside, because the Earth's ionosphere blocks out all the noise from human transmission at that frequency."

"Which is why they built it that way," Noyes cut in, "any other frequencies and they'd have had to build it on Farside, but, of course, the first radio telescope on the Moon had to be built right next door to Base One."

"Oh, I see," said Mary, slowly, as understanding dawned. "You think it can be used to pick up even the weak signal of the echo-sounder?"

"Tell me what else radio telescopes are good for," Noyes crowed, triumphantly.

"The Hipparchus Array could pick up our echo-sounder at Pluto! It's that sensitive. Not only that but . . . Boss?" Reese had taken a seat at the breakfast table once more. She had regained her composure, and the colour in her cheeks, and her expression was now one of fierce concentration.

"Bill. Mary, sit down," she said earnestly. Noyes did so. Mary was already seated. "Now, Bill have you thought out the details?" The Commander had taken charge again.

"Not yet. But first off, we have to figure out how to get Bryant to listen at precisely ten megahertz."

"How about this, Bill?" At the first whiff of hope her mind had begun racing and she had anticipated the first problem. "We send a conventional radio message to Hipparchus, or to Earth and ask them to relay it to the Moon. We make the message as innocuous as possible so it won't raise eyebrows on Earth."

"Tricky. What you got in mind?"

"We can tell Roger we're picking up ten megahertz emissions from Jupiter. Say we think there's something interesting happening in the Jovian radiation belts but we haven't got the sensitivity to tell what it is. Could he get the Hipparchus Array up and running? He can check everything's running okay by listening out for us. We tell him we'll provide a calibration signal with our echo-sounder."

"And he'll buy that? You're sure?"

"Of course I'm not sure. But what would you do in his shoes? You'd be a little puzzled at such a request. You'd sit and think about it for a while and then, when you still couldn't figure it out, you'd go fiddle with the Array. Isn't that what you'd do?"

"Yeah, I suppose I would."

"But the RN are sure to be suspicious, Frances?" Mary interjected.

"Of course." answered Bill. "They already are, for Christ's sake. But they won't *know*, and we'll just have to hope they take a long time guessing what we're up to. I think it'll take them a while. After all, Frances has hit on a pretty outlandish idea."

"Half the credit's yours."

"Well, let's share the congratulations after it works, eh?"

"Agreed," beamed back Reese. "Right. Action stations. I'm going to send the first message to Bryant."

"Careful with that wording. We don't want Ustinov down our necks."

"What do you take me for?" Already in the hatch, she stopped and swivelled round.

"Bill, make sure you can modulate the echo-sounder ready for my warning to Bryant."

"No need. We'll just switch the thing on and off. Morse code. It's the simplest and most effective way to send a message."

"Well, go and practise or something . . ." Her voice faded away as she disappeared down the corridor.

"Dinner first," Noyes shouted after her, too late for her to hear.

"What the hell's that?" He pointed at the dish Mary Xu was clearing away.

"Curry, I think. I didn't take much notice really. Want some?"

"Why not?"

She retrieved a hot dish from the dispenser and deposited it on the table in front of him.

"*Bon appétit.*"

"Yeah, thanks," he replied, prodding it gingerly.

"And good night." She launched herself towards the hatch, leaving him alone in the galley to savour the culinary delights of interplanetary flight.

# 13.

"More tea?" Kate Bryant's enquiry brought a smile and a nod from her visitor, who held out the cup to be filled. Sunlight streamed in through the open windows of the verandah, and the reassuring noise of the children playing on the grass sloping down into the valley drifted in with it. Hildy Wenzel's smile broadened, and she nodded towards the sound.

"They still get on pretty well together, don't they?"

Kate smiled in response. "I don't think Billy regards her as a girl at all. He's going through a phase, says girls are crass; but he's known Rebecca so long, I guess he doesn't count her as a female."

"She'd be pleased to know that! That daughter of mine – well, I've never known a less girly girl than her. God knows, there'll be trouble there, one way or the other, in a year or two."

But the smiles belied the expressions of concern. Hildy was proud of her daughter, tomboy or not, and it showed. Kate was equally proud of Billy; both families got on well, sharing holidays together, when Chuck and Roger were both around at the same time, hiking and camping in the mountains. Both sets of parents shared the unspoken thought – it wouldn't be right to put any kind of pressure on the kids, but one day, maybe, if Rebecca ever noticed she was a girl, well, maybe they could share a set of grandchildren, too.

"So, how's it going with Chuck?"

Hildy's face sobered, just a little. She sipped her tea before answering. Kate was worried about Roger, she knew. But this was her way – relax and socialize first, then slide the worry out into the open later, when things were quiet, and the kids were out of earshot.

"We haven't heard a lot. But then, we didn't expect to. It's so far to the Dragon – we can't expect face to face contact. Just messages, you know. Sends his love, all well, home soon."

"I know." Kate picked up her teaspoon and prodded, idly, at the sugar in the bowl in front of her.

"It's just. Well, the Moon isn't so far away. I thought they'd let me talk to Roger. After all, it's almost like being in Earth orbit."

Hildy leaned forward, put down her cup, and placed a reassuring hand on Kate's knee.

"Oh, hell, Kate. You know what those bureaucrats in Reykjavik are like. They just don't realize that it means to you. Anyway, Roger'll be back before perigee."

"I hope so."

"C'mon. You know he will. There's no reason to think anything's wrong, is there?"

Kate shook her head.

"Well, look, I tell you what. You know Kondratieff's invited all the Dragon families up to Iceland for the celebrations. We're sending recorded messages up, and there's going to be a big reception. Why don't you come, too? It'll take your mind off things."

Kate shook her head again, and smiled, faintly.

"No, you're right."

She stood up, briskly, and moved towards the window.

"It's just me, missing Roger. But I'd miss him more up there. It's better to be home, with Billy."

"Tell the truth, that's how I feel. But between you and me, this invitation to Reykjavik isn't the sort of thing you can turn down!"

Kate smiled again, more naturally, and turned to her friend.

"Royal command, huh? Come on, Hildy. Let's not sit around in here being miserable. I'll find the kids, and we can go for a ride up in the hills. Maybe Billy can find the comet for us when it gets dark."

Four days old and already it streamed a hundred thousand kilometres across space. What had begun as an imperceptible trickle of volatiles out into the vacuum was now the largest geyser in the Solar System, gushing sublimated ices at over a thousand kilometres an hour. Old Faithful, Bertorelli had christened it, after a prototype in his adopted homeland, and the name had stuck. In volume, Old Faithful dwarfed its terrestrial namesake by an enormous factor; yet the mass of expelled material was quite tiny, compared with the mass of the comet, only a few kilograms per second. No wonder the furthest reaches of the cometary outflow were reeling under the ferocious onslaught of the solar wind, twisting and breaking up as the Sun's magnetic field tore into the tenuous gas.

It was ironic that the first view of Old Faithful to be seen by Reese and her colleagues had been transmitted from Earth. From the surface of the comet stars still shone through the outflowing gas as if it were not there. Infra-red scans revealed the presence of the geyser, but, looking along the outflow, there was little to be seen. Not so from Earth.

Only the occasional whistle of surprise broke the stillness of the assembled crew in the first few minutes after the images from Earth started arriving. A resourceful engineer in Arizona had managed to get the old 15-metre multiple mirror telescope up and running, with half-decent detectors on the back end, and the stunning results were now up on the viewer for all to see.

The comet nucleus itself was still small as seen from Earth, but its halo of evaporated ices formed a spherical smudge against the star field. The growing tail pointed away from the Sun, but stretching out in the opposite direction, almost towards the Sun, was the narrowest streamer of phosphorescent gas, stabbing out to the edge of the field of view. Old Faithful, in all its spectacular glory. It really did look as if the Dragon was breathing fire.

"Well?" said Reese, offloading on to Mary Xu the sheaf of hardcopy photos. Bodies lounged on acceleration couches, spread across the rec room table (carefully avoiding Reese's line of sight to the screen) or clung at gravity-defying angles from wall rails.

Heads turned, reluctantly. "Well? Who predicted that?" Reese stabbed her finger at the screen as the latest image built up over the remnant of the last. It was a rhetorical question. No one had predicted Old Faithful, even after the seismometers had begun registering a swarm of microtremors centred on the quake region. The consensus verdict had been that the tremors were due to a belated settling of the bed ice after the quake. Even Du Toit, with his geophysics background, had endorsed that view.

She was angry. Mistakes that should never have been made were being made. Perhaps that was understandable, after all they'd been through. First they had been surprised by the quake, then Blixen and the mutiny, Valentina's sacrifice, and now this. They were all getting careless. Some acted as if there was nothing left to worry about and the job was done, while others still seemed in a state of depression. Hardly anyone was functioning normally, and only Bill really seemed to give a damn whether or not Roger got the message in time. What next? She scanned her audience, defying someone to answer her questions. "Finnegan? Perez? Saha?" She fixed them each in turn and watched them shift uncomfortably under her gaze. Let them, she thought, this must not happen again. They might all be dead next time.

Right. Time to knock some sense into everyone. Okay, they'd been working so hard they had neglected to look over their shoulders for unwelcome possibilities. Now it was time to get back some of the old NASA discipline and start looking at all the options. She prepared to deliver the dressing down needed to bring everyone back to full alertness. But before she could launch her prepared tirade, the silence broke. The voice belonged to Maria Blixen, and there could hardly have been a more unexpected interruption. In the days since Maria had been isolated by the crew, she had rarely been seen, emerging from her cubbyhole only for meals, which she ate in defiant silence. The "mutiny" – only Maria used the term – still obsessed her. After Jackson's abortive attempt at sabotage, she had been watched carefully – but what harm could she do? A search of her quarters had shown no secret equipment like the gear Jackson had used to bypass the safeties, and most of them felt sorry for her. She was so much a victim of her own delusions, so deflated, and so pathetically hopeful that her wonder man, Ustinov, would come up with some trick. They'd gradually got in the habit of letting her sit in on gatherings, like before – otherwise, someone else had to miss the meeting to be on guard duty. And, besides, she hadn't had much to say for herself lately – until now.

"I have something to say, Frances." Only Maria used the Commander's christian name, a calculated reminder that Reese was technically her subordinate. All eyes fixed on the slim figure. Maria smiled benevolently at her audience, a touch of the old Maria reasserting itself. She had seized centre stage for a reason. Blixen had lost the first showdown, but now she evidently felt she had another card to play.

"Go ahead, Maria." Softly, conciliatory, but wary. Reese steeled herself for the worst.

"I think – " she took her time, scanning the attentive faces of the crew, but avoiding catching Reese's eye.

"I think your plan is in trouble." The stress on *your* indicated Blixen's denial of complicity.

A pause to let the bombshell sink in. "Has anyone calculated the rocket effect of the geyser?"

"Old Faithful's only pushing out a few kilos per second. The effect is tiny." Mary Xu dismissed Maria's bombshell out of hand.

"But can it be ignored? Old Faithful, as you call it, is spewing material out at half a kilometre a second, and the reaction must push the comet in the opposite direction. We're no longer on a passive piece of ice dancing to the tune of gravity. This comet has its own propulsion source now, and that's going to throw all your calculations out!" Triumphantly, Maria folded her arms across her chest.

"It's a small effect . . . we can compensate . . ." Finnegan's voice was uncertain; he looked at Reese for support.

"Have you calculated it? Has anyone? Have they?" Maria Blixen's pallid face was gaining colour; adrenalin was flowing. She flicked a strand of hair away from her eyes and laid down her challenge. "The truth is, no one knows how big the effect is, and no one can predict how it will change. Old Faithful may not be that faithful. He's slowing the comet down now, sure, and you can calculate the effect – when you get around to it – and compensate. But suppose he switches off, or gets stronger, after you've made the main burn?

"Oh yes, Finnegan, it's a small effect. But how big does it have to be? A small nudge will push this comet out to miss the Moon by at least the Moon's own diameter. You only need a pocket computer to work it out. And you all know that you have to dump this lump of ice within three hundred klicks of Hyperion, or all our lives will have been risked for nothing. No Moon, *and* no spaceforce. You're wasting your time."

"Okay Maria, point taken." Reese looked outwardly confident, but inside a voice warned, Don't underestimate Blixen, don't underestimate . . . "So we hold back the capacity for a correction burn later. All we have to do is figure out the total impulse Old Faithful will give the comet before impact, and do a quick burn ahead of time to cancel the effect out."

But Maria was still smiling, an ominous, patronizing smile.

"Not so simple, Frances. Old Faithful is getting stronger all the time, and who can tell if he will change significantly, one way or the other, even after your last minute burn? Some things just can't be predicted, no matter how good a computer you use.

"And isn't there another problem? Aren't you forgetting that Secretary Ustinov appears to have had the wisdom to cut the data link? Just how well can you calculate the trajectory with no computer link?"

Reese turned, as always, to Bill Noyes in a crisis.

"Bill?"

"Well. I don't know. We certainly don't need any updates from Earth if the geyser stops blowing soon. The data we've got are more than adequate. And as long as it's a steady jet, the revisions are going to be small. Maybe we really could do the adjustments with our pocket computers here." He indicated the control panel beside him.

Maria snorted, contemptuously.

"If, If, If. *If* nothing else goes wrong; *if* the jet stays ready – how likely is that?"

She swung, suddenly, to Mary Xu. "How many core samples have you taken from this thing? Ten?"

"Twelve."

"Okay, twelve. Out of the whole comet. And they were all different, right?"

"What are you getting at?"

"This comet is about as homogeneous as a slab of chocolate ripple ice cream. We think we know why the geyser started up. The quake shook off a layer of dusty surface, and allowed the Sun to get to work on the volatiles beneath. But as Old Faithful works his way down through that layer, what happens when he reaches the next layer of dust? He switches off, right?"

"Right." It was Finnegan, getting back in on the act. "It's happened before with comets. Dozens of documented cases going back three centuries or more."

"Or", Maria's smile was broader yet, "there might be another quake. The ice and dust might shift, and we could get another Old Faithful, pushing in a different direction."

The implication was now obvious to everyone. If the future behaviour of Old Faithful could not be predicted, then there was no way its effect could be compensated for in advance. Maria hammered the point home, anyway.

"You can never be certain of hitting Hyperion. Never. Unless . . ."

"Unless?"

"Unless some of you stay with the comet. You've got to ride the Dragon to destruction, and compensate for Old Faithful by hand. You've got to fly this thing on to the Moon. And even then your efforts will probably be wasted, since Secretary Ustinov is hardly likely to switch the computers back on just to pander to your whims. Even if your story is true, he won't take kindly to being made a fool of."

Blixen still hadn't finished. One more nail in the coffin.

"Think on it, all of you. If this mission is so important, then maybe two or three of you would like to volunteer for suicide. On the other hand, it's not too late to see sense. The RN isn't going to tell anyone about your crazy scheme as long as you decide to see reason and call a halt before it's too late."

Damn her, Reese cursed silently. The mission *was* important. They all knew that, and they all knew there was a risk of not coming out alive. But there was a difference between chance of death and the certainty. She wasn't sure if she would be willing to make that sacrifice herself; and there was no way she could order anyone else to accompany her, even if they would accept such orders. And no matter how good a shuttle pilot she might be, she doubted she could fly the Dragon on her own.

There was an expectant hush. Finnegan licked his lips, and looked as if he might be about to say something. Surely he wasn't going to volunteer?

"No." Reese acted decisively. "No one's committing suicide. We'll make the best projections we can, leave the last burn as late as possible, and hope for the best. It'll be in the lap of the gods. We can't do more than that."

But in her heart she was sick. She glanced towards the hatch, but Blixen was gone. Back to her cubby to gloat. That woman had finally won a victory.

# 14.

"You think we can really start it up?" Templeton's voice came over the suit radio, as he brought the rover to a halt outside the control building.

"Frankly, no," replied Abel, "but it's what the boss wants, so who are we to argue?" He unstrapped himself from the passenger seat and leapt out into the ankle deep moon-dust. Templeton switched the rover to 'park' and did likewise. The pair of them stood a while examining their surroundings.

"Okay," Abel said, with authority. "The first thing we do is go and check the Array itself."

"What for?"

"Don't know. But it seems to me to be the most sensible place to start. Got any better ideas?"

"Nope. What I know about radio telescopes you could scratch on one side of a femtochip. Lead the way."

"Right then, let's go. Race you, Ben?"

"Don't be daft, man. This is the Moon, not Venice beach. There's a freezing vacuum out there. One false move and . . ."

"Rubbish! Surrender to an irrational impulse now and then. Live a little."

"That's just what I have in mind. Living." But Abel wasn't listening.

"Come on, Ben, last one to the ridge breaks the bad news to Roger."

"What bad news?"

"Any bad news." He was gone, in a cloud of dust. At times like these Templeton thought that Greg Abel was the most infuriating person he had ever met. The two of them were absolute opposites, like chalk and cheese. Why then, did he like the man? He puzzled over the phenomenon as he trudged up the incline.

At the top, Abel blocked his way, legs astride, hands on hips.

"You're no fun at all. Two weeks confined in pressurized tin cans and you act like an old man when you get out in the fresh air."

"Fresh air!"

"Metaphorical, Ben. Open spaces, the great outdoors, call it what you like."

Templeton glimpsed Abel's face through the tinted visor of his helmet. He had now shut his eyes and was contentedly sucking in lungfuls of bottled fresh air. Templeton shook his head. If I hadn't seen it with my own eyes, he muttered, with his radio off. He pushed on past and saw the Array for the first time.

"My God, it's enormous!"

"Four square kilometres. Two kilometres on a side," he heard Abel reply.

Four square kilometres! Templeton had somehow imagined it would be smaller. The Array stretched across the levelled floor of a large impact crater. From their vantage point, a hundred metres up on the rampart of the crater, it resembled an enormous bed of nails, dusted lightly with cobwebs. The nails were the dipole antennas, fifty thousand of them, and the cobwebs the network of interconnecting cable.

By now Abel was surveying the scene too.

"It's fixed," Templeton observed with surprise.

"Sure it's fixed. What did you expect? You steer a telescope like this electronically. Vary the phase lag from element to element. It's all text book stuff."

"Of course," Templeton replied, "how stupid of me." But

the sarcasm was lost on Abel who seemed no longer to be listening. He had evidently seen something unusual because he was pointing.

"See that?"

Templeton followed his companion's gloved finger, straining his eyes in the dim Earthlight. He saw nothing immediately. He should have asked what he was supposed to be looking at but he was determined not to appear the dummy again. So he kept quiet and looked harder. When he finally saw what Abel was pointing at he wondered how he could ever have missed it. A diagonal scar – at least it looked like a scar – cut right across one corner of the Array. And where it terminated something was glinting in the Earthlight. Yes, something was definitely there. The more he stared the more sure he became.

"What is it?" he asked, guessing that Abel didn't know either. He was right. Abel, for once, didn't have a clue.

"Whatever it is, it doesn't look too healthy," he said. "I think we'd better take a closer look." This time Abel did wait for his companion, and the two space-suited figures descended the gentle slope together.

Once in amongst the dipoles, with the cables strung seven or eight metres above their heads, they got an ant's view of the Array. The dipoles had been planted following a grid system, the rows about ten metres apart. Templeton found that the picture of a bed of nails was no longer useful this close up. The new analogy which sprang into his mind was of an orchard. An orchard on the Moon! Now that was a bizarre thought. And as bizarre thoughts often do, it conjured up a whole chain of fanciful images. Chief among them was a scene in which fruit bearing trees were sprouting from the dessiccated lunar soil. Templeton found the image hard to blot out.

As he followed Abel deeper into the Array, he half expected to scuff his boot on something partially buried in the grey dust, bend down to investigate and discover a ripe apple lying there, or a glistening orange!

165

They were now zig-zagging rapidly across the grid. Abel seemed to know exactly where he was going despite the fact that, down on the ground, every avenue of the Array resembled every other avenue. Much though it hurt his pride Templeton was beginning to believe that his friend possessed an uncanny direction sense, in addition to his other infuriating qualities. Then he realized suddenly how Abel was doing it. He was counting! The man had obviously had the foresight to note the coordinates of their destination while they were high on the rampart with the Array spread before them like a street map below. Far from cutting Abel down to size this realization only served to increase Templeton's respect for his friend. He wondered, despairingly, how many more weeks his own battered self image could survive in the presence of this man. He put on a quick spurt to catch up with him.

Abel saw him come abreast and spoke. "Not far now. Thirty rows across, and twenty-five up. By my reckoning anyway."

"Right," Templeton replied. That 'right' was intentionally ambiguous. It could easily have meant, by my reckoning too. "Look, Greg," he started, to cover himself. "Look; what do you honestly think about the message from Frances Reese?"

"Damned odd, that's what I think."

"Then you agree with Roger, that she's trying to tell us something?"

"Well, look at it this way. We're worse than amateurs as far as atronomy is concerned. None of us really has a clue how to operate a radio telescope."

"Apart from yourself."

"Text book electrical engineering, that's all I know. This is the real world. It's totally different." He paused a moment to think. "It's like giving an Amazon indian a flight systems manual and expecting him to pilot a shuttle."

He turned a corner sharply and Templeton just avoided over-shooting. "Look, say by some miracle, we actually get this thing working," Abel went on. "What useful science do you think we, a bunch of rank amateurs, are likely to get out of Jupiter's radiation belts? And who the hell cares anyhow? I mean the whole thing's a joke."

"So, if Jupiter's radiation belts are a red herring, what's she trying to tell us?"

"All I can think is that it's some practical joke at our expense. A score she's been wanting to settle with Roger for a long time. I don't know, maybe he jilted her for another woman."

"Roger? No."

"Got a better idea?"

"No, but I can't believe that. I can think of less elaborate ways of settling a score than that. Besides, Roger saved Reese's life. Why should she have a bone to pick with him? It's too fantastic."

"Have it your own way. I still think Roger knows more than he's telling us."

"You've been reading too many spy stories."

"When you've lived as long as me, Ben, you get to know what makes people tick . . ."

"Don't give me that, you're only two years older than me."

"Years? What are years? It's experience that counts."

"Yeah, yeah. And you're a man of the world, eh?"

"Jest if you like. We'll see what comes out of this affair. We'll see . . ."

"Well, at the moment we only have one responsibility. To try our best to get this Array up and running. It'll make Roger a lot happier if nothing el . . . Oh, shit!"

On turning a corner they came suddenly on the first signs of damage. Nearby dipoles no longer stood vertically. Instead they were bowed. The effect got progressively more marked further along the grid. Fifty metres ahead of the two men the regularity of the Array finally degenerated into utter chaos. The telescope had been pounded completely flat as if by an explosion.

In the clearing they found the ground littered with severed cables and broken aerials. Maximum damage had been suffered by a section of the Array some sixty metres wide. Templeton couldn't tell for sure how far it extended lengthways but he guessed it might be ten times that distance. A huge furrow seemed to run along the centre of the cleared tract. Something had gouged it deep into the lunar bedrock. Sure enough, in the distance a metallic object shone dully in the Earthlight.

Templeton broke the silence. "A surface shuttle?" he asked.

"I think so," replied Abel. "The pilot must have lost control. Christ, they were in a hurry when they left the Moon. The history tapes don't give you any idea of what it was like in those days."

"You think anyone got out?"

"It's possible. The pilot must have brought the shuttle in as shallow as he could to kill the forward momentum. Look at the size of that furrow. It must be over a metre deep and three wide."

"The excavated rock flattened the surrounding dipoles?"

"That's about it. Must have been like shrapnel. Come on, we might as well take a look at the shuttle." They set off along the furrow.

"I'll radio Roger, tell him the Array's a write-off."

"No, wait."

"What do you mean? The telescope's smashed to pieces."

"But it might not be fatal. No point in ruining Roger's day until we're sure."

"You mean to say there's a chance it'll work?"

"There's a chance. The dipoles must be isolated from each other to some extent. No one would design a thing like this and allow one element to jeopardize the entire instrument."

"But, we're not talking about losing one element, we're talking about hundreds."

"Out of fifty thousand?"

"I see what you mean." By this time the two men had reached the surface shuttle. Or what was left of it. At the end of its monumental skid it had up-ended and drilled itself into the dust. Only the rear of the silver fuselage, complete with blackened rocket motors, stuck out above the surface.

"Perhaps he didn't get out," Abel said gloomily.

Templeton stared at the wreckage a moment. "Okay then, let's take a look at the control room."

They left the Array and climbed back up the crater rampart. Race you up, Templeton nearly said. But it was the wrong moment.

A noose. She rubbed the back of her neck, imagining the feel of the rope around it. Don't be ridiculous, she told herself. He can't be on to us. And besides, it's a firing squad, these days, not nooses. But she knew why the image had conjured itself into her brain. Giving them enough rope . . .

Mikhail was an idiot. She dismissed the thought from her mind, as she had just dismissed him from her presence. The old fox wasn't that clever. It was unfortunate that the operation in California had never really got off the ground, but after all it made sense to round up such unruly elements whenever there was an excuse. And Ironfist wasn't a complete idiot, after all. But the Australian operation, now. *That* had gone like clockwork, disrupting his links with that strange comet mission, it had got people running around in a fine state of panic. Ustinov was definitely disturbed, and his disturbance was linked with the comet. This must be the time to strike, while his attention was elsewhere.

If Mikhail was compromised by the California operation – and why else would one of Ustinov's toadies have come scurrying in hot foot from the region? – we!l, even Mikhail was expendable. Anyone was expendable, as long as the finger of suspicion never pointed directly at her.

Timing, that was the key. All she needed was the moment to strike. But why had old Ironfist instructed all the astronaut families to gather here, in Reykjavik? And why was Kondratieff being held incommunicado? In disgrace? Surely not. He was the key to this whole damned comet business. For his own protection, then? And who would Ustinov think he needed protecting from?

Frowning, she leaned forward on the desk, chasing the ramifications round in circles. A cold breeze seemed to strike across the back of her neck, causing the short hairs to rise. Just a breeze, she told herself, firmly, rubbing above the line of her collar with the palm of her left hand.

If he wasn't so tired, Greg Abel would have made some quip about déja vu. It was, after all, the second time he had gathered everyone around the control console of the Hipparchus Array. Nine and a half hours earlier, to the verbal equivalent of a drum roll, he'd attempted to activate the instrument for the first time. Nothing had happened.

So, no more quips, no more drum rolls. It had been a tough nine and a half hours. He'd started out like a marathon runner, breasting the tape only to be informed there'd been a mistake, he'd have to go round the course again. Two days and nights now, working on the Array. A third of that time out alone in the buggy, troubleshooting among the waveguides. And for what? What could the Dragon team possibly have found that was so important? But Roger was convinced. If Frances Reese said it was necessary, then Roger Bryant sure wasn't going to let her down.

Well, here they were again. And he was delaying. Because he was terrified the damn thing still wouldn't work. And, admit it, because he enjoyed being at centre stage, everyone watching, waiting for him to push the key. Let the buggers wait, he thought. They'd no idea how much blood and guts had gone into this. Bryant, Russell and Higuchi had done bugger all. Just him and Templeton.

He couldn't have done it without Templeton. Amazing how that guy could dip into unfamiliar manuals and dredge out the information they needed. Templeton might not be a practical man, but Abel knew that without him he'd never have understood the Array well enough to botch up a few working connections. If he had botched them up into working order.

"C'mon Greg." It was Templeton who broke the silence. "Let's know the worst."

No more delay. He turned to the console, and typed a string of commands. Too fast. He had to retype the instructions, more slowly. The screen filled with words; the program was running. Dire threats of the repercussions resulting from illegal use or copying of the program marched across the screen, while the coordinates Templeton had supplied were loaded, and the Array was coming to life – or not.

Either way, they wouldn't have long to wait. It wasn't like a dish antenna that had to be physically pointed. The Array did its "pointing" electronically, switching phases in the different antennas.

Words – beautiful, magic words – appeared on the screen, flashing rhythmically: SOURCE ACQUIRED . . . SOURCE ACQUIRED . . . SOURCE ACQUIRED . . .

"Easy, when you know how." Abel's broad grin belied his nonchalant tone. The Array had picked up a source at just the programmed frequency, in just the right part of the sky.

A trace appeared on a screen to Abel's right. A simple XY plot, a graph showing the strength of the incoming signal. It was a beautiful, straight line across the screen, really powerful. As they watched, it fell back, disappearing into the background noise. Abel cursed, and swung back to the console. What the Hell had gone wrong now? But everything was as it should be. He looked back to the second screen, in time to see the signal jump back out of the noise, trace its line for a while, then vanish again.

Templeton was pushing buttons. "Nothing wrong here. That's genuine signal fluctuation. I'll get a hard copy."

A broad ribbon of printout began to spew from beneath the screen, carrying a continuous trace of the variable signal. On, then off; on again, for a bit longer, then off. On for a short time, off for the same time as before; on for a longer time.

It was Russell who spotted it. "It's a signal from Reese," he murmured quietly, reaching for his message pad and touching the stylus to its surface. "Morse code." He wrote quickly on the pad as he watched the trace flicking on and off on the screen. After a short time, he stopped. "It's repeating. Here, you'd better see it." He passed the pad to Bryant, who read the message in silence, then passed the pad round the small group. None of them spoke. There was nothing to say. This mission had been jinxed from the start; one more blow came as no real surprise.

*OT INFORM BUT RN MUST HEED WARNING ROGER DANGER REPEAT DANGER COMET IMPACT HYPERION EIGHT DAYS REPEAT EIGHT DAYS LEAVE MOON SOONEST VITAL DO NOT INFORM RN BUT MUST HEED WARNING ROGER DANGER REPEAT*

# 15.

Higuchi must have stopped praying on the fourth day after Bryant and the others fled Hipparchus, because that was the day the machinery broke down. In the circumstances, this was the worst possible thing that could have happened. The Mole was barely a hundred metres deep and the Dragon already filled a quarter of the lunar sky.

He had a premonition that something was wrong, a split-second before the alarm in his pocket started bleeping. For four days Hipparchus Base had been silent except for the distant rumble of the Mole gnawing at rock down in the abandoned tunnels below the deepest level. It had been a constant reassuring sound that Higuchi's conscious mind had learned to filter out – like the ticking of a bedside clock. It was a sound not worthy of attention. Until, that is, it stopped.

Higuchi had sacked a lab on level four and was staggering out into the corridor which led to lift shaft twelve with the last crate, piled high to toppling point with circuit boards. An ugly black stubble stained his features, and his eyes were tired and bloodshot. He had been unable to sleep properly since the others had left him in self-imposed solitude. With 'day' and 'night' simply being arbitrary divisions on the clock face, and the comet looming ever larger in the constant sky, Higuchi had worked more and more frantically, scurrying about the maze of corridors, almost mindlessly carrying on the task of salvage. He knew the work was futile, but it gave him something to occupy his mind and stop him counting the hours and then the minutes to impact. The pile of plunder by the foot of lift shaft twelve was a growing reminder that he was doing something constructive. And the work blocked from his mind thoughts of the gamble he had taken in deciding to stay while the others ran for the safety of the distant mountains. His survival depended on burrowing deep enough into the Moon to avoid the sledgehammer blow of the impacting comet. And he might go mad if he thought too hard about the key question – how deep is deep enough?

After running from his thoughts for four cycles of artificial day and night, Higuchi's precarious peace of mind was at an end. Silence broke like a thunderclap in the deserted corridors of Hipparchus. And then he was running, running for the lift shaft, circuit boards spilled and forgotten in his wake. Lift shaft twelve, which led down to the deepest level and the abandoned tunnels, where the spinning, diamond-toothed cutting jaws of the Mole had frozen in solid rock. And as he ran the words of Bryant and Russell came back to him. Bryant and Russell, suited up for the journey, standing at the airlock, making a last appeal to him before they joined Abel and Templeton in the balloon-tyred bus.

"For God's sake, come with us. You're crazy. If we can get to the mountains in time, we'll be shielded from the impact and we can ride out any quakes."

And Higuchi, stubborn as a child, firm in his belief that they would never make it.

"I'll take my chances here. You can run across the Moon if you think you can reach safety; I'm going to burrow as deep as I can get. Get going. Time's running out."

And they had gone, but not before telling him he was digging his own grave, and not before wishing him luck anyway. Now his luck had run out. For all Higuchi knew he had been right and the bus carrying Bryant and the rest had foundered in a ravine or ground to a halt on fifty year old batteries. For all he knew Bryant would be caught in the open, space suited and helpless, when the sky fell in. For all he knew, after four days of radio silence, they were dead already. But it didn't help, because *he was going to die too*.

The lift took an age to descend. Higuchi caught his rasping breath, and cursed himself for a fool. Better to die with friends than alone. Then he reached bottom, and was running again, down the thirty degree slope of the new tunnel. His despair was turning to anger, anger at Ustinov and the whole RN, which manipulated him and the others, trapped them here like flies in amber to be used as bargaining counters with Reese. He cursed Ustinov, instead of himself; he cursed Reese for her obstinacy, even while admiring her singlemindedness. Then he reached the Mole, lifeless at the rock face, and his anger turned once again to despair. He looked up at the roof of the tunnel, as if trying to penetrate three hundred metres of solid rock and gauge whether it would be enough to save him from the hurtling snowball from space. Could the thin layer of lunar rock protect him from a trillion tonne iceberg travelling at fifty thousand kilometres an hour?

Higuchi slumped against the wall and held his head in his hands, fighting for breath. It was over. He closed his eyes and let it all flood over him. The days of tension and lack of sleep; the weeks of uncertainty before that, helping the others to right the old bus and put it into working order, while the conviction grew that he could never risk his own life in the vehicle. Then, suddenly, ten years of training and discipline in the astronaut corps came back to the surface. Higuchi stiffened and opened his red-rimmed eyes, peering at the bulk of the Mole wedged in the tunnel. He still had a few hours left. Time to find the fault and mend it; time to dig a few metres more – perhaps the crucial few metres that would make the difference between life and death. Eleven hours. If he found the fault quickly, he could gain another ten metres. Suddenly, Higuchi wanted those ten metres. He wanted to *live*.

"Hey, Roger. Want to see the sunrise?" Abel's voice crackled over the seat intercom. Bryant, seated in blackness at the rear of the bus, jumped. The sight of the lunar terrain flashing by had mesmerized him until even the hum of the engines had receded to infinity. He had lost all track of time. A quick glance down at his chronometer confirmed that Abel was right – just fifteen minutes until the sun came up.

The voice came again; "Rog? You asleep back there?"

Bryant stabbed at the intercom button. "If I was I wouldn't be for long with you hollering at me," he said testily.

"Keep your hair on, I was only . . ." But Bryant had already got to his feet and was easing himself into the aisle of the bus. Towards the front he passed the sleeping figure of Jim Russell, sprawled untidily across a bank of three seats. No alarm call for him, Bryant thought. His pilot needed to be fresh for his spell at the controls of the bus. Had that not been so, Bryant would still have hesitated to wake him. He looked too peaceful by far.

He found Abel at the controls, Templeton beside him. Bryant lowered himself into a bucket seat behind the pair and adjusted his eyes to the dim red light Abel had on over the control console. The bus was hugging the rim of a narrow and, as far as Bryant could tell in the dim Earthlight, bottomless, canyon. "Can't you drive a bit further away from that?" he asked.

"Sorry, Roger," Abel replied, "but, believe me, there's method in my madness."

He took the bus a little further away, to perhaps twenty-five metres from the lip of the canyon. "Feel better now?"

Bryant nodded, then remembered Abel didn't have any equivalent of a rear-view mirror. "Yes. Okay," he shouted over the drone of the engines, "but why . . . ?"

"It's the bad light," Abel began but a boulder in the path of the bus forced him to take evasive action so he didn't finish. With the obstacle behind he straightened out the bus and continued, "As I was saying – "

"What Abel's trying to say, Rog," Templeton interrupted impatiently, "is – hey! Keep your eyes on the road, for God's sake."

"You call this a road! More like an assault course for giants."

"Okay, okay, but watch where you're going. What he's trying to say," Templeton began again, "is that in this bad light the canyon's the only easily recognizable surface feature. For a fifty kilometre radius, anyhow. Roger, I don't know if you realize this but this is a remarkably uninteresting stretch of the Moon."

"I can believe it." Three weeks familiarity had not dulled Bryant's fascination with the Moon. But even he had to admit, after scrutinizing the terrain for more than an hour, there was nothing in this particular region more exciting than a very minor impact crater.

"So you're using the canyon to navigate by, that's what you're telling me?" Bryant asked.

"Right. According to the map it crosses the regular highway pretty close to here. He'll be back on course before you can say muon microprobe." Abel paused a moment while he checked the status of a few of the onboard systems.

Satisfied that all was well, he continued. "I still think we could have shifted that tanker, Rog. What do you think?"

"You know what I think. If we'd squandered the batteries trying to ram that behemoth off the highway, and failed, we'd have been finished. As it is we've lost four hours making a detour. We can live with that. It simply wasn't worth the gamble and you know it. Besides you were outvoted three to one."

"All right, all right. I know when I'm beaten." He was quiet for a moment, thinking. When Abel was thinking, Bryant had often observed, you could actually hear him doing it. "How the hell do you think it got abandoned there, though?" he said, finally. "I mean, right in the middle of nowhere. Didn't they have tow trucks in the old days?"

"Who knows? I guess it was one of the last ore trucks from Clavius. The driver would have been in an almighty hurry to get back to Hipparchus for the last shuttle to Earth. Perhaps he didn't see the rubble on the road until it was too late. Most likely he put out a distress call and they sent out a surface shuttle from Hipparchus to pick him up. Who knows what it was like in the final days before they abandoned the Moon?"

"But, Christ, what a place to block the highway – across a hairpin bend, with a thirty degree slope on one side and a sheer cliff face on the other. I mean, the driver couldn't have picked a worse place . . ." He finally trailed off.

The tanker had chosen a very bad place to crash, Bryant had to admit. But the cause of the crash, half a century before, had been his least worry. When he'd suited up and left the bus to inspect the obstructing vehicle, only the fact of the tanker's existence and the comet in the sky were important. The tanker could have been dropped from orbit by a malicious god (probably was, Bryant thought wryly) but all that mattered was that he weighed up their alternatives and made a swift choice between them. Put simply, they could play heroes and attempt to budge the tanker or they could play it safe, back up the bus and take another pass through the hills. In space, heroes had short life expectancies; only those who took pains to minimize unnecessary risk reached middle age. As far as Bryant was concerned, and Russell had backed him up to the hilt, there was only one sensible course of action to take. Four hours later it was academic anyhow.

"How long," Bryant asked, "until we hit the highway again?"

"Well, it comes out of the hills over there. See that hillock?" Bryant saw it. It looked surprisingly close.

"Half an hour, a little less. What do you say?"

Abel turned to Templeton. "I'd say from the map, you're about right."

Half an hour, thought Bryant. The detour had meant that a large chunk of their safety margin had been eroded. Still, as long as they had no further mishaps, they would make it. The mountains already dominated the skyline ahead of the bus, and they were a reassuring sight. A day, perhaps a little less, Bryant estimated, then they would be safe. Or, as safe as it was possible to be in the circumstances.

Higuchi had been quite wrong about the batteries. Fifty years old they might be but they were squirting juice into the bus like they were fresh from the factory. They still retained thirty per cent of full charge, the computer calculated, more than enough to enable the bus to finish its journey. In any event, thought Bryant, with the fifteen day lunar night about to end, their chances of success had to improve. Power from the bus' solar collector could keep them on the move even if they had to dump the batteries. He felt a little happier in his mind now. But he avoided the optimism of Abel and Templeton. The bus was old and temperamental, he reminded himself. Since leaving Hipparchus they had discovered a dozen minor faults, mostly connected with the onboard computer. Jim Russell suspected that fifty years on the surface had exposed all the circuits to a fearsome battering from cosmic ray particles, principally from solar flares. Those circuits which had not been radiation-hardened had come in for the severest punishment. Russell reckoned that a scan of the parts inventory would, in principle, allow them to pinpoint the vulnerable chips. But that was a major task and, what with all the distractions, no one had found time to do it.

He asked Abel for an update on the computer navigation.

"I gave it another try back there, Rog, on a pretty smooth stretch. The forward-scanning radar caught all the small rubble, stuff less than half a metre across, and the big stuff too, but it's still missing boulders in the metre range. Probably only a few lines of firmware have been wiped out but I don't think we should risk it again. Unless, that is, you don't feel safe with my driving?"

"I feel safe. Well, safer than I would if we were relying on a navigation system which could run us aground on a rock outcrop any time."

"Am I being complimented or what?" Abel asked turning to Templeton.

"Good God, keep your eyes on the road, man," came the retort.

All minor problems, so far, Bryant thought with relief. Since leaving Hipparchus the four of them had taken shifts at the controls. There was no denying it was exhausting but, as long as they all got sleep at regular intervals, they could handle it.

The interior lights were still playing up, but the oxygen recycling plant, after making some rather ominous growling noises and forcing them to don their bulky spacesuits temporarily, was now fixed. Abel had managed to locate and remove a stray bit from the program code which controlled the plant and that had done the trick. Odd to think that a stray proton catapulted into space by an explosion on the Sun could come close to suffocating four men travelling in a bus a hundred and fifty million kilometres away. Odd, but frightening nonetheless. Bryant wondered what other systems had been damaged.

He looked at his chronometer. Nearly time. There would be no advance warning of the sunrise. This was an airless world with no atmosphere to refract sunlight, bend it up from below the horizon, and create a pre-dawn glow in the sky. No, sunrise would be instantaneous. One moment it would be a lunar night, the next the horizon would be straddled by a line of white fire, impossible to look at except through the bus' automatic polarizers.

"Where does it rise?" Bryant asked.

"Should be over that peak," Templeton pointed. "Not the one straight ahead, the jagged one to its left. Do you see it?"

Abel had now taken the bus to within fifteen metres of the

edge of the canyon. They were passing a constriction where the canyon seemed to be no wider than the bus. Far too small to be a rille, the canyon could only be a collapsed lava tube which had fed into a mare basin when the Moon was young and geologically active, three and a half billion years earlier. That seemed to Bryant to be the most logical explanation. He turned to ask Templeton's opinion but, just at that moment, Abel broke in.

"Any time now," he declared.

The sun was late. They waited a full minute and still nothing. Bryant thought he saw a glimmer of light but he knew that it had to be his imagination.

"Sure your timing's right?" Templeton asked.

"Of course I'm sure. The computer's worked out the time to $n$ decimal places. The only uncertainty is our longitude. I'd say – " But that was the last word Abel uttered.

The sun rose.

Liquid fire spilled over the rim of the world. It exploded inside the bus like a fusion flash bulb. As he clutched desperately for his eyes Bryant heard Templeton yell: "The filters! For God's sake, the auto-filters!" Then the bus was out of control, spinning wildly across the dust at the rim of the canyon. He felt pain, terrible pain. His stomach churned and he knew he was falling. At that moment the wall came up and struck him hard.

Roger Bryant followed Abel, Templeton and Russell into oblivion.

# 16.

In his dream, a man was moaning, quietly, unseen. The voice, muffled and distorted, disturbed Bryant deeply. He knew the man who owned that voice; knew him well. But recognition was beyond him. He strained his senses to interpret the moaning, but it meant nothing. Speech patterns, but unrecognizable, as if the world outside his head had been rotated ten degrees from the template he carried in his mind. Or was it his mind that had slipped out of kilter with the real world? Was he going mad?

The thought brought confusion, and he felt panic rising in his throat. But with the incipient panic rose an overwhelming desire to hold the madness at bay. With an immense effort of will, he wrenched the template of his mind until, once again, it overlayed the world of his senses.

He wasn't dreaming at all! He was in the bus, and the bus had crashed. He knew the voice. It belonged to Ben Templeton. Somewhere, in the red-black gloom of the interior, Templeton was moaning, softy, "I'm blind, I'm blind . . ."

Bryant was slumped against the rear bulkhead. He must have been flung the whole length of the bus. In Earth gravity, he'd have been dead, for sure. As it was – he felt gingerly for the back of his head, where probing fingers met warm, sticky blood among the matted hair. Still sticky, so he hadn't been out for long.

But something was wrong with his vision. The surroundings

were oddly blurred. Bryant blinked, rubbed his eyes, then blinked again. The picture stayed the same. The interior of the bus, lit only by the emergency lamps, remained fuzzy, out of focus. As if someone had dropped a pane of frosted glass in front of him. The panic started to return. If they were all blind, who the Hell would get them out of this mess? Then he noticed the breath from his mouth, clouding as it left his lips, and realized how cold he was. Either the heater was out, or the double skin insulating the bus was ruptured. Strangely, this bad news cheered him immensely. He wasn't going blind, after all. The bus interior was hazy because it was filled with a fog of ice crystals hanging in the air, where cooling and a loss of pressure had frozen water vapour out.

The realization completed his return to normal consciousness, and he took stock of the situation. The bus was in chaos. Loose fittings piled around him and on him; seats had broken from their moorings and accumulated like flotsam on one side of the bus; and the floor was no longer a reassuring horizontal platform, but an incline sloping at about twenty degrees up to the driving position.

The driver! Bryant kicked away a headrest which lay across his legs, and began to crawl forward, not trusting his dizzy head to attempt walking on the slope. His right shoulder was bruised, and his ribs hurt, but nothing seemed to be broken.

Templeton was still strapped in his seat, quiet now, rubbing his eyes with the palms of his hands. He stopped as Roger came up behind him.

"Roger? Greg . . . ?"

"It's me – Roger."

"Thank God. I thought I was the only one." He turned his head towards the sound of Bryant's voice. "I can't see, Roger. I can't bloody well see!"

Bryant placed a hand on his friend's shoulder, reassuringly. "Hell, Ben, it's only temporary. Don't worry." He surprised himself with the confident tone of his voice. "These things never last. Maybe an hour, that's all."

"You're a good liar, Roger. But you can't fool me."

"It's no lie, Ben." Of course it was – Bryant had no idea whether or not Templeton's eyesight would recover. But he had to keep him optimistic. He was relieved when a sound from the rear gave him an excuse to change the subject.

It was Abel. His face was cut and his left arm was held stiffly at his side. Somehow, he'd got covered in dust. But he was in one piece, and he was putting on a good act of being cheerful.

"Three down, one to go," he said breezily. "Who's going to fetch Russell? You and Ben okay?"

"Ben's got a temporary problem with his eyes. Stick with him for a bit."

"Okay."

Bryant found Russell still stretched across a row of seats, anchored by a belt round his waist. The pilot was rubbing the back of his neck. Looks like he's come out of this best of all, thought Bryant. If there's gonna be a crash, you can't beat sleeping through it. Or had he slept?

"Any problems?"

Russell laughed. "You tell me. Whadda we hit? Feels like somebody tried to pull my head off – whiplash, I guess. Must've been out for a few minutes."

"We're down a hole, Jim. Look out the window."

"I can't see anything."

"Yep. Either we're very deep, or the side's pressed tight against the wall. What do you figure?"

"Shallow, but tight."

"You think, or you hope?"

"Both. But mainly, if we'd fallen a long way we wouldn't be asking questions. The bus would have broken open. How wide was the fissure?"

"About as wide as the bus. And we are losing pressure."

"It figures. We're stuck lengthwise. And not too deep, though God knows if we're on the bottom or if there's a hole underneath. Could be deep enough, though."

Bryant didn't need the details spelling out. Their only hope was to climb out of the fissure, and to do that they'd need to get a line to the surface. They had explosive grapples, all right. But only about thirty metres of line. Godammit, this wasn't supposed to be a bloody mountaineering expedition.

"The first thing to do," Russell had obviously been thinking it through, "is to look out of the driver window. It should be clear."

"What are we waiting for?"

"After you, Chief."

They both began to crawl forward. Abel had moved Templeton back onto the row of seats behind the driver's position, where he lay with his eyes shut. Bryant drew level with them, Russell close behind, and reached for the seat back to pull himself upright. There was a screech and the bus lurched forward, settling more on to the horizontal but dropping perceptibly as it did so.

They froze. Nobody spoke, but the sound of breathing was loud in their ears.

"Crawl back, Jim. And you, Greg. Suit up. Carefully."

If the vibration sent them down further, so be it. They'd never get out of this by stretching out on the floor not even daring to speak. But Bryant couldn't bring himself to turn his head, and waited, listening, as they retreated down the still sloping floor.

Okay, try again. He pulled himself up, inch by inch, and leaned forward to peer through the window. By craning his neck, he could see a roughly rectangular strip of stars, and that was all. He reckoned the surface was twenty-five metres up. Or was that just wishful thinking?

"Greg, bring Ben's suit up here, and I'll slide back there with Jim. She seems stable now, but we might as well maintain the balance. Suit up, but keep the helmets open. Use ship's air as long as we can."

185

"That won't be long, Roger." Russell had been checking the gauges.

"Rear compartment's holed in a big way. There was a large pressure drop before the bulkhead sealed. And now the pressure's still dropping, so there must be a crack up here too. We'll be on suit tanks inside an hour."

Bryant nodded. It was no worse than he'd expected. The haze in the atmosphere was clearing now that they were sealed off from the rear compartment, but the ice crystals had said it all. "Then the sooner we get out, the better. I can see the top."

"You're forgetting something, Roger. We can't use the airlock." For a moment, Bryant didn't realize what Russell meant. Then it hit him.

"Shit." The expletive was barely whispered. The airlock on the side of the bus, like the windows, was pressed flush against the wall of the fissure. There was no way for a man in a vacuum suit to squeeze out. How on Earth had he overlooked anything so obvious?

"How could I be so stupid?"

"Pressure." He looked at Russell, blankly.

"Or lack of it. Slows down the old mental processes. Not enough oxygen."

So why was Russell able to work these things out, thought Bryant, irritably. Come on, *think*.

"There's always the hatch." It was Russell's turn to look bemused. The escape hatch opened in the roof, unobstructed by the fissure walls.

"The problem is," Russell responded at last, "the hatch isn't an airlock." But Bryant wasn't going to overlook the obvious again.

"So, when we crack it we lose the air from the bus. No sweat. We're gonna lose it anyway."

"But not in a rush, Chief. Blow that hatch and we'll have every loose object shooting out like popping the cork from a champagne bottle."

"All right, we'll crack the airlock open a tiny bit. Nice controlled pressure drop. The door's strong enough, after all – it should withstand the pressure while we're bleeding air out."

It was Russell's turn to move forward, testing the airlock controls, explaining the scheme to Abel and Templeton as he did so. The familiar cacophony of clunks and hisses as the air between the doors was pumped into the cabin sounded sweet. And when Russell hit the control which broke the seal on the outer door, the faint but unmistakable whooff of remaining air escaping into vacuum reached them. Now all they had to do was use the emergency overrides to open the inner door as well – a little.

"Pressure's down to almost a third." Russell's voice was coming over the suit radio. Bryant, startled, realized that the others were fully suited, while his helmet still hung open. And it really was cold! Clumsily, he finished suiting up. The taste of rich oxygen made him suddenly alert, euphoric.

"All to the good, now. If anything happens, we won't be shot out like a cork. Just a gentle fizz."

"Even so, Roger – " Russell was handing him the end of a length of rope. Well, better safe, he thought, fastening it to the suit.

"Okay. Take it away."

To open the inner door while the outer was already cracked, Russell had to operate two controls simultaneously on opposite sides of the driver's panel, one with each hand. Even though he followed the correct override procedure, the remaining lights in the bus began to flash a warning and an alarm bell started to sound, curiously distant and high pitched in the thin air.

A gentle breeze began to blow through the cabin towards the door. But it rapidly grew more intense.

Too fast!

In spite of Russell's insistent hammering on the controls, the door continued to open. The bus became a maelstrom of ice and whirling seat fittings. Abel pushed Templeton flat and laid on top of him; Bryant pressed himself against the wall, watching a steel pin fly past, only centimetres away from puncturing his suit.

But the storm was short lived. As quickly as it had begun, it died down. The wreckage was covered in frost, odd bits still falling to the floor in the vacuum and low gravity.

"Just a bottle of fizz." Abel was muttering as he helped Templeton to his feet.

"Sorry." Russell didn't seem very contrite. "Once I hit the override the door just wouldn't stop."

"Who cares, as long as we're alive." Bryant was impatient to move on. "What are you waiting for, Jim? Do the honours."

"Right." Without further hesitation, Russell triggered the emergency hatch release. There was a vibration as the charges blew, silent in the vacuum, and over their heads a square of metal lifted free and disappeared. The bus settled forward another few centimetres, then stopped. Bryant looked at the others, then upwards at the square of black velvet, studded with diamonds.

He had never been more glad to see the stars.

"This is a private report for the Secretary to the Council, under section two two six, and may not be viewed without the recorded permission of the Secretary."

The formal words from Commander Reese were followed by a statutory ninety seconds of blank tape, as recorded on the automatic monitoring system. It was a largely useless formality; tight beam communications worked one way, from Earth to the Dragon, and could be kept reasonably secure. Any competent communications engineer, however, could pick up the transmissions from the Dragon to the Earth, and decode them with a minimum of effort. But still, appearances had to be maintained.

Ustinov settled comfortably in his chair, and waited for the report to begin. Reese's face reappeared, looking strained, as she pushed a wayward lock of hair away from her forehead, obviously caught slightly unawares by the camera.

"Commander Reese, in charge of Dragon Base, with a personal report for Secretary Ustinov."

The formality continued, and the slight emphasis on the words "in charge" told Ustinov what the message would be about. He hoped she would be discreet.

"We have experienced some technical difficulties here, of a kind which I believe you may have anticipated. I need not go into details. Fortunately, our ability to complete the mission is unimpaired."

He could guess what that meant. Well, at least she wasn't sounding off all over the Solar System that the mighty Secretary to the Council hadn't even been able to organize a competent takeover, or sabotage, of the RN's own comet mission. The woman was clever – much cleverer, politically, than he had given her credit for. The rest of what she had to say might be interesting.

"In view of the changed circumstances, however, it is essential that I should immediately impart some additional information to you, and that you should discuss this with Dr Kondratieff. He can give you precise details of the orbital elements that are involved.

"You will be pleased to learn that we have established communications direct with Hipparchus Base. We understand that in spite of certain problems the chemox plant is now functioning and Bryant's team members are all well and can hold out indefinitely." She hoped it wasn't a lie. If communications had indeed been established, it was strictly a one-way affair. The computer was still pounding out the message to Roger on the echo-sounder, over and over. But if he hadn't heard it by now, he'd never get clear in time. Anyway, her words would give the Secretary something to think about. Pity she couldn't see his reaction.

Ustinov winced. How could they possibly be in direct contact with Bryant? The communications experts had told him it was impossible. They would suffer the consequences.

"This is especially important in view of the orbital details which Kondratieff will discuss with you. But in view of the difficulties I have mentioned, I must advise you that the Dragon will pass much closer to Earth than had been anticipated. Perigee will be below twenty thousand kilometres."

A frown passed across the First Secretary's face. Was this supposed to be an ultimatum? "Below twenty thousand kilometres" could well mean a direct hit. Was that what she was getting at? What did she intend to ask for in return for averting a catastrophe?

"I must stress that there is no risk of a direct impact. We are in control of the situation, and we have sufficient thrust capacity to complete the stated aim of our mission," *stated* was slightly emphasized, "and to ensure that the Dragon does not strike the Earth. But such a close approach could cause panic, and we urge you to prepare the population for the spectacular, but harmless, close passage of the comet."

There was a long pause. Ustinov almost thought that Reese had finished, but neglected to cut the transmission immediately. Then she continued.

"In view of the various difficulties I have referred to, however, there is a change of plan from our original programme."

She could say that again! The original programme hadn't exactly called for pushing the damned comet closer to the Earth than it would have been if they'd left it alone.

Reese closed her eyes, briefly, then opened them again.

"It turns out that it is necessary for one person to remain on the comet to direct the running of the fusion engines and to ensure the complete safety of the Earth and the successful completion of our primary goal."

So – the complete safety of the Earth was not the primary goal? Time to fetch Kondratieff back up here, show him the tape, and get the cat out of the bag at last. But she still hadn't finished.

"That person will require updated orbital parameters from the Tucson computers in order to achieve success. Please discuss this requirement with Dr Kondratieff and establish a direct data link for use during the close approach."

The plea was genuine; this was no terrorist bargaining for power, but a woman genuinely seeking help.

"As Commander of the expedition, of course, it is I who will remain at Dragon Base until the task is completed."

Of course. Why make a drama out of it? Then she could be taken off once the comet passed perigee, and the whole lot of them could come back here and explain just what the hell they had been up to.

"This is Commander Reese, signing off from Dragon Base."

# 17.

Strangely, the suicides stopped by the time the Dragon was as bright in the night sky of the Earth as the full Moon. Perhaps all of those susceptible to such things had already succumbed by then; perhaps it was because the event had clearly gone beyond any human comprehension, leaving only a state of numbed wonder in most people's minds. The stories that still filled the newsfax, however, sometimes raised doubts as to how far mankind had come since the troubles of the twentieth century. A young girl in the Appalachian mountains, "sacrificed" in a bizarre ceremony, her throat cut as an appeasement to the gods now making their work visible in the heavens; mass exodus from low lying regions in many parts of the world, in fear of tidal waves being swept up by the comet, in spite of numerous official exhortations to stay put, and reassurances that nothing was wrong. The inevitable con men (and women) swindling the gullible out of their prized possessions in return for useless devices supposed to ward off the imagined evil influences of the Dragon; and the inevitable lynchings when the tricksters were identified – or misidentified.

But each community responded in its own way . . .

Even in the daytime sky, the Dragon could clearly be seen, like a large, pale Moon, with streamers of material trailing back from it, pointing away from the Sun. The tall, confident woman pointed to the sky as she addressed the crowd of people in front of her, women pressing close about her feet, men on the outskirts, shuffling uneasily and glancing at one another.

"This is the sign. We changed our ways."

A low mutter from the women indicated a barely voiced response to what was becoming a ritual litany.

"We gave up the evil crops."

Another low murmur from the crowd followed each statement.

"We've gone back to the teachings of our mothers. Now we've got food. Our children can eat. The crops stand tall in the fields. And God sends his sign to us, his sign which says 'sisters, you have done well'."

The response this time was a loud ululation, clearly approving, but voicing no recognizable words.

The speaker raised both hands above her head, then brought them, palms downwards, to her sides. The noise ceased.

"I see people here from many villages. We welcome you all. But it is time now to go back, and tell your sisters what you have seen. Tell them how we have mended our ways, and made our peace with God. Tell them about the crops we grow, and the food we eat. Tell them," this quietly, almost in a whisper, "of the sign. Go now," her voice rising again, "while the sign of God's blessing is upon us, and tell them all!"

As the crowd of women began to break up and disperse, the little group of men stood for a while, uneasily. Then one of them shrugged. "Crazy women," he muttered to his companion, who nodded. The two of them turned and walked towards the shade of a hut, where they sat for a while, watching the tall woman organizing the activity of the village. Then they began playing a complex game, involving little stones and counters. Gradually, a knot of other men formed around them as bystanders drifted in to see how the game progressed. Soon, the crazy women were forgotten, left to go about their business in the fields, while the men got on with the important things in life.

Billy Bryant stole a sideways glance at his mother as she swung the camper off Highway 395 just outside Big Pine. Good, he thought with relief, she had stopped crying. He hated it when his mother cried; he felt all helpless and wished like hell his father was home. When was he coming home, anyhow? Without thinking, he opened his mouth to ask, but just in time he remembered, and clamped it shut again. When he had questioned her before, back in the motel in Bishop, his mother had disappeared into the bathroom for a long time. When she finally came out, her eyes were red-rimmed and puffy. It wasn't too hard for even a six year old to guess that his father was in trouble.

Billy peered out of the side window, across an ocean of sage brush, purple in the dim dusk light. It stretched on to the end of the Owens Valley. The sagging dishes of the old radio observatory were all that broke the surface, catching fire in places as they intercepted the last rays of the Sun, already half eclipsed by the Sierra Nevada. But even from here you could see that the dishes were broken and starting to become overgrown. Soon they would be swallowed up in the sea of vegetation. They drove on, towards Black Mountain, dark and sinister and brooding, already sprinkled with the first icing-sugar snow of winter.

He dozed, and when he woke it was already dark and the camper was jolting over a rough track strewn with splintered rocks, too uneven for the air cushion to smooth out completely. A jack rabbit froze for a moment in the unearthly white headlights of the vehicle. It stared for an eternal instant at the monster bearing down on it, then darted into the night. They came to a halt, settling with a slight tilt on the corrugated surface beneath them as his mother cut the engine and turned off the headlights, telling Billy it was time to get out. As he obeyed her, moving out of the cosy camper into the night, the first breath of the cold air felt bruising in his lungs.

They were up among the bristlecone pines, two thousand metres above the Owens Valley high desert. He recognized the spot, even in the dim light, because they had camped here many times when his dad was home. The trees were older than any other living things on Earth, his dad said, older than the Romans and the Greeks and the Sumerians and all those other ancient civilizations Miss Benton had told him about in grade school. But that wasn't why his mother had driven all this way up from Bishop, he was sure. He had some vague notion that this place had been special to his parents before he was born; so he could sort of understand that she had brought him up here so they could be closer to his dad. It made a kind of sense.

In the light of day the pines were gnarled and twisted and Billy thought they were funny. Now he thought they were spooky, so he clutched his mother's hand tightly as she struck out along the trail. The comet was already in the sky, huge and white and ghostly, a giant smudge against the stars. You could see stars right through its tail in places. Tonight eight billion people would leave their homes to look up on the sky at the sight, eight billion curious souls, many of whom had never before noticed the heavens above them. But Billy hardly noticed the comet, and neither did his mother. To them it was no more than a distraction as they climbed upwards, their shoes crunching on the frozen ground.

They sat down on a fallen pine and waited. It wasn't a long wait. The Moon rose, salmon pink and bloated against the jagged silhouette of the mountains. It crept upwards, revealing the dark smudges of the maria and rayed craters, then seemed to pull free of the mountains and launch itself into the void of stars. Billy felt his mother's arm engulf him, and he snuggled into her coat. No words passed between them, because no words were necessary. His dad was there, somewhere on that world in the sky, and his dad was in trouble. He wished he had the biggest telescope in the world, so that he could look down on the Moon base, the place they called Hipparchus, and see the space-suited figure of his father waving to show he was all right.

He felt his mother's grip tighten, and he responded in kind. Surely his father would come back, he thought, surely someone would go to rescue him if he was in trouble? If they didn't, he would go. He didn't know how, but he would go, and bring his father back himself. It made him feel better to say such things to himself, it made him feel tall, as if he could reach out and touch the Moon with his hand. So he told his mother, to make her feel better too. She smiled back and ruffled his hair, and he wasn't sure if she believed him or not. But *he* believed him.

It was hardly necessary to climb to the top of the abandoned apartment block to see the comet. Even in London, you could see it clearly from the streets. The buildings weren't that tall, the street lighting was dim, and after all the Dragon literally filled half the sky, if you included the pearly white haze of the corona, with the stars shining faintly through it. But, of course, if you were serious about such things, you could get an even better view from the top of a tall, dark building. Linda hadn't needed much persuasion; but now she was there, her interest seemed to be focused on other things.

Lying on Pete's thick coat, in the sheltered corner of the parapet at the angle of the roof, she was much more interested in the warmth of his body alongside hers, the taste of his lips, and the alarming, but delightful, activity of the fingers of his left hand, searching ever deeper into the layers of her clothing.

She shivered a little, and gasped as his cold hand touched her breast.

"Pete." Her half-voiced, half-hearted protestations were lost in his kisses. The roving fingers were working down her body now. Her body yearned for more, even while a part of her mind reminded her that this was wrong. "Nice girls don't . . . this isn't the twentieth century, you know . . . plenty of time for that when you are married . . ." the often repeated words of her mother came back to her, as they had many times before. She started to pull away, reaching with her right hand to hold and halt Pete's left hand. As she did so, she opened her eyes and saw the full glory of the Dragon, lighting up the night sky and transforming the rooftops of London into a fairytale world. Her wavering resolution failed completely at the glorious sight, and, as much to Pete's surprise as his delight, she gave herself up completely to the emotions sweeping her body.

The night flight from Paris to San Francisco was over the desolate wastes of the Canadian archipelago, cruising in the stratosphere at Mach 3, with four hundred and twenty passengers and crew on board, when the sliver entered the atmosphere. It was a small fragment of comet, no bigger than the icebergs calved off during the 'quake', so many weeks ago, when Du Toit had almost lost his life. They had been left behind long ago, following their own orbit past the Earth and Moon, while the Dragon had been gradually nudged closer to the blue planet to ensure that Earth's gravity would slow its headlong flight and steer it towards lunar impact. But in the final approach to perigee, the closest point of the encounter between comet and planet, the stresses had proved too much. Old Faithful still spurted erratically, pushing the comet one way; the fusion engines, jockeyed by Frances Reese, now alone on board the *Discovery*, pushed another; and the increasing pull of the Earth's gravity tugged it in yet a third direction. Under the strain, it was hardly surprising that the celestial ice mountain cracked and tore apart a little more. The main bulk of the comet, obedient to the laws of orbital mechanics and the carefully calculated nudge of the fusion engines, swept past the Earth at a distance of only fifteen thousand kilometres, and headed on to its fateful final rendezvous. Most of the fragments of ice broken off in the process carried on with it, along much the same trajectory. A few burnt up harmlessly in the Earth's atmosphere. Just one sizeable sliver made its major mark on the planet.

The ball of fire, trailing a thick cloud of smoke and dust in its wake, moved across Alaska and towards the Great Lakes, losing height all the time, and moving much faster than the San Francisco flight heading across its path. But, being largely made of ice, not stone, the sliver at the heart of the fireball could not remain intact long enough to strike the Earth below. Responding to the enormous heat and pressure stresses building up inside as it ploughed through the atmosphere, it exploded at 1:32 am, local time, four hundred kilometres northwest of Uranium city, at an altitude of seven kilometres, just east of the Mackenzie Mountains.

The location was as fortuitous as the impact site of the Tunguska meteorite, almost two centuries before – but then, the Earth is a big planet, and population centres still covered only a small area of its surface, even in the late twenty-first century. Windows were shattered and roofs ripped from buildings in the inappropriately named township of Fort Providence, while the Great Slave Lake and the rivers feeding it were whipped into a frenzy by the pressure waves from the blast, with tidal waves pounding and destroying Fort Resolution, Dawson Landing, and the other small settlements on the southern side of the Lake. Five minutes later, however, and it would have been the city of Winnipeg and its lake; ten minutes more, and the tidal waves would have swept Lake Michigan, with Chicago and Detroit bearing the full brunt of the ten megaton blast overhead.

The captain of Euroflight EF 221 knew nothing of this, however. His last thoughts concerned the fireball growing out of nowhere in his flight path, the sudden attempt to change course and increase altitude, while triggering the automatic Mayday broadcast which was the last the world would hear from the trans-sonic liner. When the blast wave struck, the aircraft was banked steeply to the left; the blast simply completed the job, flipping the plane completely onto its back and sending it at full power straight into the ground at 4,000 km per hour. There were, of course, no survivors.

"Hey mum, look at the sunset!" Linda's excited voice brought back to her mother, for a heart-stopping instant, the image of her little girl as she had once been, sitting on the shoulders of her father and waving excitedly at a firework display. She turned away from the cooker and walked to the door. The city of London, to the west, was outlined against a dark red glow in the sky, as if it were on fire. The red shaded gradually through all the colours of the rainbow, right to the highest point of the sky, with yellow and green tints striping the thin, high clouds.

"It's the comet dust. They said on the telly it's spreading right round the world. And it might start a new Ice Age."

"Come on, mum, don't be so gloomy. Someone's always going on about a new Ice Age, and it never happens. Just look at that!"

They stood for a while in silence, the older woman's arm draped around the waist of the young girl who was now as tall as herself. As the light and colour faded from the sky, the spectacle was replaced by another, as what seemed to be two moons rose almost together.

"Oh, look! It's even closer than yesterday. Do you think they're going to touch?"

The Moon – the proper Moon – was in its last quarter, lit on one side only. On the other side, scarcely a lunar diameter away, was the head of the Dragon, shining just as brightly, with its tail streaming behind it, away from the Moon.

"They said it might, on the box. The astronauts are coming back, now they've done their job. They said it would've hit the Earth, if it hadn't been for them pushing it out of the way. Then you'd have had plenty to worry about apart from pretty sunsets. They could've pushed a bit harder, if you ask me. Too close for comfort, that comet."

"Oh, mum, don't go on. You worry too much. They fixed it, didn't they? That's what matters. It won't happen again, never in a million years. And if it did we've got the astronauts to look after us."

She paused, gave a sigh of contentment, and squeezed her mother's hand.

"Look at the Moon. I'm sure the comet's going to touch it. It's so lovely. I think I'll call Pete."

# 18.

It was an hour since anyone had spoken. Bryant welcomed the silence. Talking used up oxygen, and the ascent was already consuming more than he had budgeted for. His best estimate was that they had ten hours left. And then what? It was too final an ending to consider; he pushed the thought out of his mind.

He brought the sled to a halt, allowing the makeshift harness to sag as he straightened up. No more than fifty metres ahead, Russell, Abel and Templeton were skirting a massive boulder, slowly. He had time for a breather before he caught up.

From his vantage point, Bryant surveyed the grey slope of the mountain and the route they had taken. Already they were a good five thousand metres above the plain, he estimated – higher than California's Sierra Nevada, although the view, he had to admit, wasn't anywhere near as good. In the Moon's gravity, they'd climbed the equivalent of a thousand metres on Earth. But they'd also had to walk many more kilometres across the plain, and up the slope.

He sat down on the thin layer of dust, propping his back against the sled. It wasn't exactly comfortable – the pressure suit was about as flexible as an inflated doll – but it made a change. Shielding his eyes from the glare of the Sun, still low in the sky so soon after lunar dawn, Bryant tried to spot the fissure where they had abandoned the bus. But it was far too small, and too far away, to be picked out in the shadows.

Seventeen hours before, Bryant had been down there, in the

shadows, peering into the gloom of the crevasse as Russell, the last of their party, was winched to safety. It had seemed like a dream, and looking back he now recognized the detachment as post-shock syndrome. Somehow, it was easier, now, to get it all in perspective, as if it had happened to someone else.

It was Russell who had got them moving, once Bryant and Abel had helped him on to the lunar surface. Like some Antarctic explorer of the twentieth century, he had stamped firmly on the ground, then set his face at the mountains.

"Right." His voice, over the radio, had been clear. "Off we go."

"How?" Bryant, in his detached state, couldn't be bothered.

"Walk, of course."

And so, at Russell's instigation, they had walked; Abel leading Templeton, Bryant and Russell each pulling a sled loaded with gear from the bus.

Well, Russell had been right on one thing. They'd certainly had no other option, except to sit and die by the crevasse, in which case it would hardly have been worth the struggle to get out of the bus. Their choices seemed to be being made for them. First, they lost the shuttle. Then, they lost the bus. Only legs were left. And those legs might yet get them to the safety of the mountains before the comet struck.

The comet . . . Bryant twisted round so he could see the blue and white disc of the Earth. By now, the comet should be between the Earth and the Moon. It would reach them in three or four hours, but he could still see no trace of it, with the Sun dominating the sky and even the Earth relegated to a second-class astronomical object.

It really didn't seem fair. Bryant caught the errant thought, and smiled to himself. Well, it wasn't fair. Here they were, lost on the Moon, certain to die in ten hours, with the only consolation that they had ringside seats for the most spectacular astronomical event since the dawn of man. And they couldn't see a damn thing! Why couldn't it happen during the lunar night?

He shook his head, and looked away, into the blackness of the sky away from the Earth. A bright star winked at him, as his eyes adjusted and the filters cut out. Nearly time to get moving. But first . . .

Hey! The stars were twinkling!

He jumped to his feet so rapidly that he overbalanced in the low gravity, and sprawled forward, stopping himself with his hands and standing, ungainly, like a four legged spider in the dust. Hauling himself upright, he chinned the radio switch.

"Jim! The stars are twinkling. Look out about twenty degrees from the Earth!"

"Where? What?" Even Russell's voice came across tired and irritable.

"I can't. Hang on . . . well, holy shit!"

Bryant's eyes, now well adapted, showed him the astonishing sight. The stars were twinkling, as nobody had ever seen them twinkle from the airless surface of the Moon. They could be twinkling for only one reason, because he was viewing them through a tenuous layer of gases. It could only be the halo of the comet.

All along, there had been a part of him that didn't really believe it, a part that needed hard evidence, the evidence of his own two eyes. Well, now he had it. There could be no doubt left.

The comet was really coming.

Russell's voice shattered the silence inside Bryant's suit. "Roger! I see it! I see it!"

"Stay where you are!" Bryant grabbed the reins of the sled and began to bound towards the others in the leaping, slow motion, lunar version of running. It was a stupid thing to do, part of his brain noted. Running tripled the rate of oxygen consumption. But seeing the comet had changed everything. Oxygen conservation was no longer his highest priority. If they didn't find some cover in the mountains, somewhere to shelter from the ejecta when the comet hit, it wouldn't matter how much, or how little, oxygen there was left in their tanks. Dead men don't need oxygen.

The sled was too heavy, and the slope too smooth. Stumbling and sliding, he was forced to slow his pace. But as he passed the big rock, he was surprised to see how little ground the others had covered while he was daydreaming.

Oddly, the tight little huddle of men and equipment was below him on the mountainside. Russell and the others had descended a steep bank on to an expanse of rock that ran horizontally, a kind of natural viaduct that stretched around the bulk of the mountain ahead, and seemed to penetrate far into the mountain range proper. The upheaval that had thrust these lunar peaks skyward, eons ago, had crumpled the skin of the Moon to create the semblance of a winding highway, twisting around the neighbouring peaks. Some long-ago lava flow had filled long gone valleys, then been thrust upward, bodily. The three black specks below had been moving along this easier path.

Bryant nodded, happy with their diversion. Safety lay ahead, with the peaks of the mountains wrapped around them. But, as he looked beyond the foreshortened figures of his companions, Bryant's heart sank. They had ventured into a landscape built for giants. The monumental highway of the lava flow dwarfed them, and they had less than three hours to cross it. Like a great mountain glacier, the surface that seemed so smooth at first sight was pocked and wrinkled by features larger than a man. Three hours, in which to find a spot surrounded by the high peaks on all sides – or else they might just as well have stayed at Hipparchus, like Higuchi, digging their own graves.

Stifling his negative thoughts, Bryant pushed on, down the slope. He let the sled run on ahead, and out on to the surface of the lava flow. Bounding after it, zig-zag down the slope, he came up rapidly on his companions. His spirits began to rise again; the surface of the lava certainly was scarred and pocked, but the ridges were almost too big to be a problem, great sweeping undulations that scarcely made him break stride.

He switched the radio on to the common channel, catching the end of something Abel was saying.

". . . like, like someone draped a gossamer curtain across the sky."

Astonished, Bryant barely avoided stumbling. My God, he thought, has Abel turned into a poet? The same Greg Abel who given a choice between William Blake and a shuttle manual would choose the latter for light reading any time? Well, the proximity of death was said to concentrate the mind . . . what else was he saying . . .

"And that's about it. Okay, Ben?"

"Thanks." Templeton's reply lacked enthusiasm. "You'd make a great guide dog."

Bryant laughed out loud as he realized his mistake. Even at this distance, he could see, now, that Templeton and Abel were standing close together. Templeton was staring at a blackness much darker than space.

"What's so funny?"

"I thought . . . no, nothing. Just lightheaded." It wasn't worth the explanation.

Russell was watching him. Although he could see nothing of the pilot's face through his darkened visor, Russell's whole stance betokened disapproval. "Screw it, Jim." He got in a pre-emptive strike. Make it clear who was still boss around here. "Forget the goddamn oxygen. Let's get our butts into gear while there's still some time."

Suddenly, Bryant was among them, fatigued but on an adrenalin high, with a new-found sense of purpose. He'd get these bastards moving again, if it was the last thing he did. What was the point in holding back? Time to go for broke. And now, they had only to look up to see what they were running from. If that didn't put a light under them, nothing would.

The adrenalin kept them going at a stiff pace for an hour. But the changing vision of the comet began to slow them down, as the temptation to stop and gaze grew stronger with every passing step. Several times, a man dropped back, head tilted to stare at the sky; each time Bryant had to chew him out with a stream of abuse over the radio. He tried, now, to concentrate only on the pitted plain in front of him, on each successive step. But even he could not resist the urge to peek from time to time. Once, he too gave in to the sight, before Russell, in his turn, broke in on his reverie.

The comet had turned space white.

Between the stars, in every direction, the sky was glowing. It was a soft, pearly light, but it was growing in strength moment by moment. The fierce Sun had failed, after all, to spoil the show. If anything, the sunlight that refracted through the swathes of cometary material enhanced the display, contributing to the bizarre luminescence.

Another hour passed, at a slowing pace, before Bryant admitted to himself that they weren't going to make it. They could march another eight kilometres, maybe. But when the comet hit, they would still be exposed. They had to stop somewhere, and it might as well be here.

The situation wasn't quite hopeless. Although the flat curve of the lunar horizon was visible behind them, mountains now hemmed them in in almost all directions. And there were some boulders nearby, large ones that might offer some protection. He waved the exhausted band towards them.

They dropped their gear among the rocks, and sat. Nothing but the rasping of breath sounded over the radio. As their breathing eased, each in turn – except for Templeton – looked up at the sky, taking stock. Barely half an hour to go. The comet was close; Bryant fancied he could pick out the nucleus, a knot of darker material in the bright clouds, still high in the sky. He said nothing, though Abel, clearly, had spotted the same thing. When Russell looked that way, he'd see it too. And when it struck, it would gouge into the crust, spewing ejecta far and wide. Was it getting visibly bigger, or was it his imagination?

There was a sudden movement at the edge of Bryant's vision. Russell was climbing to his feet.

"Roger – Skip – I'm just going to take a scout around, if it's okay with you."

"Okay." Why not? Whatever kept him happy. Up to Jim how he chose to spend his last few minutes. As for Bryant, he was just going to sit here and admire the view.

The rumble of the *Discovery*'s fusion engines died, together with those of the cannibalized craft out on the ice plain. Frances Reese cleared the control screen, for the last time, and began massaging her aching, strained eyes. She had spent the last twenty-two hours tweaking the fusion motors and she'd made it – on her own, in spite of the self-doubts, but only with the aid of Jackson's programming. Now, her job was done. Whatever Old Faithful did in the next few minutes, the Dragon would hit its target.

Strangely, she felt no sense of achievement, only overwhelming relief that, for her, the mission was finally over. It seemed she had been holding her breath for nearly a year in anticipation of this moment, hoping, praying all the while that they could pull off the impossible and save one world by creating another. Now, as she held her head in her hands, the strain seemed suddenly to dissipate, leaving behind only a mental numbness and a dull physical fatigue.

She was free at last of the awful responsibility. She turned her back on the cramped control room, and propelled herself wearily to the main access shaft. No longer *Commander* Frances Reese, she was free. Her life was now her own, to do with as she wished.

In the deadly hush of the ship it dawned on her, for the first time, how complete was her isolation. The voices of Bertorelli and Mary Xu, imploring her to get off the comet before it was too late, seemed dreamlike recollections from a former life. It was obvious why; she had ceased to be part of their world just minutes after static had drowned the last transmission from the two departing, overcrowded spacecraft.

An invisible but inviolable barrier had dropped, dividing her from the rest of humanity. She had become a jockey, with no choice but to ride the Dragon down to the Moon . . .

Reese pulled herself, hand over hand, up through the hatch which connected the *Discovery*'s upper and lower decks, then jack-knifed to the left and headed for the airlock. She fumbled in the pocket of her tunic for a stimtab, but when she pulled one out decided abruptly against it and tossed the capsule away. This was a moment when she didn't want her senses tampered with. Besides, she rationalized, her weariness was fast disappearing of its own accord, to be replaced by a mounting nervous excitement. Her pulse rate was already quickening as she thought of what awaited her beyond the thin titanium skin of the *Discovery*.

She suited up quickly, efficiently, although her hands were trembling. Taking the prepared flare canister from a wall rack, she strapped it to her tool belt. She picked up the jet pack, slung it over her shoulders and clicked the fasteners shut, fumbling just a little with the last one. Then, helmeted, she stepped into the lock and started its cycle.

Outside, a violent blizzard was raging, flakes of icy topsoil swirling in a maelstrom. Reese cowered in the airlock long after the outer door had slid back into the skin of the hull. Her helmet beam illuminated a hemisphere no more than ten metres in radius, and it was clear that if she ventured further than that from the *Discovery* she would be hopelessly lost.

It was several seconds before she realized that something was wrong; something peculiar. What was it? Then her brain recognized the strangeness being recorded by her eyes – the snow was falling the wrong way! Superimposed on the apparently random turmoil was a steady drift of flakes – upwards! Of course, the blizzard was being driven out from the comet by the heat of the Sun. But somehow Reese had not made the mental adjustment immediately; her Earthbred intuition had proved, not for the first time, inadequate in space.

But she could delay no longer. It was just because she knew that visibility would be bad that the jetpack was pre-programmed. She took a deep breath, stepped forward, and initiated the automatic sequence.

In an instant she was flying headlong into an impenetrable wall of snow. Her first instinct was to put up her hands to shield her face from the sleet spattering her visor. But that was a stupid instinct. She was quite safe. The suit radar would detect any particles big enough to be a danger, and throttle back the moment it spotted one. The programmed parabola would take her to the summit of Mount Fuji, the largest lump on the irregular surface of the Dragon, in six and a half minutes. All she had to do was lie back and enjoy it.

Reese shut her eyes and let her arms relax, her limbs spreading out into the star shape of a pressure suit in space, held out from her body by the slight stiffness of the joints and the pressure in the suit. She made a vain attempt to focus her mind on the mission, on the gargantuan task that she and the crews had completed, but she found that she could no longer recall the faces of her companions, while their names seemed to blur into a dyslexic confusion. The mission, which had dominated her waking and sleeping thoughts for so long, now belonged to another, impossibly remote, time.

Onward she flew. She opened her eyes again, but there was still nothing to see. Her universe had shrunk to a ten metre sphere, lit by the helmet beam, and within that sphere was only featureless whiteness. It hardly made any difference whether her eyes were open or closed. Perhaps she was dreaming the whole thing. How could she tell if she were awake or asleep? How could she . . .

Something flashed close by. It had to be a number changing on the helmet display. She focused on the near field. Four minutes! Her body responded by pumping adrenalin into the bloodstream; the dreamlike state vanished to be replaced by one of alertness, ready for action. Beneath her suit Reese's skin crawled, every nerve-ending roused to fever pitch.

The minutes blurred past. Bill's face flashed briefly in her mind. A twinge of regret, then nothing. He would find someone else, Reese felt sure. Their love had smouldered all these years like a slow burning fuse, but it had never really ignited. Only with Jay had that happened; Jay, who died in the '75 quake in California, and took with him a part of her soul. Perhaps, soon, she might get that back. Was that why it had been so easy to decide to stay with the comet?

One minute! She felt the change in the thrust from the jetpack, saw a slackening of the sleet on her visor. She was set down, lightly, at her destination, boots sunk into soft slush. Beneath her feet was Mount Fuji, three hundred metres of jagged ice thrust spaceward during the quake, so many weeks before. It was the highest point on this small world, reaching up through the haze of sublimated ices, a bridge extending to interplanetary space.

Reese stood on top of her world and the fog of snow swirled about her tiny, spacesuited figure, driven ever upward into the vacuum. Dust rained down on her, plucked back from space by the comet's weak gravity. It spattered her suit, streaked her visor. She pawed at it with a gloved hand, peering upwards towards the light, the watery light which dimmed and brightened erratically. She would wait a few more moments, then, if a break did not come, she would use the flare anyway.

It came. Suddenly. A statistical fluctuation in the outflow, a transient eddy. Blackness and the curved limb of the world. So brief it was almost subliminal. Had she seen it? Had it been a dream?

Shakily, she unclipped the flare canister and set it down among the loose snow and ice. Activating the heater element she retreated ten metres, to the limit of visibility.

The white glow of magnesium burning in oxygen suddenly expanded her range of vision. Heat rising, swathes of vapour wrenched suddenly in a violent updraught, convection doing its work even in the weak gravity of the Dragon. A fountain formed, a hole punched through the shroud of the comet.

And Reese saw space and stars, and a world that filled half the sky, grey, crater-strewn and terrible. She was a tiny figure caught between colliding worlds – and she could not tear her eyes away from the beautiful sight.

# 19.

It seemed an age before Abel's voice broke into his thoughts. That lump was the nucleus, and it was getting bigger.

"Roger! Roger! He still isn't back – and he's off the air!"

Bryant shook himself back to alertness. "How long, Greg?"

"He's been gone twenty minutes. I can't leave." He gestured at the still figure of Templeton.

Bryant sprang to his feet. Twenty minutes! What in God's name had possessed him, to let his pilot wander off unaccompanied?

The fog of the comet was visible in all directions, now. They were inside the damned thing!

"Stay with Templeton." Abel acknowledged. Just outside the group of boulders, Bryant found Russell's tracks. They headed straight out on to the lava flow, but with this foggy light all around, he couldn't see more than a couple of hundred metres. One thing was clear. Russell hadn't been scouting around, he'd gone off at a fair lick, in a beeline for something. Why had he gone?

Fifty metres out on to the plain, he had his answer. The oxygen bottles were stacked, upright, where anyone following the tracks couldn't fail to find them. The crazy bastard.

"Greg." Bryant's voice was quiet. "How long can a man survive on the suit recycler, with no reserve?" He knew the answer.

"Ten minutes, maybe fifteen." Abel's voice was puzzled.

"But why?" Maybe there was still time. Reason told him there was no hope, that Russell had sacrificed himself in a useless gesture, giving his friends a temporary stay of execution. It was pointless. They were all done for anyway. But he'd be buggered if he'd let Jim get away with it.

"Follow me out, Greg. You can easily pick up the tracks. Collect two oxygen bottles, from about fifty metres out, and get back to Ben. I'm looking for Jim."

Greg's puzzled acknowledgement scarcely registered, as Bryant began to bound forward along the tracks. But as he hit the ground, the ground itself moved up to meet him, and he was knocked flat as the mountains rocked to a terrific concussion. A wave rippling through the tenuous gas that surrounded them seemed to make it lift for a while, increasing his range of vision dramatically. The first quake was over quickly, and he scrambled to his feet once more; but the rolling aftershock nearly laid him out again. Staggering drunkenly, lurching forward all the time, he caught sight of a small, black silhouette against the pearly sky.

Russell! He screamed into the radio, trying every channel, but to no avail. The figure was a long way off; he must be surviving on willpower. How fast could Bryant run to him? Even as the thought was forming, another, bigger aftershock struck, tumbling him to the ground. Run? He couldn't even bloody well crawl. And when he looked upwards, he could see the sky falling.

Rocks, melted in the impact at Hyperion, were raining down on the mountains. The sky was criss-crossed by glowing meteor trails, molten rock scorching through the cometary gases. Something hit, less than a kilometre away, in a blinding flash that hurt his eyes. When he could see again, Russell had vanished.

The ground seemed to be staying where it belonged, now. He got to his feet, determined to pursue Russell to the end. But shrapnel from the local impact began to fall on him, together with a fine rain of dust which smeared his visor and reduced visibility to a few metres. It began to bury the tracks, here, on the surface of the Moon, where no erosion had occurred in a billion years. Other bolides were striking all around, increasing the chance of getting his suit punctured. One of his crewmen was out there, almost certainly dead already. Two of his crew were waiting back at the boulders, one of them blind. Bryant's mind cleared. His duty pointed one way only. He owed it to Jim, now, to eke out those last few litres of oxygen to the last possible minute. If nothing else, they'd leave a proper eyewitness record of what had happened, for whoever came here to find them – if anyone came to find them.

Instinctively, but uselessly, lowering his helmeted head against the rain of dust, he trudged back towards the shelter of the boulders.

When the worst was over, they crawled carefully out into the open, staying close to the boulders but raising clouds of fine dust that seemed to take an inordinate time to settle, even for the Moon. They sat quietly, scarcely speaking, as Bryant and Abel watched the sky clear. Abel had given up his running commentary; Templeton, alone with his thoughts, no longer seemed to want it.

Bryant's oxygen, hardly surprising, was the first to be exhausted. He felt no more than a passing pang as he connected up one of Jim Russell's cylinders in its place. Jim had wanted them to live; they would live – at least until the oxygen ran out. Bryant was quietly recording an account of the impact, for the benefit of posterity, when Abel broke in.

"Sorry to interrupt, Skip."

"It's okay, Greg."

"Looks like I'm out of oxygen, too."

Well, it wasn't surprising. Greg had been pretty active on the hike. Only Templeton, through no fault of his own, had been conserving oxygen by moving slowly and sitting around while the others worked on the sledges and equipment.

"You know what to do."

He watched while Abel took the other partly-used cylinder that Russell had left for them. There was no real way to tell how long they'd last. When Templeton's oxygen was exhausted, Bryant or Abel could go on the recycler for a few minutes while Templeton used their oxygen, then they could all swap round again. There wasn't really much point, but that way they'd all go together. Bryant was sure the others would feel the same; nobody wanted to be the last alive, still breathing oxygen and watching his friends suffocate. Maybe Jim Russell had taken the best way out, after all.

"Roger."

It was Templeton, breaking in to his thoughts. His voice sounded different, slightly hysterical, not the calm monotone of the hike. Christ, he'd better not be cracking up.

"Yeah?"

"Roger, I think I can see something!"

"What?"

Bryant and Abel both turned towards Templeton. In the shade of the boulders, his visor was only on partial filter; they could see his eyes blinking, as he held his hands up in front of his face.

A broad grin spread across his features. "There's a lot of red; left eye's not too good, but the right one can see you two bastards all right. Hey, let me see the view, before it's too late!"

He stood up, suddenly, swaying slightly, and lifted his head to the sky.

"Where'd it hit, Roger?"

Bryant stood, more carefully. He pointed.

"Over there, Ben. How much can you see?"

Templeton's voice lost some of its enthusiasm. "Not a lot, to tell the truth. But it beats being blind. I'd hoped to see the stars twinkling. But I guess the old eyes won't recover in time."

Abel interrupted. "Look about twenty degrees left, Ben. There's a really bright star over there, twinkling like hell. 'Bout as bright as Jupiter."

"Jupiter?" Bryant frowned. "Wrong direction for Jupiter . . ."

He looked anyway. What the hell . . . "Well." There seemed nothing else to say. Abel had realized it too. Only Templeton still couldn't pick out the bright object, glinting in the Sun.

"What's going on?"

"It's only a shuttle, Ben, that's all. Frances kept her promise!"

"Then, don't you think – I mean, it's only a suggestion, and you're the Skipper, after all – but wouldn't it be a good idea to activate the radio beacon?"

Abel leaped to the pile of equipment. Crazy! They should have had the damned thing running all the time. But who would've thought it? Who could have possibly have been around to respond to the call?

While Abel was at work, Templeton continued to babble. Relief was making him run off at the mouth. But part of what he was saying brought home to Bryant how much they owed to Jim Russell.

". . . and, by the way, I've just gone on to the recycler, but I guess there's plenty of time now, just watch that beaut coming in. Hey, Roger, can you recognize the ship yet? I wonder if . . ."

Bryant, watching the shuttle descend in a graceful arc, was too lost in his own thoughts to take much notice. At first, he thought his eyes were deceiving him, but now it was clear. The underside of the shuttle was glowing, a dull red. How could a space vehicle get hot landing on the airless Moon? Even as he pondered the question, the answer became clear. That was why the dust took so long to settle. The comet had been destroyed in the impact, but it had left its mark. The Moon had obtained a trace of an atmosphere.

That must be it. That was what Frances had been up to! If only his father could have lived to see this!

The suited figure met them halfway between their abandoned camp and the shuttle, parked about a kilometre away on a flat stretch of the lava flow. They were unable to talk until they got close, using sign language to indicate the radio channel, and only then by being patched through the shuttle's communications.

"You guys sure picked a helluva place for a touchdown. I'm Bill Noyes. You," he picked out Roger, standing just ahead of Abel and Templeton, "must be Bryant. Frances told me a lot about you." He looked around at the desolate scene. "God, you guys must have a story to tell, huh? We were told there were five . . ." he trailed off, tactfully.

The others didn't seem to want to speak. Bryant had no choice.

"We lost one. My pilot, Jim Russell. And Higuchi . . ." It was Bryant's turn to trail off. Poor bloody Higuchi. He'd have a hell of a time explaining how he'd come to abandon one of his crew members. He changed the subject.

"How's Frances? I can't wait to get the story behind all this." He waved a gloved hand around the desolate scene.

Noyes stopped, almost at the shuttle.

"Roger, I'm sorry. Someone had to stay with the comet for final approach. She insisted."

"Stayed with the comet?" It took a moment to sink in.

"I'm sorry Roger. I know how close . . . I mean, I knew her too, and . . ." but he didn't finish.

"Yes."

In the awkward silence, a female voice broke in on the circuit.

"Bill, it's Mary."

The nagging, logical part of Bryant's brain noted the casual disregard of official communications drill. These guys must have been through a lot, too.

"Any problems?"

Casual, maybe, but efficient and alert.

"I don't know. I can't make it out. We're picking up a distress signal from – from Hipparchus, of all places. Surely there can't be anyone . . . ?"

"Higuchi!" Abel yelled. "The little devil! My God, the son of a bitch made it! He made it through!"

Roger Bryant was the last to enter the shuttle, and stood watching as the hatch slid shut. Higuchi was alive; he, Ben and Greg were alive. The last thing he saw through the hatch, above the grey desolation of the Moon, was a bright star, twinkling mischievously. Goddammit, the Moon was alive! And Frances? As long as the Moon was alive, Frances was alive.

*Goodbye Frances*, he mouthed, silently, before he made to strap in for the journey to Earth. And *au revoir* Moon, he thought, as he settled into his seat. Even Ustinov won't be able to stop us coming back here now.

# Epilogue

"It's the best way, Kondratieff, but don't think I am pleased." The Secretary turned from his balcony, where the Moon, nearly full, was visible just rising above the horizon. "You have given us the Moon, whether we like it or not. I would like to think that your subterfuge was unnecessary. If you had come to me openly two years ago, we could have achieved just as much, without this wasteful loss of life. But yes," the Secretary held up his hand to forestall interruption, "would I have accepted your mad scheme after all? Perhaps I am glad that you made the decision for me." And I am certainly glad, he thought, to be presented with those noble martyrs to deify.

He turned again, to look out at the Moon, clear above the horizon in the still night. Unobscured by cloud, yet faintly indistinct, seen as it had never appeared before during human history; not quite fuzzy, yet not sharply outlined; a sister planet in the making.

"Within five years, we will have bases up there. In fifty we will be adding to the atmosphere. Already Roger Bryant is pestering me with his plans to revive the Lagrange station.

"You expect me to be mad, perhaps? To accuse you? To dismiss you even? Not at all. I'm not saying you weren't wise to keep me in the dark beforehand; the risk was too great. But now there are opportunities, and we must grasp them."

"Opportunities? But, sir, you always dismissed the notion of opportunity for mankind in space."

"I dismissed the projects I was offered, Kondratieff, and with good reason. Tin cans in orbit, as far away as the Moon. What opportunity is there in a tin can? How many could Lagrange One have taken, even if it hadn't been for the accident? A few thousand, an élite, something for the masses to resent. The O'Neill colony was never more than an élitist concept, taking resources from the masses and building a plaything for the few. A whole world is different. It might even be worth using that tin can to help service a new world. You talk of a new frontier, and you speak the truth better than you know. One sixteenth of the area of the Earth – one-fifth of the land area of our planet – is waiting there now for us to tame. It will take far longer than it took to tame the so-called new world here on Earth. But that's all to the good. The longer it takes the better, because when it's done we'll only have to find another new frontier, to save ourselves from stagnation. Yes, indeed, David, you have done well."

And, thought the Secretary to himself, although the risk might have seemed too great to take officially, I know how to seize an opportunity when it arises. Martyrs for the masses to idolize; a project that actually justified some sacrifices, in the short term, here at home; already, with only a little prompting, the news media were publicizing the possibility of power satellites and mining the asteroid belt for raw materials. The euphoria wouldn't last, and it would be a generation before any real benefits accrued. But the wave of enthusiasm for space would see him comfortably into old age, if not to the grave. And he'd be leaving his successors at least a glimmer more hope for the future than he had inherited from his predecessors.

Side by side on the balcony, the two architects of the new world gazed upon their creation.

## TITLES AVAILABLE FROM
# VGSF

The prices shown below were correct at the time
of going to press (August 1989)

| | | | | |
|---|---|---|---|---|
| ☐ | 04008 4 | HEGIRA | Greg Bear | £2.95 |
| ☐ | 04090 4 | STRENGTH OF STONES | Greg Bear | £2.95 |
| ☐ | 04009 2 | ANGEL WITH THE SWORD | C.J. Cherryh | £2.95 |
| ☐ | 03988 4 | THE OTHER SIDE OF THE SKY | Arthur C. Clarke | £2.95 |
| ☐ | 04199 4 | BUY JUPITER | Isaac Asimov | £2.95 |
| ☐ | 03995 7 | WITCH WORLD | Andre Norton | £2.50 |
| ☐ | 03996 5 | WEB OF THE WITCH WORLD | Andre Norton | £2.50 |
| ☐ | 03999 X | YEAR OF THE UNICORN | Andre Norton | £2.50 |
| ☐ | 03998 1 | THREE AGAINST THE WITCH WORLD | Andre Norton | £2.50 |
| ☐ | 03997 3 | WARLOCK OF THE WITCH WORLD | Andre Norton | £2.50 |
| ☐ | 04000 0 | SORCERESS OF THE WITCH WORLD | Andre Norton | £2.95 |
| ☐ | 04365 2 | SPELL OF THE WITCH WORLD | Andre Norton | £2.95 |
| ☐ | 03989 2 | TO LIVE AGAIN | Robert Silverberg | £2.95 |
| ☐ | 04038 6 | UP THE LINE | Robert Silverberg | £2.95 |
| ☐ | 04040 X | THE TIME HOPPERS | Robert Silverberg | £2.95 |
| ☐ | 04022 X | MISSION OF GRAVITY | Hal Clement | £2.50 |
| ☐ | 04096 3 | MEDUSA'S CHILDREN | Bob Shaw | £2.50 |
| ☐ | 04090 4 | WHO GOES HERE? | Bob Shaw | £2.50 |
| ☐ | 04011 4 | EARTHWIND | Robert Holdstock | £2.95 |
| ☐ | 04010 6 | EYE AMONG THE BLIND | Robert Holdstock | £2.50 |
| ☐ | 04023 8 | IN THE VALLEY OF THE STATUES | Robert Holdstock | £2.95 |
| ☐ | 04125 0 | QUEST OF THE THREE WORLDS | Cordwainer Smith | £2.50 |

### Also available: VGSF CLASSICS

| | | | | |
|---|---|---|---|---|
| ☐ | 03819 5 | THE SIRENS OF TITAN | Kurt Vonnegut | £3.50 |
| ☐ | 03821 7 | MORE THAN HUMAN | Theodore Sturgeon | £3.50 |
| ☐ | 03820 9 | A TIME OF CHANGES | Robert Silverberg | £3.50 |
| ☐ | 03849 7 | THE CITY AND THE STARS | Arthur C. Clarke | £3.50 |
| ☐ | 03850 0 | THE DOOR INTO SUMMER | Robert Heinlein | £3.50 |
| ☐ | 03851 9 | THE REPRODUCTIVE SYSTEM | John Sladek | £3.50 |
| ☐ | 03978 7 | A FALL OF MOONDUST | Arthur C. Clarke | £3.50 |

Continued overleaf

| | | | |
|---|---|---|---|
| ☐ 03979 5 | ROGUE MOON | Algis Budrys | £3.50 |
| ☐ 03981 7 | MAN PLUS | Frederik Pohl | £3.50 |
| ☐ 03993 0 | INVERTED WORLD | Christopher Priest | £3.50 |
| ☐ 04061 0 | FLOWERS FOR ALGERNON | Daniel Keyes | £3.50 |
| ☐ 04122 6 | JOURNEY BEYOND TOMORROW | | |
| | | Robert Sheckley | £3.50 |
| ☐ 04144 7 | DANGEROUS VISIONS | ed. by Harlan Ellison | £6.95 |
| ☐ 04123 4 | BABEL-17 | Samuel R. Delany | £3.95 |
| ☐ 04127 7 | GLADIATOR-AT-LAW | | |
| | | Frederik Pohl & C.M. Kornbluth | £3.95 |
| ☐ 04121 8 | BRING THE JUBILEE | Ward Moore | £3.95 |
| ☐ 04134 X | BEASTS | John Crowley | £3.95 |
| ☐ 04195 1 | RENDEZVOUS WITH RAMA | Arthur C. Clarke | £3.50 |
| ☐ 03994 9 | THE SPACE MACHINE | Christopher Priest | £3.50 |

All these books are available at your shop or newsagent or can be ordered direct from the publisher. Just tick the titles you want and fill in the form below.

VGSF, Cash Sales Department, PO Box 11, Falmouth, Cornwall.

Please send cheque or postal order, no currency.

Please allow cost of book(s) plus the following for postage and packing:

UK customers – Allow 60p for the first book, 25p for the second book plus 15p for each additional book ordered, to a maximum charge of £1.90.

BFPO – Allow 60p for the first book, 25p for the second book plus 15p per copy for the next seven books, thereafter 9p per book.

Overseas customers including Eire – Allow £1.25 for the first book, 75p for the second book plus 28p for each additional book ordered.

NAME (Block letters).............................................................

ADDRESS...........................................................................

.......................................................................................

.......................................................................................